Created by M. Drewery

Co-Authored, Edited and Published by the

Rokeby Writing Team

Senior Co-Authors

Year 8	Year 7	Year 6
Liam Anderson	Radamir Averin	Angus Stephens
Oscar Heath	Alex Scrivens	Will Boon
Luca Sanderson	Hyon-Soo Pak	Rafferty Martin
Finn Pleasance	Aaron Kim	William Watkinson
Ethan Harrington-Myers	Alex Reynolds	Rahul Mawji

Co-Authors

Year 8	Year 7	Year 6
Edward McBride	Byron Broulidakis	Tetsuya Boeringer
Leo Satchell	Jack Wingate	David Chong
Toby Chohan	Teddy Harding	Gabriel Palazzo
Ethan Qian	Devan Patel	James Tully
	Ethan Smith	Joshua Dunn
	Maximillian von Grundherr	Tristan Oliver
	Adam Claudet	Christopher Kim
	Charlie Ellis	

Cover Designs by Byron Broulidakis and Rafferty Martin

The Tribes of planet Ontaria

Frayan Tribe

Strength is the
foundation of
society

Volant Tribe

In the sky,
you are truly
free

Pura Tribe

Water is
life

Stimuli Tribe

Sensing is
connecting

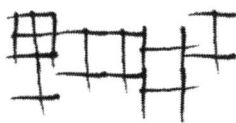

Animalis Tribe

We are all
animals

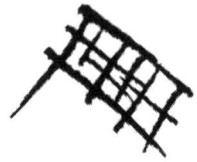

Swift Tribe

Be everywhere,
become speed

Tomb Tribe

Do not fear
certainty

Morphosis Tribe

Be all, know all

Astral Tribe

We are one

Intelligen Tribe

Knowledge
grants conviction

Motus Tribe

Make nothing beyond
Your reach

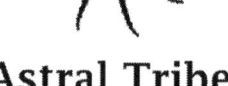

Mend Tribe

To share
is to heal

Tredicim

The goal
of all

4

THE PRISON KEY

First Published in 2021 by **M. Drewery** with www.lulu.com and the

Rokeby Writing Team

Text Copyright © M. Drewery 2021

ISBN: 978 1 365 92152 0

For more information, visit www.mdrewery.co.uk

ACKNOWLEDGEMENTS

Well done everyone who took part in editing

and creating this book.

You are on your own literary journey now, and

one day you will be writing your own stories

and creating new worlds.

Congratulations to the

Rokeby Writing Team

To,
David, Nathen
Merry Christmas

I hope you enjoy this book that I helped write

Lots of Love,

Liam

2

Prologue

Edeps Swift paced back and forth, muttering to himself as he walked across the same patch of floor repeatedly, leaving light clouds of condensation in his wake. He shivered, rubbed his shoulders and arms, then ran on the spot for a moment. He looked down at the thin, skin-tight fabrics that he wore, which revealed bony protrusions on his arms and legs, and highlighted his wiry, muscular frame. *Why didn't I bring a jumper?* He thought.

The room he strode across over and over, was oval shaped and mostly undecorated, except for bland military designations stencilled on the walls. Rows of screens and terminals hung off the far wall.

From all around him explosions, muffled by metres of stone and metal, shook the building. The computers rattled on their stands and the ground vibrated, causing little chips of concrete on the floor to bounce around. Edeps also felt this through his feet shaking him to his core.

He instinctively ducked when a thunderous blast hit somewhere above him on the roof, and shook the lights dangling from the ceiling.

Edeps looked at one of the screens. "How long?" he anxiously asked.

"Huh. What?" a woman who had her back to the camera said. She spun in a swivel chair and the light of her monitor illuminated her lined and tired face. Her golden hair, with streaks of grey, elegantly fell over her left shoulder as she turned to him. Then as if it had a mind of its own, her locks wriggled off her shoulder and dropped down her back.

"Did you forget we were here?" Edeps asked incredulously. He scratched the recent stubble on his chin and ran his fingers through his greasy, unwashed hair. It stood on end for a second, before settling back down on his scalp.

"Of course not, General Rowep was just giving me an update on the situation outside your little fortress."

Edeps' eyes flicked to another screen displaying the architecture of the fortress. He saw several layers of reinforced walls and defence turrets. A scrolling readout showed the damage taken from the bombardment.

Several red dots were scattered over the map and occasionally half of them would suddenly disappear and reappear in another room.

As he stared at a dot in the centre of the fortress, which he knew to be him, the bony protrusions on his arms started rising and falling like they were aerofoils on a plane's wings. "Please tell me enough Tredicim are outside and we can finally get on with this mission. It sounds like they are close to breaking through the walls!"

As if on cue, the entire building shuddered around him. The woman on the screen turned away to check something. Edeps looked into another screen and watched a feed from cameras around the building. Balls of light fired from Grav-Tanks struck the walls, but caused only minimal damage. "This Fortress the Intelligen designed is impressive, but it's been withstanding fire for far longer than we thought it would have to," he said to the woman's back.

Soldiers outside, who appeared as dark shapes occasionally silhouetted by bright blasts of weapons fire, marched around the perimeter. *No doubt searching for weaknesses in the walls*, Edeps thought. Insectoid like ships plunged down from above to strafe the fortress with bombs. The defence turrets responded with automated fire, blasting some ships from the air and the mangled wreckage dropped onto the army below.

"Not yet," the old woman said, finally turning back to him and answering his earlier question.

"Commander..." he began, then placed his hands either side of the screen and bent down, "...they are going to breakthrough. Once they do that, we might not have a chance to enact the plan," he said, his voice rising on those last few words.

The Commander's eyes narrowed as she meet his gaze. "Aren't you the one who has boasted to me all his life that he was the fastest member of the Swift tribe on the whole planet? Suddenly, you fear you're not fast enough?"

"If I had known that one day my speed would put me in the most dangerous place imaginable, I would have slowed down a bit these last few years."

"Hold on," the Commander said, holding up a finger to the screen like an irritated teacher. A nine-foot tall man, wearing a helmet that covered his face, marched up to the Commander and bent down to say something into her ear.

"Thank you General," she said to the man, and then turned back to Edeps. "We've done a rough count of the number of ships and Tredicim in the crater. We calculate 80% of their forces and support elements have gathered for this assault. We have another incoming blip on the sensors, a ship may be nearby, we want to wait and catch it too."

"How long till it gets here?" Edeps asked.

"Five minutes."

The fortress shook once more and Edeps stood up and ran his fingers through his dark, red hair again, expelling a long breath through clenched teeth.

"Calm down," the Commander said.

"I am calm," Edeps replied quickly.

"Your plates are moving," she said.

Edeps looked down at the bones on his arms that were still rising and falling. "So?"

"Your plates always move like that when you're nervous."

Edeps crossed his arms and clamped the plates down, yet they still twitched under his hands. "You're not the one in the centre of this trap."

"Let's go over the plan again, it will occupy your mind," the Commander suggested. "Have you got the crystal?"

"If I didn't this would be for nothing," Edeps replied. He plucked a small box off the top of a nearby computer, then held it open close to a camera for the Commander to see. Inside was a piece of ruby red crystal. It shone with an inner light that broke through its surface into various fractal patterns.

"Check," the Commander said. "Are the doors leading out of the fortress still stable and ready to go?"

Edeps punched a few commands into the computer. A list of checks appeared one after the other. "Good to go," Edeps said.

"Then you and the others are ready when the time comes," the Commander stated.

Edeps put the box down and then stood still, tapping his feet.

"You can all make it in time," she said reassuringly.

"I know we can make it from here to where you are before we too are trapped, the problem is if we are chased," Edeps said.

"Who cares if they chase you, you'll always stay ahead, the team you selected are the fastest Swifter's on Ontaria."

"What happens when all this is done?" Edeps asked.

"The war will be over and we will celebrate," the Commander replied.

Edeps stared off into space. "No, I mean after, after," he added.

"You'll be back on the farm no doubt, a peaceful life again."

"I was hoping to stay in the military," Edeps suggested.

The Commander looked over her shoulder quickly, then leaned in closer to the screen. "The tribal council won't allow it, in accordance with the Dusk Laws of the Patriarchs they gave you special dispensation to serve militarily, but with the war's end they will terminate your service."

"Surely they can make an exception…" and he let that last word hang in the air.

"They won't," the Commander replied.

Edeps stared into space as his mind wandered a little further, but before he could voice his thoughts, he heard another rumble, although this time it came through the speakers next to the computer screen.

The Commander looked up at the ceiling of the room she was in. "The ship we were waiting for just passed overhead."

"Did they detect the hidden base?" Edeps asked.

"No, the time has come, we'll see you all in a moment," the Commander said. "When we detect the shield activation we will open the portal for you to gain access."

Edeps bowed his head slightly and closed his eyes. He uttered a short prayer to himself, then he looked up and nodded at the Commander. He took the crystal from the box and plugged it into a special aperture on another computer. It logged the exact composition of the crystal, all its internal flaws, atomic arrangement, and geometric lines, then saved the sensor readings.

Once it was complete, Edeps typed a long string of numbers and words into the computer. He then checked the sequence once more memorizing it for later then hit enter. He boxed up the crystal and put it in a backpack that he slung over his shoulders. The fortress then started to power up. Edeps waited, listening to the humming of the power plant within the building.

On the computer, three options appeared for him to confirm or deny. One read, **Activate Shield Number 1?** The second **Activate Shield Number 2**? And lastly **Timed Open and Closure of the Fortress?**

Edeps then pressed a button on the console and held it down. "Fortress Team everyone return to the control centre now. It's time to abandon this place."

Seconds later several Ontarians ran into the room, all wearing red uniforms like Edeps. They were all roughly the same height as him, and they too had bony plates on their arms.

One had distinctly grey hair and longer arms than the others. He grasped Edeps on his shoulder, then the old man joined the rest of the team. They all scanned the screens on the walls. Some were biting their lips, others stretching and bouncing and taking deep breaths.

One of them stepped up to Edeps' side and turned to face them. He was an imposing man, with short, red hair and a sharp angular face. "Calm down Swifters, in a moment you'll be running faster than you ever have before."

"Yes Lieutenant Acer," the group said as one.

"We've trained for this, you'll be fine as long as you focus on the finish line," Edeps added.

The Swifters nodded and they all stood to a loose attention, muscles less tense and still.

Then a second group walked into the room. They were all a foot or more shorter than the shortest Swifter. They wore loose fitting robes that hung off thin frames. They hunched over with tired looks on their faces.

Edeps looked down at their leader. "Captain Levi are your squad ready?" he asked.

The woman leading the group lifted up her head. Her grey hair, which was twirling around itself tightly to her skull, like the tentacles of a nervous octopus, framed her young haggard face. "We are," she said in a whisper.

"I apologise now for the indignity about to befall you," Edeps said with a smile.

"It's fine," she said with a slow wave of her hand. "Better than the indignity of you fellows crashing into a wall of Tredicim," and she looked up at the Swifters and smiled.

The Swifters chuckled.

"I for one definitely don't want to crash into that kind of wall, the last thing to pass through my mind to be my feet," Lieutenant Acer said, to general laughter.

Edeps pointed at five Swifters, "You will carry our Motus Battering Rams. The rest of us will be right behind, picking up those who fall. Clear a path and we will get through this," he instructed.

The Swifters he had pointed at picked up the Motus tribe members and raised them up onto their shoulders.

Edeps turned back to the computer and his finger hung over the button for the third option.

Everyone else stiffened.

This is it; this is my moment Edeps thought. He knew what lay in wait for him if he succeeded, if he got his crew to the finish line it was the end of the war. They would get glory, fame, acknowledgment, and peace at last. He did not think about failure…not an option.

"Four years of war are about to end," Captain Levi whispered.

The Swifters all faced the doors and crouched a little.

Edeps looked at his team, brave women and men all, and he was going to lead them to victory. For a moment, he wished he could have done this alone rather than risk their lives, but they had needed a crew, to trick the Tredicim outside that the fortress was fully manned. Now he was responsible for getting this crew out of here. He smiled to himself. *I'm fast, the fastest, this is no problem at all.*

He stretched a little, took several deep breaths and rotated his shoulders.

He then pressed the button.

A double door unlocked on the far wall of the room he was in and parted automatically.

The Motus tribe members raised a hand in front of them, palm out as if they were pushing the doors open.

Beyond, another set of doors parted then another, and another, the only gaps in a concentric ring of several walls. Edeps had been counting the unlocking doors in his head, and when the sixth opened he pressed the other two buttons activating both shields. The seventh door unlocked.

The fortress detonated a series of mines around its main entrance, blasting any Tredicim there away, keeping them from the main door.

Then the console started beeping.

Edeps eyes went wide and looked down, "The automatic system has stalled."

"Captain?" Acer began.

"Go!" Edeps commanded. "I need to reset the system."

"Captain."

"That's an order, go," he barked at his second in command.

The seventh and final door opened and through the unlocked doors, the battlefield outside came roaring in. First the heat of weapons fire, then the smell of explosives and then the sounds of Tredicim cheering in celebration, assuming they had got the fortress open.

Acer nodded gravely and repeated the order and the Swifter's rushed from the fortress.

Edeps was left alone as he frantically tried to reset the system. He stabbed buttons and willed the system to reset. He stared at the screen with clenched teeth as a small candle icon shrank then reformed and repeated. Edeps wiped his forehead, "COME ON," he shouted.

Automatic System Reset, the computer finally told him.

The first set of doors started closing, but Edeps was already through them and they slammed shut behind.

The second set closed and he made it through, just barely.

He pushed himself harder, to run faster.

He exited the fortress missing each door closure by millimetres.

Edeps smiled, he did not encounter a single Tredicim on his way out; they had not even made it to the fortress' main entrance yet.

I am the fastest, he thought to himself.

Then a Tredicim officer stepped in front of the exit, filling the doorway completely with his heavily muscled body. Edeps had met him before on a different battlefield.

The creature was tall, almost seven feet with rough, dark green skin. He had pure white eyes and a head crowned with tentacles writhing about all over his skull. He wore a dark, blue military uniform. A small, golden chain hung from his neck, what was on the end was held to his chest beneath his shirt.

"WHAT IS THIS?" the Tredicim bellowed at him.

"No time for you Trettan," Edeps said, and he flung himself forward and raised both legs, which slammed into Trettan's stomach.

Trettan howled in pain and was sent flying backwards.

His sharp claws swung at Edeps, catching his arm, tearing at his clothing and flesh, and the two of them tumbled out of the fortress.

The last door shut behind them, sealing the building once more. Edeps had made it outside and found what he expected to find. In front of him the Tredicim army and beyond, an ash covered landscape.

He quickly assessed the situation. There was a gigantic hole in the front line of the Tredicim and in the distance his squad was breaking through the next using the Motus' powers as a battering ram.

Edeps picked himself up, Trettan was on all fours and he looked at him with grinding teeth and a penetrating gaze. Then the fortress lit up as a giant bubble of energy expanded from within, breaching the outer walls as it grew. It then stabilised, forming a solid wall of energy around the whole building.

"A shield, ha, it won't take us long to get through that," Trettan gloated.

"That's only the first one," Edeps said with a smile, and then sprinted away following his team, just as a second bubble of energy started expanding out from the fortress.

Trettan looked up at it, then his face fell. "Come back here," Trettan called out and he licked Edeps' blood from his hand. Bony protrusions erupted on his arms, legs and back and he gave chase, matching Edeps' speed.

They both cut through the lines of the Tredicim surrounding the fortress. The second shield then started growing at a rapid pace behind them.

Edeps caught up with his team, they had been stopped by a Tredicim squad on the edge of their army, who were also using Swifter powers. As he approached he saw two Swifters and a Motus on the ground, clearly dead. The others were battling for their lives, trying to detach themselves from this obstacle.

The Swifter who held Captain Levi was jumped by two Tredicim, but he held up Levi like a trophy. The captain, through gritted, bloody teeth raised both her hands. The air shimmered and a wave of energy erupted from her extremities. The heads of the Tredicim shot back and even from this distance Edeps heard their necks snap.

Lieutenant Acer was beset by a burly Tredicim. Both stood their ground trading blows, occasionally trying to side step the other.

"Acer, duck," Edeps said, as he came rushing in.

Acer dropped without missing a beat and Edeps close-lined the dumbfounded Tredicim, who was slammed into the ground.

Edeps helped Acer up and then pushed him to the side as Trettan came bounding in.

The two of them tumbled over until Edeps managed to get his legs into Trettan's stomach and he pushed him off.

Edeps got up on all fours and looked around in a daze.

He was vaguely aware of the bubble of energy that had been chasing them. Out of the corner of his eye he saw the bubble become a dome as the sides touched the floor of the volcanic crater the fortress sat in, a blighted, black landscape of noxious gases and malformed rocks. Then it started fanning out. First it washed over and expanded beyond the first shield then over the Tredicim army.

The Tredicim shouted in surprise as it grew, filling the crater of the volcano. They were unharmed as the shield passed over them, yet they howled in fear when it did, all of them knowing immediately what it was for.

Those not already swallowed up by the bubble turned and fled.

"YOU TRICKED US!" Trettan shouted and leapt forward and clawed again at Edeps.

Then the grey, haired Swifter came running in on all fours like a cat and shoulder barged Trettan.

Edeps screamed in pain as claws slit across the back of his right leg in the calf muscle, just as Trettan was knocked aside.

He went down on one knee. The shield was mere meters from reaching him and the air crackled as if it was burning.

"Go," the old man said and leapt at Trettan again before Edeps could command him to go on without him.

"Come on sir," Acer said and he pulled Edeps upright and the two started running.

Edeps concentrated on a small pinprick of light a few hundred meters away, a doorway in the lip of the crater. It lay beyond an encampment surrounding the army, supplying the warriors of the Tredicim tribe. Already the others were entering the small doorway.

"We have to go back for him," Edeps cried out, turning around. The man who had saved him from Trettan was now within the shield.

"No sir you can't, you have the Key, it's too late, don't let it be in vain," Acer said, and pushed his Captain on.

Edeps remembered the backpack he wore, and inside the key to this whole trap. He didn't care, he pushed Acer off and ran back.

He passed through the shield and his eyes were blinded for a moment as he crossed the threshold. When his vision returned he saw Trettan standing over the old man who was cowering before him.

Edeps lent down grabbed a rock from the ground, forced his exhausted body to burst forward and threw it.

Trettan looked up just in time to see the projectile strike his chest and he crumpled around it.

Edeps rushed to the man's side picked him up and pushed the man forward. "Go, go," he said. The man was in shock, but he obeyed and he went down on all fours and sped off and Edeps followed him on his two feet.

They both caught up with and burst through the expanding shield running just ahead of it.

Edeps winced as pain shot up from his leg with every step, but he ignored it. He felt the hairs on the back of his neck start to rise as the energy field followed him.

He pushed himself to his maximum. His whole body told him to stop, that he was tearing himself apart. Finally, he reached the lip of the crater and he flew through an archway of stone into a command centre, just as the shield reached its outer edge and stopped expanding with a final crackle, like a miniature lightning strike.

He was caught by Acer and the old man who were waiting for him. The old man then held him by the shoulder. "You shouldn't have come back for me, you had the Key," he said between deep breaths.

"I wasn't going to let you die, besides I know how fast I am, there was never any danger."

Even though Edeps was the man's superior officer the old man scowled at him. "Never do that again, you had the key, you were responsible for making sure we trapped that army. The whole of Ontaria matters more than just me."

"Relax Grandfather we made it, I will always make it."

"This time yes, in the future though don't do it again you must make sacrifices for victory, there might not be another way. I was willing to die for my people. If you had failed to rescue me, we both would have been dead and where would we be?"

Edeps smiled with his hands on his hips and he looked around the room, where other Ontarians were looking at him in awe for making it back safe from the fortress, it filled him with confidence. When he turned back to his elderly relative, he saw the man's serious expression. "Ok Grandfather you're right," he finally said.

"I am grateful though," the old man added and opened his arms.

Edeps hugged his elder. Then they both turned their attention to the doorway he had passed through. The shield wall was visible in the arch, like a film of shifting, glowing glass.

"Begin phase two," Edeps heard someone call out, "the shield is stabilizing."

The energy spikes rippling across its surface began to fade. The static energy that had filled the room was dissipating.

Trettan then leapt through the shield the moment it stabilised.

He made straight for Edeps and with a roar he threw him to the ground and held him down.

"Restrain him," the Commander ordered.

"I will tear your skin off," Trettan cried out in a high-pitched voice twinged with rage. He raised a clawed hand above Edeps' head.

"RESTRAIN HIM!" the Commander said with rather more urgency.

Before Trettan could gut Edeps, two armoured giants a full two feet larger than him, stepped forwards and grabbed his arms.

"Watch out, he has my speed," Edeps warned.

Trettan growled and spun on the spot at high speed sending his attackers flying away from him.

He tried to run, but Edeps kicked at his knees flooring him, then Trettan was bundled by four more giants who held him down. Trettan bit down on one of their arms drawing blood and in seconds his body increased in size and his muscles bulged.

He tried to lift the four giants off him, however they were far stronger and after a brief struggle, he was contained and chained.

"Stop struggling Tredicim, you have lost," the Commander said.

"Lost? LOST? That shield won't hold us."

Weapons fire then struck the part of the shield wall that was visible at the end of the command centre.

The shield had no more sparks of energy rippling across its surface. It was now like the skin of a soap bubble, yet not nearly as fragile, it resisted all attacks against it. Blurry, dark shapes stalked around on the opposite side, ferociously attacking the barrier.

Everyone's focus in the room then turned to a giant monitor fixed to one of the walls. It showed a view of the crater from above now engulfed in a dome of energy, and beneath a smaller dome around the fortress. Fuzzy, but visible though the shield was the army of the Tredicim. Even their ships prowled under the bubble, unable to soar as the second dome reached high into the sky.

"I have to admit that trapping us in a shield is a cunning plan, but do you think that will hold us? That fortress was imposing, but it cannot possibly generate enough energy to power two shields for very long. My brethren, my Family, all they need to do is wait. When the first fades we will tear down that fortress and destroy the emitter for the second shield," Trettan declared. "We'll be free in days."

"Watch," the Commander replied, "Edeps, lock the pylons."

Edeps nodded and limped over to a nearby console.

"Pylons?" Trettan growled, "what are they for?"

"You can project power through a shield if you know its exact frequency," the Commander explained.

Edeps reached the console and inserted the same crystal key he had used before. He tapped at the buttons on the keypad so fast that no one knew exactly what he was typing, then he turned to the view screen.

Around the mouth of the crater, pylons rose from the ash covered ground, like skeletons rising from the grave.

"No, NO," Trettan screamed as the pylons sent beams of energy through the shield and straight towards the fortress.

The beams passed through the smaller shield around the fortress and when they hit the building, dishes on top absorbed the power. At first nothing seemed to happen then the smaller shield protecting the fortress turned completely opaque as the shield strengthened considerably. Then the bigger shield encompassing the entire crater did the same, turning the shield a dark blue that crackled with extra energy.

"You're powering the shields from the outside," Trettan gasped.

"Yes an impractical way to power shields from a tactical point of view, but brilliant in order to energise your people's prison, forever," Edeps commented. He then took the red crystal from its slot and brandished it in front of Trettan's face.

"This Key is the only way to shut down the system and this is the last time it will be in this room," Edeps said to Trettan.

"A dome within a dome, the generator sealing your people in cannot be reached, the Tredicim are trapped forever," the Commander said. She took a deep breath, "The war is finally over," she announced.

The technicians, giants, all the people in the room cheered. Raising fists into the air and leaping into one another's arms.

People slapped each other on the back and shook hands.

The noise was deafening. The Commander hugged Edeps' grandfather; Acer lifted and hugged Captain Levi. Edeps was patted on the back so much he was afraid his heart would come tumbling out his mouth.

"HOW DARE YOU, WE ARE YOUR RULERS," Trettan cried out, silencing everyone. He struggled in the grip of the giants who held him, "Let me go, I must get back in there, he needs me." The gold chain around his neck flew free and a locket bounced on his chest as he struggled. His clothing started to rip as he tried to pry himself free. His efforts were in vain though; the giants holding him were too strong.

"Not anymore," Edeps said.

Trettan's head whipped around to face Edeps. "YOU, you will suffer for this," he said.

Edeps looked back and shrugged.

"You don't believe me...?" Trettan growled.

"Take him away," the Commander said. Trettan struggled furiously as giants led him out of the room. Before he was taken out of sight, his eyes gleamed as they locked onto the key that kept his people's prison sealed. Then he was ushered out of the room.

"The secret of the Key must be maintained," the Commander said walking up to Edeps.

"And it will be, you have my word," Edeps replied.

"Where is it to be stored?"

"The council deemed only one place in the entire solar system where it would be safe."

"Where?"

Edeps smiled back at her. "Planet Earth of course."

"The council won't let you drop it off, not if your only reason is to have a little sightsee of the human world," the Commander remarked.

Edeps then leaned in to whisper to the Commander. "I'm a hero now, I imagine they'll let me do anything."

"Don't be so sure," the Commander said, with a playful smile.

Edeps winked then turned to the room, everyone started to clap. He brought his team together in one big group with him at the centre as the praise grew louder.

It's good to be the hero, he thought to himself.

Chapter 1

Present Day

Ryan Barns wiped water from his forehead. It bombarded his head from above, running through his black hair and down his face like a waterfall. His saturated clothes clung to him like a second skin, which made him feel clammy, yet also cooled down his body from all its recent exertions.

Boys around him, some wearing red shirts others wearing blue, squelched about slowly, their feet heavy with mud. A few were groaning about it, raising their hands to the heavens to curse the rain. Ryan however smiled.

He bent down and tightened up his shoelaces. He stretched a little and rocked his head from side to side. He looked over at the Coach. She was holding up her left hand showing three then zero.

Thirty seconds till the whistle, Ryan thought to himself.

He looked along the line at his teammates, all giants with bulging muscles or stomachs, while he had a tough, thin physique. They were all crouched and poised. "Come on, why doesn't the ref just blow the whistle?" a teammate muttered.

Ryan, just waited. Although absentmindedly he scratched the scars on his right arm, he also had identical ones on his left.

His grandparents had told him he had received them as a young boy who, while trying to get sweets from the top of a kitchen table, ended up knocking a teapot onto himself, causing scalding hot water to burn his arms and legs. Although hidden by his rugby shirt, there were more burns on his back, running down the length of his spine.

He made no effort to hide any of his scars, freely displaying them. They intimidated most people. He caught one of the opposition staring at them, eyes focused on him not the game.

His team occupied the lower half of the field. They were on fifteen points the opposition were beating them with seventeen, they needed a try or drop goal to regain the lead. Not so difficult you would think, but they were about to polish off the last thirty seconds of the game. If they were going to win this they would have to pull off something special.

"For the cup," someone on the sidelines yelled.

"Come on lads," shouted another.

Ryan stared down the field at the opposition's try line, which was at least three quarters of the pitch from where he stood,

Impossible that he, the right-winger, could reach it and score a try. Ryan knew that he could do the impossible though.

A scrum was forming to his left, eight of his team members, fellow students from his high school, were taking up their positions. They all knew what was at stake, they had to get the ball to their wingers, specifically their star winger.

Ryan breathed in deeply. For over an hour he had pushed himself very hard. That was strange for him it never usually hurt to go at top speed, but he could not worry about that now.

The referee brought the scrum together.

All the players on the pitch went still.

All the spectators on the sidelines went quiet, the only sound was the rain beating down on umbrellas like a hysterical drummer.

The shrill of the ref's whistle cut through the air.

Ryan, far from the action close to the sidelines, found himself almost deafened by the roaring of the crowd.

"COME ON GET THAT BALL," shouted a group of seventh years.

"GO ON BILL, COME ON MATTHEW," some parents called out.

"CHANNEL THE BALL, CHANNEL THE BALL," bellowed the coach, a PE teacher called Mrs Thatcher. She had her hands cupped to her mouth screaming at her players. She then turned her head to look down the line at Ryan.

"Get ready for the ball," she said to him, "it's all on you."

No pressure then, Ryan thought.

He started moving into position, the rain smacking against his face as he jogged through what felt like a curtain of water.

The players in the scrum were shouting at each other, edging themselves to do better, pushing on the opposition, and digging their feet in.

Ryan could only just see the ball, and luckily, his players had control. Time was running out though, they had to hurry.

Finally, the ball came completely into view and the real action started. The player who picked up the ball swung his arms and twisted his hands to make the first pass, sending the ball through the air like a spinning top. The ball left a pretty, circular shower of water behind it, Ryan watched the water, to him it was moving in slow motion. The first winger was already moving and caught the ball then went careering past the scrum and up the pitch.

The opposition players pushed forward with a roar, one stepped up for the tackle, but before he could even reach his target the winger passed.

The second winger for Ryan's team caught the ball and fumbled with it slightly.

The crowd gasped as one, as it looked like the player would make a fatal drop.

However, the student grasped it firmly and ran for a gap in the line and the crowd roared its approval. The opposition closed in on him quickly, and for a third time the ball sailed through the air as the player tried to get it away from the enemy.

Now it was the crowd who supported the opposition's time to cheer, as one of their players suddenly intercepted the pass and was now taking it back down the pitch.

One of the former members of the scrum was in his way, and was going for a tackle, so the opposing player passed to a fellow player practically right next to him.

This was Ryan's chance. He drew upon the latent power in his body and it tensed every muscle. His legs felt like coiled springs as they launched him forward. Accelerating faster than anyone could have imagined. He sped towards the ball; running through his own line of defenders rushing to tackle, and was between the two opposition players from twenty meters away in a matter of milliseconds.

The ball was muddy and his hands came together as it slipped free.

Ryan concentrated. To him the rest of the world slowed down while he moved normally. He even had time to whip his head around and evaluate his position, identifying a way through and up the pitch. He then repositioned his hands, gripped the ball, checked it was firmly in his fingers and everything returned to 'normal' speed.

The cheer from his supporters was one of surprise and outright celebration at a one in million move. He wondered what they had seen, to them had his hands moved in a sudden blur for a fraction of a second?

He refocused on the game. Super-fast he tore up the pitch with mud flying out behind him, whipped left and right by his legs that pumped like pistons.

"GO, GO," the crowd shouted.

The opposition closed in on him. While their feet made sucking noises as they pulled their boots from the mud, Ryan moved his legs so powerfully the dirt could not grip him. They moved like they were running through treacle while nothing stopped Ryan for finding each gap in the line and powering on through. He ducked under arms and moved through gaps that might as well have been a mile wide.

In a few seconds he was clear of all the other players, heading for the try line.

He smiled and turned around, and while he trotted backwards he saluted to his team, passed over the try line and planted the ball down.

Five points, the whistle blew.Final score, 20-17 to his team.

He had just won the match.

Ryan then started coughing uncontrollably, his lungs were suddenly burning. He panicked and grasped his chest, never had he felt tired, not even once after using his super speed for his entire life. He was thinking about all the other times he had run at speeds no other human had even reached, how easy it had been and now was he suddenly paying the price?

Gradually the coughing stopped and his lungs cooled off.

Ryan stood up straight and looked as his team's supporters.

Everyone was cheering, all the exhortations directed at him, and he soon forgot about his laboured breathing and drank in the praise.

His heart beat fast and euphoria flooded his system.

It felt great.

Chapter 2

"RYAN, RYAN," his teammates shouted as they crowded around him on the try line to shake his hand and pat him on the back. Even the weather seemed to thank him as it stopped raining that very moment and the sun came out.

Their cheering started to trail off. "Best move ever right?" Ryan shouted, and the team erupted again in cheers.

"Well done Ryan," someone said, in stern authoritative voice.

The crowd parted and the coach, who stepped into the void, beamed at them all. "Well done team," she added, "I've got it in my mind to request you be given no more homework for the rest of the term."

"YEAH," the team shouted, Ryan included.

"You all did very well, be proud of yourselves."

"We are the best team in the borough," chanted one of the big flankers of the team.

"NUMBER ONE, NUMBER ONE," the whole team shouted.

The opposition team, now leaving the pitch, looked over giving venomous glances at the Ryan and his fellow players.

"Now, now," said the coach patting the air, she then clapped her hands together and said, "I just want to say this was a hard match, you played your best and you deserved this victory, congratulations."

There was one last collective cheer and then everyone went back to exchanging more praise with each other on their performance."

"Did you see that try?"

"Did you see that conversion in the first half?"

The comments kept coming and after a while the team broke up with shouts of triumph by their supporters on the line. Parents hugged and praised their sons for an excellent game and students congratulated their friends.

Ryan's smile faded as his friends turned their backs to him to embrace and receive praise from their parents, leaving him alone in the middle of the group. His eyes lingered on Barry, whose father embraced him and patted his back, which his son heartily welcomed.

Ryan bit his bottom lip and darted his head around squinting through the gaps between families. He finally spotted who he was looking for. He wandered out of the circle of friends and parents, over to an old man waiting patiently for Ryan's attention. He stood on the edge of the pitch with his hands in the pockets of his heavy raincoat, smiling broadly.

"Well done son that was a great run there at the end," he boomed.

"Thanks grandad, but I got lucky," Ryan replied as he walked up to greet him.

"Now don't say that my boy, you know as well as I do it was all you out on that pitch," he said, "I won't have my grandson demean himself." The old man then leaned down and whispered to him. "You may be faster than most, but it's nothing to hide, you know that right?"

Ryan thought about that remark.

He was by far the fastest player on the pitch, far above the others in fact. He did not always run at top speed and he never completely held back if he did not have to. His grandparents knew all about his super speed and they encouraged him to use it, but covertly of course.

Ryan had always wanted to tell his friends the truth, but then he knew that could lead to awkward questions, not to mention they might tell others.

He was glad his Grandparents let him cut loose with his speed, it is not like he was cheating. His abilities were natural after all. He had first run at speeds unmatched by any other human when he was eight. He had been playing catch with his grandfather in their garden and after running for a long throw he somehow ended up sprinting out of their back garden and a mile into the Yorkshire moors.

He came out of his thoughts and looked back at his grandfather who was waiting for an answer, "Yeah you're right, I shouldn't be ashamed," he finally replied.

"That-a-boy, now go change, I'll call your grandmother, give her the good news," he said, and he started trudging off towards a pay phone located next to the pavilion.

Ryan walked down the pitch back to his teammates, who were still chatting about the match. People came up to him to shake hands, parents he knew and students he did not, who just wanted to say they knew him.

"Ryan, brilliant play, how do you run so fast?" Barry, his best mate, said pushing his way through the crowd. He was a black haired boy as tall as him, but wider, and friends with Ryan ever since the start of secondary school.

"Hey Barry, if you're jealous then lose some weight then maybe you'll be able to catch me in practice," Ryan joked.

"This girth helps us win," Barry responded pointing at his large stomach. "People just bounce off me."

"Come on let's go change we've got celebrating to do," Ryan said and he and his friend started out for the pavilion as did the rest of the team.

"Man, I didn't think you were going to make that run Ryan," said another one of his teammates called Bill, a short, stocky boy with long hair.

"Me too it was close, but when I get going there's no stopping me," Ryan boasted.

Everyone laughed.

Ryan started coughing as he joined in.

"You alright mate?" Barry asked.

"Yeah, sure – just - you know - still haven't got my breath back," Ryan answered, in between coughs.

In truth though he wasn't alright, he was panicking, grasping his chest as if he could reach inside his body and cure himself.

"After sprinting like that I'm not surprised," Barry said.

"I was fast wasn't I?" Ryan said, trying to ignore the pain.

The team reached the pavilion. As they stepped off the muddy ground onto the concrete, they all slipped their boots off and banged them together to free them of the mud they had accumulated.

Their opposition were already going into the changing rooms. As the last members of their team shuffled inside, they were still giving Ryan intense frowns or sneering.

"Watch out mate I don't think they are too happy with you right now," Barry warned.

Ryan smiled and even waved at the opposition, and through his forced smile, he said to Barry, "Watch what happens next."

His team then entered the changing room filled with row after row of benches and clothes hooks. Dried mud covered the floor and steam from the hot showers wafted across the room. The other team had taken up the benches closest to the shower block.

As Ryan's team entered the room the chatter stopped, the other boys all turned towards him and his friends.

Both teams stared each other down.

No one in his group spoke, they all looked to Ryan and held their tongues. "Problem?" Ryan asked, still smiling.

A six-foot tall boy stepped out from the rows of benches and looked across the changing room straight into Ryan's eyes.

The rest of his team shrunk back a little, while Ryan stood straight and poised. When the world passed you by at a hundred plus miles per hour, feeling fear and doubt only slowed you down.

He stepped away from the group to stand a few meters in front of the boy. They stared each other down as their fellow teammates crowded around behind them, both as back up.

Ryan broke eye contact to size up his opponent. The boy was massive and a bit fat. At some point he had broken his nose, which was slightly crooked. His other features seemed too small for his large head. It was like someone had drawn small eyes and a mouth on a balloon then inflated it.

After a few seconds of slowly sizing him up Ryan resumed eye contact, "Do you need something? Tips about playing Rugby perhaps?" Sniggers erupted from behind him.

The tall boy opened his mouth to speak, but did not immediately say something, obviously trying to come up with a witty retort.

"Do you want help with some of the words?" Ryan interrupted.

"Shut up!" the boy said, "how did you do that?"

Ryan sighed theatrically and crossed his arms, "Do what?"

"That interception, no one runs that fast especially a skinny boy like you," the boy replied.

Ryan then shrugged his shoulders, "Whatever, thing is we won you lost."

"I think you cheated," the boy said.

"You can think? It doesn't look like something you're capable of doing," Ryan shot back.

The boy's eyes narrowed and he looked behind him at his mates who did not looked impressed. The boy had had enough of this mental sparring and stepped forward raising his fists and hunching over like a boxer.

Barry then stepped out from the crowd, "Err fella, maybe not take on this guy, he does Taekwondo, unless you want another broken nose, let this go." Barry then smiled appreciatively at the giggles his comments generated.

The boy paused, then sized up Ryan again.

He didn't believe Barry, as he tiptoed forward again his arms still raised. "Come on then..." he declared and threw a punch. Ryan moved forward under it, came around behind the boy and placed his foot at the back of the boy's left knee, however he did not push down. He did not need to fight it rarely solved anything when he did, he just wanted to make a point. The boy gasped and froze with his punch extended and looked over his shoulder at Ryan who still had his foot planted on the back of his knee.

"I'm fast and I didn't cheat." Ryan said. "Do we have to do this?"

The boy's face contorted as a number of different emotions and thoughts passed through his mind, if they could find it. He finally straightened up and nodded. Ryan walked back around him towards his team.

As soon as his back was to the boy his opponent moved again to grab him. Ryan had time to sigh, shake his head and move out from under the boy's arms and then stick his leg out and trip him up.

Their opponents stepped forwards to help their teammate now groaning on the floor, but Ryan turned his head and glared at them.

Without the big guy to lead them, they all froze.

"I've had enough and now so have you!" Ryan ordered. He brought his foot back ready for a swing at the boy's side.

The boy cried out and closed his eyes.

Ryan paused when he saw the boy cowering. He let his foot drop and his smile faded and he slumped a little.

"Sorry," Ryan said, "forget about this, I didn't cheat and that was a good game," he muttered.

The boy got up and walked back to his teammates with his arms hanging by his sides and now somewhat smaller than he had been a few minutes ago.

His team, who were all smiling smugly, greeted Ryan warmly. "Well done mate, he was no match for you," Barry said.

Ryan nodded, the praise and adulation warmed his heart and he fist bumped a couple of boys.

Then he grasped his chest.

His lungs were on fire again and his throat was swelling up. He had to get dressed and out of the changing room as quickly as possible.

He rushed to his bag and pulled out his clothes, he intended to change right now and get out of there.

"You're not going to have shower?" Barry asked.

He never got the chance to answer because he burst into another bout of coughing, putting his hand to his mouth in a vain effort to stifle the fit.

"Pat on the back's what you need," Barry said.

"Get me - a drink – of - water," Ryan gasped.

Bill fished a bottle from his sports bag and gave it to Ryan who spluttered it down as he drank it quickly, spilling loads down his top.

It did not help he just kept coughing.

"Someone get the first aider," Barry yelled.

He started to lose focus of the world around him. In the background, he could hear the opposition team start to jeer and in a daze, he watched as his friends closed in around him.

"I don't think - the magic sponge will help – me," Ryan joked.

Then his chest tightened up and he stopped breathing.

"Call an ambulance," he heard Barry shout just as he blacked out.

Chapter 3

Ryan's eyes shot open, and he immediately had to scrunch them up again because he had looked straight at the light in the ceiling. He then opened them again, slowly, raised his head a little and let his tired eyes scan the room. He saw plain white walls, covered in various posters that were encouraging people to get themselves checked out for multiple diseases. There was an intense smell of lemon in the room and it practically burnt his nostrils.

He raised himself up slightly more and discovered that he was on a hospital bed, and at the end near his feet were his grandparents. They both sighed as he focused on them, and his grandfather put his hand on his grandmother's shoulder and she grasped it smiling.

"Are you alright Ryan?" his grandfather asked.

"Fine," he muttered sitting up, "what happened?"

"You passed out," his grandfather replied.

"Oh we were so worried," his grandmother said, ambling up to the side of his bed and hugging him. Her fluffy white hair brushed against his cheek and made him itch. Tears, magnified by her thick glasses, streamed from her eyes. She was a big frumpy woman, as tall as his grandfather and she practically smothered Ryan with her hug, he felt out of breath again.

He looked over her shoulder and saw his teammates peering through the window in the door to the hospital room, and laughing. They were making stupid gestures and taking the mickey. Barry even pretended to press a lift button and disappear out of sight.

His face turned red, "I'm fine Nan," Ryan said, and he squirmed on his bed.

"How are you feeling?" his grandmother asked stepping back and pulling her cardigan around her body.

"Fine," Ryan answered, "did anyone…?" he started and he raised his eyebrows and tilted his head towards his arms and legs.

His grandparents looked over their shoulders at the faces of his friends, then leaned towards him.

"No one had time to do any...difficult...medical procedures on you son. I was there in the ambulance to make sure of it," his grandfather whispered.

Ryan could tell they were both relieved that none of the doctors managed to examine him thoroughly. His super speed had certain biological traits that he did not want people to see.

His feet were crammed with more tendons and muscles than a normal human in order to give him more power when running. His ankles and leg joints had softer than normal cartilage that regenerated very quickly, to allow for shock absorption and friction. There was also this power within like extra energy to keep him going, to dampen the effects of muscle fatigue.

Ryan and his grandparents kept such details to themselves. They did not want anyone to know he was so different, after all people would ask questions, tricky questions.

The door to the room clicked open, "Hello," said a high-pitched voice and entering the room came a young doctor. She had tied her hair up and it had various pens sticking out of the bun. She practically danced into the room bursting with energy Ryan wished he had right now. "How are you feeling?" she said almost singing the words.

Ryan did not want to repeat himself, however out of courtesy he replied, "Fine, can I go?"

The doctor seemed to ignore the comment and she plucked a clipboard from the end of his bed and perused the details on it through pink-rimmed glasses. She then took a pen from her hair bun and started adding notes.

"Mr Ryan Anrib Barns," she said reading his name, enunciating each word. "Hmm odd middle name," she remarked. "Let's see now, shortness of breath and you blacked out," she read from the clipboard.

"Shortness of breath? More like a complete lack of," Ryan commented remembering his lungs crying out for oxygen.

"I don't feel comfortable letting you go since I still don't know what happened," the doctor said, ignoring his complaint, "Do you have asthma?"

"No," Ryan replied.

"What else might have caused it?" Ryan's grandfather asked.

"Well, it's a strange thing Mr Barns, your grandson is very young and fit, and although he physically exerted himself immediately prior to the incident, it shouldn't have caused such symptoms that are more commonalty associated with an allergic reaction. According to the paramedics nothing restricted his air way and your grandson is not allergic to anything. It was as if your body, for a short time rejected oxygen."

Ryan looked at his grandfather who eyes darted downwards and squirmed in his seat after receiving this new information.

"He's alright now isn't he?" his grandmother asked.

"Oh yes," the doctor replied with a broad smile.

"Then he can come home?" his grandfather said.

"Yes I suppose he can," the doctor admitted with a sigh, as if she wanted him to be ill.

"Then let's go," his grandfather said hastily, and he was up and headed for the door.

"Thank you," Ryan said to the doctor and slipping off the hospital bed. She left and his friends piled into the room.

"How are you doing mate?" Barry asked.

"I'm fine."

"I thought they were going to have to take you into surgery or something," Bill said.

"Cheers," Ryan replied.

"Shame really, we missed a chance to see them cut you open," Bill added.

"Well, if Ryan's done faking his death, we've got celebrations to get started." Barry said.

"Not tonight," Ryan's grandfather cut in, "you can celebrate tomorrow," he added.

"Bu..."

"No! Not tonight," his grandfather said, his voice rising.

Ryan was ready to argue, however something in his grandfather's eyes made him realise though that now was not the best time.

His grandfather extinguished any disapproval from Ryan's friends with a fierce scowl then turned to him and his grandmother, "We are going home!"

•

Ryan sat in a wheelchair biting his bottom lip and fidgeting. He had to be wheeled through the hospital to the exit, instead of being allowed to walk himself.

A porter in the hospital pushed him while his family and friends trailed behind. He heard giggling and snippets of jokes from his friends. He tried to ignore them.

It was embarrassing and pointless, but apparently hospital procedure, and he had no choice.

He used the time to think of an argument that would convince his grandparents to let him go out tonight.

Ryan felt as he always felt, with boundless energy and strength. The last time he had been in a hospital was when he was almost five years old. The event only vaguely imprinted in his memory and most of what he could recall was pain. It was the surgery required to fix his burned arms, legs and back. He had woken up from that catastrophe in a hospital ward with his extremities bandaged. His grandparents always told him that if his mother had not been a doctor the burns would much worse.

That was over ten years ago, and he had never needed a doctor during that time for anything.

Ryan did not consider that odd at all, it was just another fact that made him brilliant. Surely his grandparents could see he was healthy, there was no reason to stop him celebrating his team's victory.

After a minute or two Ryan reached the exit and the porter indicated for him to vacate the chair. He almost was not quick enough and the porter nearly tipped him out like he was emptying a wheelbarrow.

Ryan stood up straight and stretched, then rotated his arms.

"I feel great, I don't need to go home," he said to his elderly relatives.

"You are going home," his grandfather growled. Before Ryan could object, the old man marched towards the car park.

His grandmother gave him a pleading look then followed her husband. Ryan stood with his friends to say his goodbyes. "Tough luck Ryan, I guess we'll have fun without you," Barry said.

"Yeah what a shame, never mind have a glass of milk on us when you get home," Bill added. "And a cookie before bed."

"Jerks," Ryan muttered.

The group laughed at his misfortune and strolled out of the hospital together, then Ryan went one way and his friends the other.

•

Silence dominated the drive home, which surprised Ryan. "So that was a great game right? Did you see that interception I made?" he said. Having to raise his voice a little because the heater was on full blast, turning the inside of the car into an oven.

No response.

"If I hadn't done that interception we would have lost," Ryan said, and waited for the praise.

His grandfather just grunted.

He huffed and slouched on the back seat with his feet up on the other passenger seat staring out of the window at the darkening moors of Yorkshire.

His grandparents lived in an old cottage right in the middle of the moors. The old grey stone house was on its own on the shallow slopes of a valley, in what seemed like the loneliest place on Earth.

Any other fifteen year old would have hated to live there. Ryan was miles from his friends, and the type of scene where people his age usually hung out.

For him though it was heaven, a nearly empty place on the British Isles for him to run to his heart's content.

Most teenagers had to be forced out of bed, but Ryan loved getting up early, right at dawn, when the light was bright enough to see, but it was still too early for people to be up and about. It was the perfect time for him to run, as fast as he could without being spotted or more importantly caught on a camera phone. Eating up the miles faster than most supercars.

Ryan squirmed on his seat with his arms crossed and huffed. He had just earned a stunning victory that most of the school had witnessed, everyone was going to be talking about it. Ryan had hoped to bask in the glory for a whole evening.

Now he had to spend it at home.

"Come on Grandad, I'm fine. Remember when I first starting running fast and I hit that dry stonewall. That should have broken bones. I think this minor hospital trip doesn't mean anything. That doctor, she reminded me of mum, said I was fine."

His grandparents remained silent. Ryan wondered if he shouldn't have mentioned his mum. She would have let him go, she was a doctor, she would have seen that he was alright. He tried to think of something to change the subject in case they were now cross at him for name-dropping her like that.

"I think my performance today means we should think about my sporting future. We've got to get my name in front of scouts for under 18s or even some of the big clubs. They are going to be falling over themselves to sign me. Think of it, I'll be a sporting sensation, maybe I could even run in the Olympics. I'll be able to buy you an extension for your house."

"That's nice dear," his grandmother replied, but she didn't turn to speak to him, she just stared out of the window up at the night sky.

"We don't have to worry about my secret coming out, there isn't a test in the world that would reveal my special powers."

"We're nearly home," his Grandfather just barked out in response.

Ryan huffed, threw himself back into his seat with his arms crossed, but they didn't respond, so he just slumped back and dreamt of wealth, fame and glory.

As images of himself accepting the sportsman of the year trophy played out in his head, the car pulled into the driveway and the sudden braking shunted Ryan out of his head and back to reality.

He opened his car door and stepped out on the gravel driveway. The small stones crunched under his feet and the security light on the front of the house came on and lit up the driveway. Ryan paused with his hand on the car door, he could hear a low level humming noise, which seemed to fluctuate in rhythm, like a heartbeat. He looked at the security light and wondered if its bulb was going, but the sound did not seem to be coming from there. He looked up into the sky, there were no stars or clouds just pitch-blackness.

He turned towards his grandparents, about to try and feign more illness, then pretend to go to bed and then sneak out, however, he stopped when he saw them already by the front door with it wide open. They stood either side of the door as if ushering him in first.

"What's happening?" Ryan asked, smiling. Were his grandparents about to throw a surprise party for him? When he was out-cold did they plan this? Had his friends beaten them to the house and set something up? Maybe to congratulate him on his victory and make him feel better after his illness.

"Ryan, I'm sorry about this but there is someone you need to meet," his Grandfather said, bowing his head solemnly as he held the front door open.

Ryan strolled up to the door and beamed at his grandparents. They had planned a surprise for him, and he wasn't falling for it. As he entered the house he walked slowly, expecting people to jump out at him and shout 'surprise!'

A number of lights in the house were on, *Surely everything should be dark, it would be easier to hide*, Ryan thought. There was a sudden

metallic rattle of stainless steel on stainless steel, someone had just dropped some cutlery in the sink. He frowned, this was not what he was expecting.

He went into the kitchen. Sitting at the table in the centre of the room, was an old woman. She had greyish hair braided into multiple locks, which were writhing around like snakes down her neck and back. She wore blue trousers and a jacket that had a distinctive military look to them, they were made of many small inter locking plates, like fish scales. While her clothes were unique her most distinguishing features drew Ryan's immediate attention. She had bony plates covering her neck running down to the top of her shoulder blades.

The woman looked up from the steaming cup of tea she held in her hands. She sighed when he entered the room and put down the cup.

Ryan did not say anything, he just looked back at the woman in confusion as if he had just caught a burglar with his hands in the safe who then asks politely, 'where's the silver?'

"Nice of you to visit," his grandfather said, with a sneer.

"Don't start you two," his grandmother scolded his grandfather.

"This is usually the only reason I'll come down onto this planet," the woman stated, holding up the mug of tea. Her English was impeccable, each word pronounced so perfectly. Ryan suspected the Queen did not even speak it so well. "This leaves in hot water has an extraordinary taste, but let's talk about why I have come today." She took a long draught from the mug, "I want to know what has gone wrong with the boy?"

Chapter 4

"I'd also like another cup of this tea," the woman said.

"I'll get you one," Ryan's grandmother replied and she filled a saucepan with fresh water and put it on the boil.

Ryan's grandfather took off his coat, put it on the back of a chair, and then sat down opposite the stranger.

Why are my Grandparents welcoming this complete stranger? Ryan thought. *What is wrong with her, why did she have those plates on her neck?* He could not stop staring at them, they were freakish, not to mention her writhing hair.

His Grandfather made no comment as he took his seat opposite the casual intruder into the house, sitting as straight as he could with his arms crossed.

Ryan noticed that the two of them seemed to be engaging in some sort of mental battle. His grandfather was staring at the woman, his brow set in a frown. His eyes darted over his enemy, carrying a hint of suspicion. The stranger did not seem to notice and seemed to be winning the battle, by looking aloof and un-intimidated by the stares she received. Every now and then her eyes cast a glance at Ryan, not liking what she saw.

"On this planet it's traditional to wait for an invitation," his grandfather finally said.

"Mine too, however we both know there is no need to wait, this is important," the stranger replied. "We knew this might happen, unfortunately, and we need to talk about it as you would say ASAP."

Ryan's grandmother placed two mugs on the table, one for his grandfather and the stranger who immediately took a gulp without waiting for it to cool.

"Thank you, the last time I had this kind of drink was a year ago and I have missed it."

"Well maybe we would have sent you some, Admiral, or you could have visited," Ryan's grandmother suggested with a coldness to her voice. "It would do well for you to visit Ry..."

"I don't fraternize with humans," the woman interrupted, "unless it can't be avoided."

"Admiral?" Ryan said. "Who is this, what's going on here?" he added.

"Ryan dear this is Admiral Tarms," his grandmother said standing behind her husband rotating and nursing her own cup of tea.

"Who?" Ryan asked again.

"Admiral Tarms, Commander of the Core Planets Wing of the Ontarian Tribal Fleet. I'm here to take you home," Admiral Tarms said bluntly.

Ryan looked at the stranger, this Admiral, like she had escaped from somewhere. "I am home," Ryan replied. "See this house?"

"Your new home then," the Admiral said, ignoring Ryan's sarcastic comment.

"Now hang on, the boy deserves to know what's going on and you can't just take him like that," and his grandfather clicked his fingers to illustrate his point. His old gnarled hands still managed to produce a decent snap that cut through the air. He did it right in front of the Admiral's face, which caused the Admiral to frown.

"I need to take him now, his Ontarian physiology is asserting itself, and he needs to come with me to-day," Admiral Tarms reiterated.

"He has friends, a life here and one I'm sure is better than you can provide, even if you were willing," Ryan's grandfather said.

"What are those?" Ryan asked and pointed at the plates on the woman's neck. He did not even feel remotely awkward or guilty for pointing out an obvious physical peculiarity.

Everyone else in the kitchen turned to look at him.

"And that hair, why does it move like that?"

"No Ontarian can fully control their hair, it's technically a separate organism," the Admiral answered.

"What?" Ryan blurted back at her.

His grandfather gestured to an empty seat at the table, "Take a seat Ryan," his grandfather said.

"What's all this about?" Ryan replied without sitting and he skirted around the table standing between his grandparents and this Admiral.

The Admiral sat back in her chair and looked at her mug, her fingers drumming on the side. She then took a breath and fixed her full attention on Ryan, "You're only half human," she stated flatly.

He did not quite understand this comment. *What could the other half possibly be*? He thought.

"Perhaps we should explain," Ryan's grandmother said, her calm voice smoothing the tension that was filling the room. "Your mother Ryan, our daughter, was of course a human being, your father however was not." She drew out the last half of that statement. As if the words were not hers and she did not quite recognise them or where they came from.

Ryan did not understand how that would explain everything. He loved his grandmother very much, but right now, he was thinking she had lost it.

If his father was not human, what was he? He thought. "Are you trying to say I was a test tube baby?" he asked.

"No silly boy she means **he wasn't human,** he was an alien," the Admiral said.

Ryan scoffed at the Admiral.

"You're an alien," she repeated.

"This is a joke," Ryan declared. He looked into his grandmother's eyes and saw her honesty. She would never lie and not joke like that, she was telling the truth.

"It's not true," he stated raising his voice.

"I can see he doesn't have our intelligence or emotional control," the Admiral commented. "Have you never wondered about the source of your super-speed?"

"Aliens don't exist," Ryan said.

"I think they do," the Admiral replied and she tapped her plates for emphasis.

The Admiral nodded at the scars on Ryan's forearms, "How did you deal with his?"

"His mother performed surgery on him," his Nan answered.

Ryan looked down at his arms, "Wait, what? Mum did surgery on me?"

"She did this?" he asked motioning towards his scars, "you told me..."

"You used to have plates there, kind of like the Admiral's. To fit in on Earth they needed to be removed," his Grandfather explained.

"Fit in?" Ryan said.

"Ten years ago it was decided you would remain on Earth instead of your father's homeworld. You needed to look as human as possible so the plates were removed from your body," his Grandfather added

"Listen Ryan, you are half-human, half-Ontarian that's the name of your father's race," his grandmother said.

"My Father's race, listen to yourself..." but Ryan trailed off. For the first time in this conversation, he actually confronted the fact that he still had a father. He wasn't dead, he wasn't washed up somewhere or chilling in another part of the world. He was an alien…from space. That's why he wasn't around.

His head started to hurt, his gut tightened, he felt cold and he started breathing deeply. His brain in a desperate attempt to save him threw up a quick retort to this mad conversation.

"There's no such thing as aliens," Ryan said, repeating his earlier comment, but with further emphasis. However, the words sounded forced even to him, more a denial than a statement of pure fact.

"Human ignorance and arrogance," the Admiral said, "I'm living proof, as are you."

"You're not an alien you're a freak," Ryan shot back. "So my dad was an alien? Come on, how is that possible?"

"He came to this world and met your mother. That's how it's possible," the Admiral said.

"That doesn't explain why you're here?" Ryan said, "Why are you telling me this now, my dad disappeared years ago?"

"Weren't you listening? Because your Ontarian side is starting to assert itself. Your physical makeup is half that of this world and half that of another. While one side of you can live on this planet the other needs the environment of the planet we, the Ontarians, live on. A unique combination of genetics are battling for supremacy inside you and the Ontarian side is winning," the Admiral explained.

"I'm not leaving my home," he said.

"You have no choice!"

"That is out line," his grandfather replied slamming a palm on the table, "He needs time to assimilate and understand this information."

Ryan stepped back a little from his grandfather's outburst and smiled in pride at being defended by the old man.

"You can't just uproot him," his grandmother said.

"You understand why this is necessary? I told you it could happen when the boy was delivered into your care," the Admiral retorted.

"Why wasn't I raised with the Ontarians?"

"We didn't want you," the Admiral bluntly said. "You should never have been born."

Ryan gritted his teeth. "What does that mean?" he replied.

"Our race is not meant to fraternise with yours. Humans know nothing of our species and we prefer to keep it that way, and we certainly wouldn't want humans on our world."

"But you want to take me to your planet."

"You're still half Ontarian and we…still have a duty of care…I guess. You will come to our world to live there, so you can survive. Your human side will be medically adapted to our planet's conditions, you'll find you'll integrate sufficiently."

Ryan did not like the sound of that. It seemed like no life at all when put so coldly. "I'm not going with you," he said, "I have school tomorrow, exams, rugby and friends. I want to stay here."

He turned to his grandparents. His nan was looking worried, staring at her grandson as if he could fall over and expire at any moment. His grandfather looked torn between wanting to keep his grandson safe, while also keeping him at home.

"Ryan you have to go," his grandfather finally said.

"You've known I might have to go to this planet. You never told me?"

"We knew all about your past, your father, we went to your parent's wedding of course. The Admiral here was the one who gave you to us, she explained the whole thing. We never told you because you never asked."

"Never asked? You didn't think that maybe you should have just told me?" Ryan said.

"You were almost five when we took custody of you, as you grew up we were prepared to tell you when the time came. We assumed you would want to know and ask us when you were ready. Your unnatural speed was so unusual, we were surprised you never did ask."

Ryan turned his face away, they were right. He never did want to know where everything that was strange about him came from. He feared it would change his life forever. Now he had been proven right, and his life had turned upside down and he was about to be relocated to a different planet.

"I don't have time for this," the Admiral said and she got up off her chair. She looked down at Ryan's grandparents, nodded curtly, then said to Ryan, "I'll wait outside, while you discuss this," and she went to the counter and put her mug down.

At that point she turned her back and Ryan's eyes went wide as he noticed the plates on the Admiral's upper shoulders and neck ran behind her skull covering the lower part of her head, which was bulging.

Instinctively Ryan felt the back of his neck, his scars ended where his shoulder blades were, they did not touch his skull.

When the Admiral turned around Ryan dropped his hand to his side.

"You have an hour to decide Ryan," the Admiral said, using his name for the first time.

She left the kitchen and Ryan heard a door open and slam. He turned around to his grandparents. They both sat at the kitchen table staring into their mugs of tea. Ryan knew he would have to be the one to break the silence. This was indicative of the relationship Ryan and his elderly relatives had. They were not his parents; on some level they did not feel like they had the authority to dictate the way his life should be.

Could he make this decision though?

"Say something," Ryan begged.

"You have to go," his grandfather said immediately.

"What about everything I have here," Ryan said. His mind started skipping through all the things he might have to do on this new planet, make new friends, live in a strange place, did they have *PlayStations*? "Do you have any idea what I'll be facing?" he asked.

"Afraid not, we don't know much about the Ontarians."

"Did you ever get to know my father?" Ryan asked.

"Of course, your parents were married on Earth, but it was only until after you were born we found out your father's background. He never spoke of his planet, though to be honest we never asked, it was all so much to take in and he was a fine man," his grandfather said.

"How do you think I feel?" Ryan said. "I can't imagine it, I can't see a different world of different people. I don't want to face it. He looked away out of the kitchen window. It had been obvious throughout his life that he was very different to his friends, he had never once thought he was an alien though, more just a different type of human.

He used to think about it, try to understand his super speed and scars. The only answer he had come up with to explain it was that he was a freak, a mistake blessed or cursed with remarkable physical traits. He had always hidden those traits, however he often wondered what would happen if someone found out about him. What would these aliens say about his human side when he met them?

"You know you have to go…right?" his grandfather said.

"I'm not going, sorry I can't do this," he said, he felt his eyes sting with the prospect of tears.

"Ryan," his grandmother said softly.

"I want to stay, I want to stay where mum lived," he added, then sped out of the room before his grandparents could stop him, slamming the kitchen door behind him. He stopped in the hall though, waited, they didn't follow.

He had this feeling that something had not been said, that they were keeping something back from him, to spare him.

He looked through the keyhole in the door.

"We should have told him," His grandfather said.

"It will freak him out, more so than he already is," his grandmother replied. "He'll see. The changes will convince him."

"Do we want to take that risk, do we want to risk him…dying before then."

If his grandparents had noticed his eye, framed by the keyhole, they would have seen it widen in shock.

Ryan backed away from the door.

I could die, he thought to himself. *No! I feel fine.*

He rushed up stairs and into his room.

Looking into his mirror he saw his own fresh face, full of colour, full of life. *No, I'm fine. I'm strong, fast, I can get through this.*

Chapter 5

Ryan woke up the next morning, looked at his phone, saw that it was seven o'clock and sighed. After rolling out of bed and creeping down stairs, he grabbed some cereal and downed a whole bottle of high-energy drink, something he knew he would need to get to school on time, and then he changed.

He slung his backpack over his shoulder opened the front door closing it as silently as he could and strolled out across the drive to the road. It was forty minutes by car to his school and he had half an hour to run it. He usually went to school with his grandfather who drove him, because that looked more normal. After sneaking out of the house though, he needed to run it himself.

Before he could start off, the front door clicked, and he turned and saw his grandfather pull the door open. The old man was red faced and his dressing gown hung off one shoulder. His grandfather looked relieved to have caught him before he left for school.

"You can't go," he said, panting a little.

"I'm not going with them grandad," he replied.

"Ryan you need to go with them," his grandfather said. Ryan then heard his grandmother descending the steps coming down to also talk him out of it.

"Grandad I have a life here. Do you know how many friends in high school I have? I'm going to go on and be the best player the England Rugby team have ever had. I'm going to be an Olympic gold medal winner for sure. I'm going to get money and fame. You think I'm going to give that up?"

His Grandad sighed and looked away.

"Yeah this other planet doesn't sound too good does it? How could it compare?"

Ryan then sped off.

He zoomed down the road passing a few slow moving cars on the way, but he was going so fast the passengers would probably think they had something in their eyes, certainly not that a fifteen year old boy was passing them at sixty miles an hour. Eventually he reached Whitby. It was a nice seaside town famous for being the home of Dracula and where Captain Cook set sail to explore the world. The famous Whitby Abbey stood on the south side of the river Esk, which cut the town in half. The smell of fish rolled out of the harbour and into the streets, a pleasant and familiar smell to Ryan and a sign he was where he was meant to be. As he worked his way deeper into the town he had to slow down when he thought he might get spotted. Eventually he caught a bus the rest of the way, so he would make it to school on time and not get spotted pelting by a pedestrian at super speed.

Waiting for him at the school gates was Bill.

"Ryan," he called out.

"Hi mate, what did you do last night after we parted company?" he asked.

Bill waved him off, "We ditched our plans in the end, it just didn't feel right to celebrate without the man who won us the game. Here's Barry," he then said, nodding his head over Ryan's shoulder.

Barry's dad's Range Rover came to a jarring halt by the pavement rocking on its suspension. Ryan peered through the windscreen and saw his friend's dad turn in his seat to speak to him. It appeared as if they were having some cheerful banter.

For a moment Ryan's smiled drooped and he felt a pang in his chest as he watched father and son talk. He thought about his own dad. Ryan had always thought his dad lived as far away from him as possible, maybe drunk somewhere, maybe a free bachelor. He blinked and stared off into space for a moment, realising that he was actually right, his dad was as far away from him as it was possible to be. Ryan looked up into the sky, wondering where the planet where his father lived was.

Barry finally got out of the car said, "Bye dad," and walked over to Ryan and Bill. "You feeling better today?" he asked Ryan.

"Much better," Ryan replied.

"Good, we need you for future games, plus no one wanted to hang with us last night without you around."

"Well, we'll have plenty of time to hang tonight," Ryan replied, as the trio turned away from the gates to walk into school. "Anyway, I think people have forgotten about the game don't you?" Ryan said, waving Barry's praise off, however he eyed the small groups hanging around the entrance to school waiting to become a part of his inner circle, and smiled again.

"Well done Ryan," a random 8th year student said.

"Cheers," he said over his shoulder.

"Heard about the fight you had in the changing room," said another who raised his fists and did some mock jabs like a pro boxer.

"Alright make way, make way," Bill cried out like he was a herald for some medieval knight.

Those in the younger years parted as Ryan led his friends across the school grounds to their form room. Chatter accompanied them wherever they went, girls darted looks and teachers congratulated him on his amazing try from yesterday.

"Your grandad was right angry with you last night, what was his problem?" Bill asked.

"He just thought I shouldn't be going out, what with the hospital trip and everything," Ryan replied, pleased that he was starting to forget about last night's revelations.

"Great game though, we thrashed that other team," Barry said.

"We'll celebrate tonight," Ryan said.

He and his gang reached the form room and some of the students were already going inside. Ryan saw their usual seats at the back of the room, which were currently occupied by other pupils.

Ryan coughed a little when his group reached their seats.

The pupils already there shuffled aside quickly.

"Thanks guys," Ryan said, as they found other places. He dumped his bag down on the table as did his mates. They occupied their places, displacing more students as they did so and talked loudly over everyone in the room.

It was then that the fun stopped and the form tutor strolled in to take the morning register.

Ryan sat next to Barry in silence, bored to tears and resting his head on his hands. He only perked up when the teacher called his name.

"Yes," he replied, then sank back down onto his arms.

He lifted his head again when his arms started to itch. He scratched his forearms, which helped a little.

The form tutor then got up and started reciting from a list of school notices and Ryan's boredom increased.

His right arm then began to tingle, he felt every muscle in his arm tense, then all those in the right side of his body, and he jerked in his seat.

"You alright?" Barry asked, after his sudden convulsion.

Ryan tried to look relaxed and said in a slightly slurred voice, "Ok."

There was then a shooting pain in his left arm, then both his legs. Ryan was glad to be at the back of the class and that everyone was looking forward, because his left arm jerked in the air involuntarily. He looked around sweating, seeing if any students were looking his way, thankfully no one had spotted his bizarre behaviour.

His right hand escaped his control and he hit Barry on the leg.

"What?" he asked.

Ryan desperately tried to cover, "What's...erm...the first subject of the day?" he asked.

"Geography," Barry answered.

Ryan used his left hand to control his right and held on tight, hoping that this would end before he had to leave for the first lesson.

Eventually it did stop.

Ryan rubbed his arms to relieve the tension and pain.

"And finally, the cricket tour is postponed until the 19th," the teacher said. "Ok, go on get to your first lesson."

All the students got up and started for the exits, "Let's get to the humanities block," Bill said.

Ryan nodded and wiped a film of sweat from his forehead.

As they walked through the school grounds they passed the toilet block.

"I'm just going to duck in here," Ryan said.

He did not wait for a response from his friends and just went inside.

The toilet was almost empty and he went into a cubicle and locked it. Then he rolled up his sleeve on his left arm to inspect it.

He was shocked to find that his scars were gone. The skin had healed completely.

Then for the first time in his life he felt the bone in his arm. The feeling felt completely alien, sensing the presence of his own skeleton inside his body. It was such a surprise that Ryan shivered.

The bone then sent lances of itself through his arm's flesh and pierced the new skin where his scars had been.

He whimpered, he actually whimpered and put his hand to his mouth. He didn't want people in the school to pass around gossip that he had cried in the school toilets. However, the pain in his arms was hard to take and he started writhing as if trying exorcize it from his body.

He watched as the extensions of bone started to grow and combine with more slithers of marrow.

The pain was excruciating and Ryan could barely hold back his cries of anguish. He listened out to see if the toilet was empty and when he reckoned no one else was in there he allowed himself a little cry, and he shut his eyes to try and block the pain.

The agony finally subsided and when he steeled himself to actually look at the end result, he involuntary shrieked in alarm. The bones had formed interlocking plates across his forearms. He flexed his arm to have a better look and he got goose-bumps as the bones slid over one another then suddenly flipped up. They reminded him of ailerons on plane's wing, providing down force and steering.

He thought the ordeal was over, but then his legs and remaining arm joined in with the first.

He had to sit down on the lid of the toilet and brought his arms and legs into his chest as the pain tensed every muscle in his body.

Five minutes later, sweating and panting Ryan's body relaxed.

He rolled up his trouser legs and inspected the result. The same plates had grown on all his limbs.

Ryan stretched out his body in an attempt to relieve the tension. As he rolled his head back he felt on his neck something he had never felt before. It was not the stiff starched collar of his school shirt it was something on his back. He reached up and felt more bone on his spine. As he felt further it continued down his body.

He became aware of the silence around him, of a school hard at work. The morning classes had begun, and Ryan was now conscious that he was late and most likely in trouble.

But he could not go back to class, not like this, he needed to escape the school and get help.

He left the cubicle and washed his hands out of habit then headed for the school gates. His kept his eyes down yet he imagined faces in every window looking at him.

He wanted to run as fast as he could, but he could not risk it, not inside the grounds.

He turned one corner and almost went head first into the deputy headmaster.

"Ryan Barnes isn't it?" the deputy head said gruffly, looking down at Ryan. The deputy head was a stern man with black, immaculate hair and thick glasses enlarging his dark eyes. He also had an excellent memory for every student's name, no one escaped his attention.

"Yes Sir."

"You should be in a geography class shouldn't you?" another unsettling habit of his, he seemed to know where every student should be at any given time.

"Yes sir I'm on my way there now."

"Then that way boy," he said, pointing behind Ryan.

"Yes Sir," Ryan sighed and he went back the way he came. He would have to take the long way around to the school exit. He could hear the deputy following him, making sure he went to class.

Ryan had no choice, he had to risk it.

He turned a corner then ran at full speed towards the next, disappearing just when the deputy head turned the corner himself, losing Ryan completely as he doubled back towards the main gate. He quickly crossed the playground towards the exit and walked through the school gates, briefly wondering if he might ever return.

He did not care if anyone saw him as he rushed home, all the way from Whitby across the moors to his grandparent's house. It was nine o'clock when he arrived.

He went through the front door and dropped his bag in the porch going straight for the kitchen.

To his surprise sitting there at the table was the Admiral sipping on a cup of tea.

"I knew you would change your mind," the Admiral said.

"I haven't," Ryan said.

"You will."

"I won't," Ryan shot back.

"You have to Ryan," his grandmother said.

"I won't, even if you do this to me," Ryan said, pulling back his sleeve and showing the Admiral the interlocking plates on his arms.

His grandfather came over to him and tapped at the bony plates. "Did you do this to him?" his grandfather asked.

"Of course not, I told you his Ontarian physiology is asserting itself, everything you have tried to hide about him will once again manifest," the Admiral explained.

"Like what?" Ryan asked.

"The plates will become more pronounced and tougher; your speed may increase and I expect that a frontal plate will emerge."

"A frontal plate, what's that?"

The Admiral merely tapped the area of her chest where her heart would be.

"Oh, come off it," Ryan sneered.

"We won't be able to hide that," the Admiral said then she sipped her tea in an infuriatingly calm manner.

"She's right Ryan, we can't hide these plates for the rest of your life," his grandmother said.

"We won't have to, these aliens can take them off and make sure they don't grow back," Ryan said.

"Just because Ontarians are more advanced than humans it doesn't mean that we can perform those kinds of miracles. Your mother was able to remove them when you were young, because they had just started growing. We cannot just separate half of what you are from the other half at your age, you have to come with me."

"I don't want to!" Ryan shouted then he stormed off up to his room.

He practically ripped his blazer from his body and threw it at his desk chair. Then Ryan dropped his bag hard on the floor and stomped around the room as he removed his shoes and tie. He paused as he started on the buttons of his shirt, he undid a few then did them up. He then huffed and finally removed the whole thing, letting himself see in the mirror his new features. The new bones were not exactly conspicuous.

Ryan's skin tingled, he did not like the touch of this bone. He then went to his mirror and turned around, the back plate went all the way down to his waist.

A shrill ringing then echoed around the house and Ryan twisted to face the door of his room. Ryan heard it ring twice before someone downstairs picked it up. He went and looked down the staircase and saw his grandmother talking into the receiver; she then covered the mouthpiece and whispered into the kitchen. "It's his form tutor," he heard her say.

"Err yes Mr Harwood, Ryan's here at home…Oh no he's perfectly fine he wasn't feeling well and decided to come home."

Ryan did not like what he overheard, not just the fact that she was lying, but that already there were going to be questions, and people might never stop asking them.

"Yes I know, we already had words, he should have informed you, however he thought it was serious. Yesterday at the Rugby Game I think you know, he had a funny turn."

Great now I am a dork, Ryan thought.

"Yes, don't worry, he'll have a doctor's note to hand into you tomorrow, yes, thank you, bye," and she quickly put down the phone.

Ryan closed the door to his room. He looked at the clock on his wall and he noticed that it was ten thirty, which meant it was break time at school. A thought then struck him and he looked at his phone and sure enough right on cue it chimed, indicating an incoming text message, then another and another.

He picked up the phone and pressed a few buttons.

"Mte whre r u?" one read, it was from Barry.

"U wrn't at class! Teach was mad :)," said the next text message.

Ryan texted back to Barry that he was ill. Barry's reply came through quickly.

"We're going out ltr join us in town if yr feeling betr," his friend's final message said.

A few more came in, all the same, so Ryan turned his phone off then lay down on his bed and stared up at the ceiling. He spent the next few hours considering his options.

He brought his right arm up and held it out in front of him. The plates flipped up and down at his command, like a foot operated bin lid.

It was so...alien...to see the plates there. The strange feeling in his arm was unbearable so he grabbed one of the plates and pulled at it. Pain flared up his arm as he tried to pull them off, it was like trying to wrench a nail from a fingertip and he gave up.

He was stuck with these plates.

Ryan wondered if there was a doctor somewhere he could talk to about this, but then he realised that if he showed these to anyone he would be in the newspapers inside of an hour, and trending on Twitter in two. For the briefest of moments, he toyed with the idea that maybe he should go with the aliens then pushed it out of his mind immediately.

He did not want to go anywhere and he did not want anything to change. So he considered all his options, trying to come up with a strategy. He revaluated the whole doctor thing. There were loads of back street doctors weren't there? And they wouldn't think his condition was so bizarre? Ryan remembered those stories he had heard of, of people with weird diseases.

Yes this could be passed off, he thought. It would be embarrassing if it came out, but people wouldn't care in the long run, he would be called a freak then they would be removed, problem solved. Maybe people would be more sympathetic to him, then he would be like those amazing para

Olympians, who overcame huge odds and still became sports stars just like he intended. *Yes, everything was falling into place*, he thought.

These plates would not deviate him from the choices he had already made. After sitting for hours contemplating all the variables, Ryan was sure he was safe. He got up and took off the rest of his school uniform and put on some fresh clothes.

He was going out. He did not care about the Admiral or his grandparent's concerns. Earth was his home and he was going to stay here.

Chapter 6

Three very tall people, who wore a mismatch combination of black human clothing, stood in the grounds of the Whitby Abbey. It was dark and the moon's pale light cast ghostly shadows of the crumbling building over them.

They were unused to the clothing they wore that was not from their own home-world, nor were they used to the shapes they had assumed.

"I hate human bodies, so unsuited to our abilities," one of the men said. He was six feet tall with a fully shaven head, and bladed tattoos crawling up his neck to his chin.

"Well don't worry, we don't have to assume them for long," said the second man who was identical in appearance to the first.

"Let's get this over with," said the third man also identical to the other two.

"Yes Trettan," they both said, reverently.

"Now when our target gets here he will no doubt use his powers to escape. He is not a full-blooded Ontarian so I am not expecting too much speed. We will utilise these powers..." he said, opening his jacket to reveal three syringes, "...to insure success."

The other two men eyed the syringes with glee.

"Remember the plan. We must give chase, make a scene, and herd the boy right where we want him."

"No problem," the two men said.

"These...disguises will wear off soon," Trettan said.

"Shame we didn't keep the source alive," one of the other men said.

"He struggled too much Tredici," Trettan replied looking over his shoulder.

A man who had a fully shaven head and tattoos on his neck lay in the grass, his eyes looked up at them, but they were vacant and empty.

"Humans break so easily."

"That they do Trinact," Trettan commented, he then removed from his jacket the three syringes and held them out for the others to take.

"What are they? Which tribes made the…" Trinact said, and then smiled "donation?"

Trettan's eyes glowed yellow. "The first, fourth and eleventh donated these powers."

"Frayan, Stimuli and Motus," Trinact said.

"I'll be taking the Stimuli vial." Trettan said.

"I'll take Motus," Trinact said.

"Leaving me with Frayan," Tredici commented.

All three of them looked at the syringes they received, which contained a small amount of blood that toiled and shifted of its own accord in the glass vials.

They all rolled up the sleeves of their jackets to reveal the crook in their arms. They then injected the blood into the most prominent vein they could find.

The blood had a profound effect on all three of them. Tredici's muscles bulged considerably. Trinact's posture slumped and his expression was as vacant as the man lying nearby.

As the last drop of blood entered his veins Trettan stared off into space. Small nuggets of bone then shot out of his head connected by cartilage. It was like he was growing bony dreadlocks. His pupils dilated to twice their size and he stood much taller than he had before. A long tongue snaked its way out of his mouth and tasted the air.

Trettan breathed in deeply through his two nostrils, plus two more that appeared beneath his eyes like slits in his cheeks.

"Humans," he said turning to his right, towards a white hut on the edge of the abbey grounds. Three humans were exiting the hut and walking across the grounds of the abbey. They all wore dark green jackets with a badge of the abbey sowed into them. They held flashlights and were calling out to Trettan and his companions.

"Hey you can't be here," they shouted. "Abbey grounds are closed to tourists in the evening."

Trinact gestured with his hand and some of the stones lying around in the long grass that had once made up the walls of the abbey, rose off the ground. Dirt and moss fell from them as they hovered above the holes they had left in the soil.

"What the?" the lead human said.

The stones then flew at them striking one of them in the head and knocked him to the floor as the others ducked. A giant piece of rock, once a foundation stone of the medieval building shot in the air then came down on the fallen man and crushed him.

Tredici was then suddenly amongst the other two humans and he grabbed one by the clothes he wore then tossed him into the sky.

The man screamed as he flew upwards and then when gravity resumed its hold on him the man landed on his back with a sickening crunch. He lay spread-eagle on the walls of the abbey.

The third human ran for his life amongst the ruins of the abbey.

Trettan followed him, bounding over the walls and stones with perfect balance. The man tried to hide in the maze of the ruins, but Trettan went straight to him without missing a step.

"You can't hide from me Human," he said.

The man screamed in terror as Trettan fell upon him.

When the man was dead the three of them re-grouped.

"It's good to feel this kind of power again," Trinact said.

"Now to the centre of the town, that's where the boy will be," Trettan ordered. Tredici and Trinact nodded and set off.

Trettan paused and fished out a locket from his pocket. The gold chain that once held it around his neck had snapped, leaving a few links attached to the top. He opened it and looked inside, smiling at the face he saw within. His eyes glanced at the town beyond, he looked into the sky and using his senses he searched for Ontarian ships.

He sniffed the air and only smelt humans and one Ontarian.

"Soon," he said to the locket.

He tucked it away and then set off after his fellow Tredicim.

Chapter 7

Ryan had forgotten all about the Admiral, his arm plates and his health. Right now, he was having fun with his friends.

"I can't believe you pulled a sicky," Barry said to him.

"And in front of the deputy head," Bill added.

Ryan shrugged, "I just thought I deserved a break."

"No doubt," his friends agreed.

Ryan and his friends were standing around outside the Whitby Library and he was still enjoying the glory of his rugby win the other day, and also his daring truancy from school.

"You should have said you planning on getting out of school," Bill said.

"It was flash of inspiration, when I realised I could milk the hospital trip for all its worth," Ryan said, hoping he could cover his tracks about what really happened.

They seemed satisfied with his comment and conversation returned to more normal topics such as the games, music and school gossip.

He had met them here at the library, a surprisingly common place for teenagers in the town to gather. His friends always seemed to congregate at the library despite their virtual non-interest in books. But it was just about the only place in town they felt they could go and sit down out of the cold. There was no youth club open for them during the week and they had nothing else to do.

Unfortunately, they had made so much noise inside the librarian had shooed them out. So they stood around outside just beyond the front door right on the fringe of the library, out of the staff's jurisdiction making as much noise as they had inside.

A group of girls from his high school stood nearby leaning on the rails that lined the road.

A few of them were smiling at Ryan and inching closer to him as the conversations drew the two groups together.

Ryan was enjoying the attention.

"Can you please leave the library?" he heard someone say.

Ryan turned to see a librarian standing in the doorway waving his hands as if to shoo them along.

"We're not in the library," Ryan replied, and there were sniggers amongst the group.

The Librarian opened his mouth to reply, then realised that he was not going to be able to convince them all to leave so he turned around and went back to the main desk and picked up the phone.

"He's calling the police, I bet you," Ryan said.

"Do we leave?" Barry asked.

"Nah, let's wait until the community support police get here, that's who they will send," Ryan said.

"Not even a real policeman, why should we listen to them?" Barry said. He then looked over Ryan's shoulder and a broad smile spread across his face.

He then leaned in close to Ryan and whispered, "Tanya Fields is checking you out," he said.

Ryan looked over his shoulder and caught Tanya tearing her gaze away from him.

His face flushed with excitement and he smiled. Tanya was the girl all the guys at school wanted to be with. She was funny, popular and above all stunningly beautiful. He went pale though and looked away from her when he remembered that he had bony plates hidden under his jacket sleeves. If they fooled around, she would discover them.

Involuntarily his eyes drifted to his arms, feeling paranoid that someone might see them. He convinced himself that no one knew they were there, but they were, like a deep dark secret.

How could he possibly go out with a girl and keep them hidden?

On the other hand, it was Tanya Fields and Ryan did not feel like passing that opportunity up.

He turned around to face Tanya and the group of friends surrounding her. Her girlfriends immediately starting whispering to her when they saw Ryan focus his attention on Tanya, there were a few giggles and she waved them away.

Ryan was about to walk over and start chatting to her when he noticed three men standing across the road looking straight at him.

They were three of the strangest looking men he had ever seen.

Out of the corner of his eye he saw Tanya, who had turned to greet him, scowl as suddenly he appeared to forgot all about her.

Ryan assumed the men were triplets since they were almost identical in appearance except for some very weird characteristics.

One was clearly overdosing on steroids as muscles rippled under his clothes. The second was obviously unwell, perhaps a druggie, as his arms drooped down by his sides and he held himself as if he was about to collapse. The third was the weirdest of all. At first Ryan thought he had dreadlocks, but then he realised that they were pure white dreadlocks and made of what appeared to be bone.

Ryan turned back to Tanya, giving her his full attention and she shot him one of her dazzling smiles as a reward. But he could not help himself, despite that beautiful face, and looked back at the men who had moved across the road in the blink of an eye. They were now standing on the pavement just behind Tanya and her friends.

That was fast, he thought to himself, *how did they...*? He began to ask himself, then the answer was in his mind before the question had fully crystallized in his head.

Ontarians? They're super-fast just like me. Why are they here? Ryan asked himself, *are they going to force me to go with them*?

Then all three of them came for him pushing his group of friends to one side and making their way up the steps.

"Hey what do you think you're doing?" one of the girls cried out.

The men ignored them.

Fat chance I am not going with them, Ryan thought and he immediately leapt over a nearby railing.

He heard the screams and shouts of his friends then the rapid footsteps of all three men.

They were chasing him.

Ryan gathered his speed and started running.

Chapter 8

Ryan turned right and sped down Windsor Terrace.

The cold evening air whipped at his face as he accelerated to top speed.

He had to dodge to the left as an old lady ambled down the street towards him. He spun around and ran backwards to see the three men close behind, so he turned around and continued running.

As Ryan sprinted away he thought about his pursuers. He did not expect much speed from the one who look dead tired or the brawny one on account of his weight. The one sporting dreadlocks looked to be the fastest and so Ryan would match himself against him.

Houses and cars and people passed him by at blurring speeds.

The only things that caught his attention were the shocked faces of the people he left in his wake.

His phone started vibrating in his pocket.

Ryan, who long ago learnt how to run and text, took out his phone and saw a message from Barry.

"Where r u going, who r those guys?" his text said.

Ryan pocketed his phone, no time for that now, but he still wondered how he was going to explain what was happening to his friends.

The pavement was not affording him a lot of room to manoeuvre so he cut between two parked cars and into the road. He looked over his shoulders and saw the tired one leading the trio, and just reaching the same cars he had passed through.

The man raised his left hand as he ran.

In response the two cars lifted off the ground and flew into the air.

Ryan couldn't believe what he was seeing as one of the cars fell over the wall bordering the road and down onto the railway line, while the other careered into the other parked cars. Glass smashed and metal scrapped on metal as the cars tumbled over and over, tossed like salad without the man even touching it.

Ryan doubled his speed and came towards a bend in the road.

A car swerved right into Ryan's path and beeped its horn. Ryan dumped all his speed into a jump and leapt up onto the roof of the car in his way. After sliding down the rear window, he kept running and snuck a glance into the wing mirror of a parked car as he passed by. He spotted the heavily muscled man that was chasing him, bring his hand down on the bonnet of the car Ryan had just leapt over.

His fist caved in the bonnet of the vehicle and shattered the suspension. For a second its momentum lifted it into the air and its back tyres rose of the ground. It teetered for a second before gravity pulled it back down.

The man then shoved the car aside as a rugby player shoves aside an opponent and continued after Ryan. His companions followed in his wake.

The car's horn continually sounded, people all around were screaming in terror, tyres squealed as other cars came to a stop.

Ryan was heading up the road away from them, but a car came out of nowhere smashing down in his path. Ryan skidded to a halt and had to turn left down another road. He clipped a car on his way and winced grabbing his shoulder as he ran.

He ran down a grass verge running parallel to the road and towards the railway line.

Using his speed, he knocked down two temporary fences that bordered a construction site next to the line. Then he clambered over a wall lining the and leapt off the top landing in the middle of the railway tracks.

The line was still, there were no trains.

Then he jumped to try to clear the security fence on the other side of the track. On the other side he rolled roughly across an uneven patch of pavement bordering a car park.

A sharp pain shot up his leg as he grazed it on rough stone. He had no time to worry about it and headed straight for the rows of parked cars.

He crouched low and hid among them, running as fast as he could to put distance between him and his chasers.

Eventually Ryan found a large four by four to duck behind. He risked a glance around its front end. The muscle man shattered the brick wall next to the line then tore down the metal security fence as easily as he might tear paper. The other men followed in his wake.

They strolled from the ruined security gate down to the car park.

Through the windows of the cars Ryan saw them look around, they had no idea where he was.

The man sporting dreadlocks led the trio into the car park. Ryan froze in surprise as the bony dreadlocks suddenly locked together forming giant ears behind the man's normal ones.

He tried to remain still without making any noise. This man had suddenly developed radar dishes on his head.

Ryan's phone then vibrated again in his pocket.

He flinched expecting to hear it ring and give away his position, and then he sighed as it only vibrated.

But its slight trembling was enough.

The man turned all his attention towards Ryan, his glowing eyes focusing right on him

The tired looking man gestured with his hand and several cars between the trio and Ryan rose into air to float above him.

Ryan backed off as the four by four he stood next to lifted off the ground. He spluttered in shock as he watched the cars hang in the air by invisible strings.

This is unreal, he thought.

The raised cars had created a straight path towards him that the men immediately exploited.

They rushed towards him underneath the flying cars and as soon as the men passed under them, they dropped to the ground, which blew out tyres and smashed windows.

Ryan pulled himself together and headed through the car park. He crossed over the road on into the grounds of the harbour.

The river blocked his way so he headed left back towards the road.

In his dismay, he saw that it was not going to be that easy.

The Endeavour, an old sail ship that floated in the harbour as a tribute to Captain Cook, was in his way as was twenty metres of harbour.

He had no choice he was going have to hope a super speed jump from the ship would help him clear it.

Ryan leapt from the dock and hit the deck of the old boat then focused on the other side.

But he bottled it, slowed down and hit the rail of the ship.

It was too far he would never make it.

He heard three impacts behind him on the deck.

Ryan spun around, the three men took up separate positions on the vessel, covering him from multiple angles.

"I'm not going with you." Ryan said knowing it was going to be his last act of defiance.

They said nothing.

"Why are you chasing me?" Ryan asked.

"Revenge," one said.

"HEY YOU GET OFF THAT BOAT," someone shouted.

Ryan and the three men turned their attention to the speaker. It was a policeman, standing on the harbour wall pointing a flashlight onto the ship, illuminating each one of them in turn.

"Human Authority," one of the three men hissed.

Ryan took his chance while they were distracted.

He sprinted for the bow, ran along the mast extending over the figurehead of the ship, and jumped the five or so metres from the bow of the ship to the harbour.

He then sped away back into town passing surprised members of the public.

•

Trettan watched the boy escape and smiled. He then turned his attention to the uniformed human who was standing there, his mouth open like an idiot.

The human then composed himself and concentrated his attention on Trettan and his men.

"YOU THREE STAY THERE," The human shouted.

"Our mission is over, Trinact get us out of here," Trettan ordered.

Trinact stepped forward to the centre of the ship and raised his hands in the air.

The ship they stood on, no more than an old wooden wreak in Trettan's opinion, bobbed in the water. The wooden deck plates vibrated and the sails above them billowed as Trinact's borrowed powers took control of the human vessel.

It started to turn in the water. The ship pulled away from the harbour under Trinact's guidance.

The uniformed human's jaw dropped again.

Ropes tying the vessel down snapped as the ship heaved against them.

"Take us down river, we'll ditch this ship on the beach and make our way in land from there." Trettan ordered.

"Yes sir," Trinact said.

The Endeavour groaned as the ship turned in the water and headed down river towards the coast.

"THEY'RE STEALING THE ENDEAVOUR!" The human cried out.

Trettan chuckled in delight; the weak humans were in disarray. "If we've done our job right, our brothers will soon be free." Trettan said.

"Trettan, we were able to keep up with the boy?" Tredici commented.

"I know," Trettan responded.

"How is that possible?" Tredici asked. "We already had the blood of another tribe."

"The boy is an aberration, who knows what the combination of human genes and our own create," Trettan said. "We will explore this development; it might be useful in the Tredicim's future."

"For the freedom of the Tredicim," the other two chanted together.

"For the freedom of the Tredicim." Trettan echoed.

•

Ryan found his way back to the main high street in town, he quickly darted down an alleyway and hid in the shadows.

Those three had to be from that planet Ontaria the Admiral had talked about. Ryan had seen videos about that on *TikTok*, how children were taken, he had seen it in films. Were they trying to do the same to him, force him to Ontaria, by just abducting him like aliens do?

He also did not understand how they managed to do the things they did, he thought they would be fast, not super strong, telekinetic and be able to track him wherever he went.

The laughter and voices of a crowd walking down the main street caught his attention. It was his friends; they had moved on from the library.

He came out of the alley ready to re-join them, wondering how he should explain what just happened, without telling them the truth.

By why not tell them, he thought, *maybe they would think it was cool. That I was even cooler for being and alien for being special.*

He stood up straight, dusted himself down then exited the alley way just behind the group, "Hey guys."

Everyone turned at the sound of his voice and he smiled. Their mouths fell open at his dramatic entrance and his mates offered up fist bumps and high fives. "You out run those losers," Barry said.

"What did they want?" Bill asked.

"I have no idea, maybe they thought I was someone else?" Ryan replied. "Hey guys can I show you something?" he said and paused while simultaneously holding his breath.

He mates looked around at each other, they both shrugged.

"Sure, mate go ahead."

Ryan swallowed then grabbed the sleeve of his jacket and starting rolling it up. His friends smiled at each other as if wondering what kind of gag this was, or what was the stunt he was about to pull.

Ryan reached the plates on his right arm.

Barry leant forward.

"What the hell is that?" Bill asked.

Ryan suddenly realised that he did not want to reveal the whole story so he plumped for half the truth.

"I don't know exactly, however they grew on my skin yesterday," Ryan exclaimed.

Barry reached out and touched the nearest plate.

"Why are you wearing armour?" Bill asked.

"It's not armour look at it," Ryan said. He then made the plates flex up and down. They backed away.

"What is this some sort of joke?" Bill asked. "Cause I don't get it," he added.

"Look guys this is me, really me, I'm just different, you know."

"It's a bit freaky."

"It is isn't it, I have these on my back too," Ryan added.

"This is a weird gag to pull Ryan," Bill said.

"Yeah give it up," Barry said and he grabbed the plate Ryan was showing him and pulled at it.

Ryan screamed and he backed away. Tears filled his eyes, it was such a sharp pain that it had really shocked his entire system.

Blood squirted out around where the plate touched the skin of his arm. Barry released the plate and took his had away as if trying to avoid a mousetrap shutting on his fingers, he then looked at the Ryan's blood covering his fingers. "Fake blood?" Barry said, Bill shrugged.

"Well, I'm not wiping it on my clothes," and he lent forward and wiped it on Ryan's jacket.

Ryan slapped his hand away.

"That hurt," he shouted back at his friend.

His friend's gaze looked at his arm again, blood was running through Ryan's fingers where he held the plates.

"Wait that's really real," Bill said.

Ryan managed to stifle the pain enough to look into his friend's eyes. There shock there, fear. He had expected that, they had never seen anything like this before after all. But he saw something else too, Bill's lip turned up like he had smelled something awful or disgusting. They were not taking this revelation well.

"Get out of here man," Barry said.

"What?" Ryan cried out.

"Get out here we don't want anything to do with that," Bill added.

"Guys I need your help," Ryan replied.

"With what? Look Ryan, get rid of those things man, people don't want to deal with stuff like that. You've got a disease of something. Stay away from us because we don't want it either," Barry said, gesturing for Ryan to leave.

Bill actually checked his arms to make sue he wasn't growing anything on his fresh. He then shivered, "Yeah I don't want growths on my arms."

"Guys these aren't growths, I'm part alien. This is how I look."

He expected them to think that was cool, to be shocked, but crack a funny joke about it like in the movies. Instead, they look at him like he was crazy.

Ryan was struck with a sudden and horrifying epiphany. This reaction was not unique to them. Others from school would be freaked out too, it would make him an outcast and as an outcast he'll have no friends, no one to stand by his side or defend him.

What if he changed in a dressing room before rugby and everyone else saw his plates? What if he was in the news or on some reality TV show about weird growths on the human body? He wouldn't be a celebrity, just a curiosity.

How can this be happening? He thought and looked down at his bloodied hand. Then he thought of the Admiral, those would be abductors.

This was their fault! He started running again, not caring who saw. He just wanted to get home.

Chapter 9

Ryan rushed home without even looking behind him even once.

The house lights came into view as he shot across the moors and in a few minutes he was at the front door. He got out his keys and fumbled with them in the lock.

His attention was distracted for a moment, as he was certain he could hear a faint humming noise all around him, just like yesterday.

He ignored it and opened the front door. He heard his grandparents talking in their kitchen along with the Admiral.

"Aren't you going to speak to him?" he heard the Admiral say.

"Why don't you, after all…" his grandmother prompted.

"I do not have to involve myself in these petty family affairs," the Admiral replied.

"You don't have to," Ryan said.

He stood in the doorway to the kitchen, his face was bright red and he was sweating profusely.

He held his palm up for everyone to see, the blood had dried, but the wound was still fresh. "I was just attacked in Whitby by members or your species," Ryan said pointing at the Admiral. "They tried to kill me," Ryan said.

The Admiral eyes went wide and her hair suddenly went very still, she stood up sending her chair flying backwards, "What did they look like?" she asked.

Ryan thought that was an odd question, *did the Admiral not know they were after him*? He studied the old woman's reaction, it had been so immediate and sudden, *maybe she didn't know*. "They all looked the same, like triplets except one had muscles as big as blown-up balloons and another one had bony dreadlocks," Ryan answered.

"The Tredicim," the Admiral said, she then reached into a pocket in her clothing and pulled out a device and spoke into it. "Get some security down here now and surround the house," she ordered.

"What are you...?" Ryan asked, but three loud bangs outside interrupted him.

"What was that?" Ryan said.

"Drop-Pods," the Admiral said pocketing the device.

"Why would they be interested in him?" Ryan's grandfather said frowning, then suddenly his eyes widened when he thought more about his own question. "Wait I know why, this is his mother all over again, you have to take him to Ontaria."

"What?" Ryan said.

"You have to go with the Admiral now Ryan, you're in danger," his grandmother said.

"In danger? From who?"

"They are called the Tredicim, they're Ontarian Terrorists," his grandfather said.

"Your grandparents are right, it's time to go and for you to stop your childish opposition to this fact," the Admiral said.

"What are they after me, one of them mentioned revenge, revenge for what?" Ryan asked.

"Probably against your father," the Admiral said.

"What did he do them?" Ryan asked.

"We can explain later, you need to come to Ontaria now, we can't look after you on planet Earth, we have better security on our homeworld where we can move and act freely," the Admiral replied.

Ryan would normally have objected there and then, but the chase in Whitby and the Admiral's words questioned his desire to stay on Earth. For the first time it occurred to him that he was breathing very heavily and aching all over. It was becoming a recurring problem. He was definitely getting sicker and sicker as his body started to change.

"What will my life be like on this planet of yours?" he asked.

The Admiral drank the last of her tea in one big gulp, then looked down into the cup for a moment. Then she turned to Ryan. "You will live with your extended family. Our society is very different to yours, much more ordered for example. There are no countries, only one government, no schools and one, well, what you would call a religion. We still have fun, we are not unemotional, there is unfortunately no television, which I believe humans watch intensively. In short it is like nothing you have ever seen. The planet is also very different than Earth, wilder, stranger animals."

"Where is it?" Ryan asked.

"Ontaria orbits the same star as Earth, on the same orbital plane only on the opposite side of the sun."

"What, how come I haven't heard of it before, why isn't there a planet named Zeus or Hera or whatever on a picture of the solar system?"

"Ontarians discovered space travel many years before humans, we've managed to keep our planet hidden from your scientists for years," the Admiral explained.

"How…?" Ryan began.

"We'll cover this later," the Admiral said, pinching the bridge of her nose. "I know enough about humans to know that change is only difficult because you hold onto the past, and forget that you can adapt easily. You can live amongst our people Ryan as long as you are willing to make changes."

Ryan looked at his Grandparents. His grandmother spoke up first. "Your mother would tell us constantly about Ontaria, your father told her about it. It's not a horrible place; she always wanted to go there. Ryan you cannot stay here not any more, like it or not you have to go."

"You can't resist this change, you need to come with me, your life is in danger," the Admiral said. "When you have a choice like this there is one option."

"Maybe to an alien," Ryan shot back, "I like it here, and I don't mind the hard work it will take to stay," he added.

"You are an alien on this world, more so than me Ryan," the Admiral said, "A child of two races."

"You must be able to stop this?" Ryan said rolling up his sleeves and indicating his freshly grown bony plates.

"It's genetics boy you can't just reverse it, it's part of your very being," the Admiral replied.

"I don't want it, I liked things the way they were before," Ryan cried out.

"Things change," the Admiral said.

Ryan scowled at the Admiral, it was such an obvious comment to make and an insult to his intelligence, of course things change, but they did not change like this, not in the real world.

"You will come with me," the Admiral said, "We will not allow you to die."

"It doesn't sound as if you care that much," Ryan shot back.

"You are a very unique person; the first of your kind, your presence on my homeworld will be problematic, but necessary. You must make the decision quickly; even now the very air you breathe becomes toxic to you."

Ryan could feel his own resistance falling away. He had noticed other problems lately, the back of his throat felt rough as if he had been shouting all day, there was also a tiredness in his limbs as if his body was unable to maintain its energy levels.

He remembered his moment in the changing room, when he had almost died from a lack of breathable air. He knew his body was rejecting the very planet he lived on. He did not know what it was like to die, but he was sure it felt like what he went through in that changing room.

"Fine I'll go," he muttered.

"Go pack your things," the Admiral said, "you won't need much. We have to go now, especially with the Tredicim out there," the Admiral said.

Ryan turned to his grandparents for some back up, but he saw no help there.

He went to his bedroom and quickly packed everything he would need into two suitcases. It was mostly all clothes, so much that made up his life would not be going with him. Texts books from school, photos, birthday presents, music, books, the sort of things that clutter a teenager's bedroom.

He also changed into a new, fresh pair of jeans and t-shirt, he then put on a warm jacket.

He was definitely taking a rugby ball mostly for his own entertainment, also magazines, his tablet and mobile phone. He had no idea what he needed for this trip to a new world or what to expect from his new life. He still could not believe it was happening, maybe he was dreaming?

He closed his eyes, "Wake up, wake up," he said to himself.

Nothing happened.

Giving up, Ryan lugged the suitcases downstairs thirty minutes later. Right now, he was trying to think about all the good things he would experience, to build himself up for the journey. For one thing all his homework would not matter anymore, the world's problems did not matter, and there were many things he did not have to worry about now.

At the bottom of the stairs were his grandparents, waiting for him, smiling, but they were forced smiles. "Put this in your rucksack," his grandmother said handing him a sealed envelope.

He took it and looked at the back, there was no name written on it. "Who's it for?" he asked.

"Your father," his grandmother said.

"My-my Father?" Ryan said.

"He's on Ontaria, you'll see him when you get there," she said.

"I will?" Ryan said. He had not been expecting news like that.

"He was not allowed to maintain direct contact with you," the Admiral said.

"Why?" Ryan said.

"You'll understand when we reach Ontaria," the Admiral replied.

Ryan shook his head, "Ok then," he replied still in a state of shock he was actually going to meet his father, his real father.

He looked at his grandparents, "Well I'm guess I'm really going."

"You'll fit in son, everyone likes you on this planet, it would be impossible for these aliens not to like you too," his grandfather said.

"Thank you," Ryan said.

Suddenly the enormity of the situation struck him, he was about to leave his friends, his family, York, England and Earth behind, "I am going to see you again, aren't I?" he asked.

"Of course, your father, with medical assistance, could survive on this planet for short term periods, I don't see why visits are out of order," his grandmother said, flashing an angry expression at the Admiral.

Ryan turned to the Admiral for confirmation of that, she nodded. "Yes once the changes to your body have locked in you will be able to make quick visits to Earth." She then left the house.

His grandmother kissed him and his grandfather hugged him.

"You need to go," they both said.

Ryan forced his own smile, unlocked the front door stepping out onto the driveway, which was illuminated by the security light. He carried one suitcase in his hands out the door and his grandfather dragged the other.

Ryan winced when he stepped out of the house and held a free hand to his ear as a humming sound assaulted his senses.

"What is that noise?" he groaned.

The Admiral was not alone on the driveway. Standing next to her was someone he had not met before. The guy was huge and all muscle. A helmet covered his face and his clothing was like a suit of armour, padded with metal slabs.

"You are ready?" the Admiral asked.

"Yes," Ryan replied.

The huge man stepped forwards and took the suitcase Ryan was holding, which he lifted with just one hand. Ryan noticed that this man didn't have any bony plates on his arms and legs, *did that mean he's an Ontarian or not*? Ryan thought, *does that mean there are there more alien races out there.*

These thoughts continued to run through his mind as the big man took the other suit case from his grandfather in the same hand as the other. Ryan decided now was not the best time to ask questions about this display of strength.

"Let's depart," the Admiral said.

"Just how are we going to get there anyway?" Ryan asked, there was not any other form of transport around other than the car, and he was not expecting them to be driving to this new planet.

The Admiral just looked straight up into the sky.

Confused, Ryan looked up as well.

His eyes went wider than saucers.

At least he now knew the source of the humming.

Hanging above him floating in the sky was a huge object with sets of lights along its sides. It must have been longer than three rugby fields.

He knew what it was straight away.

The only way to get to another planet…a space ship.

Chapter 10

The ship had the shape of a bird of prey. Its nose pointed downwards like an eagle's beak. Its wide wings swept upwards and pointed forwards rather than back like a plane's. Its rear section was a nest of engines that jutted out of the ship like a tail. On its underside were three blisters surrounded by four pods each. The hull of the ship was a series of panels that flexed like feathers.

Ryan could not understand how it stayed in the air, there did not seem to be any rockets or engines that kept it hovering a hundred or so meters above the house.

"Duodecim, please send down another drop pod for pick up," the Admiral said into her communication device.

One of the pods surrounding one of the three blisters detached from the underside of the ship and plummeted down towards Earth.

Ryan instinctively backed away as the pod head ed for the house.

"It's going to crash," Ryan cried out. He looked around at everyone close to him, who were not worried in the slightest, even his grandparents waited patiently for the craft to land.

Ryan looked back at the pod, which was seconds away from bursting through the roof of his grandparent's home. He looked away, he could not bear to watch.

However, there was no crash, no earth-shattering impact.

Ryan opened his eyes, the pod hovered over the house. It then floated over the drive and set itself down on the road with a thud.

The pod sat silently for a moment then with a hiss it cracked open and one side dropped to the ground creating a ramp that led up into its core.

"On board," the Admiral ordered and she stepped onto the ramp followed by the giant armoured man carrying the suitcases.

"Is that how we are going to get onto that thing?" Ryan exclaimed pointing at the pod then the space ship hanging above their heads.

"Yes," the Admiral said irritably.

"What, no teleporters?" Ryan asked expecting something extremely high tech.

The Admiral rolled her eyes, "Such technology does not exist. This is the safest way to travel from surface to ship," she added, and then continued on into the pod followed by her companion.

Ryan breathed in deeply, this was it, he was going to go with this Admiral to another planet on board a giant space ship. There was no way he could stay, too many changes were happening to his body. A part of him wished his friends were here to see him off. Then he remembered their reaction to his plates. No, they wouldn't be here wishing him well and happy they knew an alien. They had already rejected him.

He turned and looked at his grandparents. They came over to him and hugged him. His grandmother sniffed and his grandfather wiped away a tear.

"You'll be fine Ryan," his grandfather said.

"Look after yourself," his grandmother added.

They separated and Ryan nodded and smiled at them, "I will," he replied.

He looked into their eyes and saw that they had been prepared for this moment for a long time.

Ryan however, was not prepared. There were a million different things that he was worried about. His only choice right now though, for the dignity of the human race, was to suck it up and deal with it. For the time being he was going to pretend that he was going on holiday. He figured that if he did not like this planet then he could come back...somehow.

"Good bye," he managed to say.

"We'll see you again, don't worry," his grandmother said.

"Definitely," Ryan said.

"Ryan," the Admiral called out.

"You have to go," his grandfather insisted.

Ryan took one look at the house; he could not force the smile anymore and a tear welled up in his eye. He turned away from his grandparents and headed for the pod.

The tall muscular Ontarian, Ryan guessed that what he should start calling them now, stood with his suitcases by his side with the Admiral. As soon as Ryan stepped into the vehicle, the ramp started to lift up off the ground and seal the pod.

Ryan turned around quickly, his rucksack swinging about inside the pod barely missing the Admiral. He starred at his grandparents who were slowly disappearing as the ramp started to block his view. His grandfather waved as did his grandmother, standing on tiptoes to keep him in sight, her eyes filling with tears.

He waved back until they were completely out of view and the pod's ramp snapped shut sealing him inside.

Ryan let out a long breath, staring at the ground, feeling trapped. He noticed the giant and the Admiral looking at him, so he stood up straight and cleared his throat. "Let's go already."

The Admiral snorted.

He examined the inside of the pod that it was very spacious, however it also seemed to be devoid of any controls, or anywhere to sit. He saw a few buttons fixed next to a speaker and something that looked like headphones. However, there was no steering wheel or anything that could drive the pod through the air. Up against the far wall of the pod was a ladder, leading up to the top of the craft. Two lights lit the inside in dim white light.

The Admiral plucked the head phones from the wall of the pod and put them over her ears then pressed a button on the wall and held it down.

"Recall Pod," she said into the speaker.

Ryan suddenly heard a loud blast of static. It was coming from the headphones the Admiral wore. The sound was unbearable for him to hear, but the Admiral didn't seem to mind, in fact it looked like the Admiral was listening to the static and deriving a meaning from it, since she stared forward deep in concentration and was tapping the buttons next to the speaker.

The floor started to vibrate, and Ryan's legs felt they were rising up into his body. He felt heavy and the force of the pod rising into the air almost made him go down onto his knees. It felt like he was riding in a very powerful lift.

For about half a minute, Ryan had trouble standing while the big Ontarian next to him stood as still as statue. His eye less helmet looked forward without displaying any emotion, while the Admiral ignored them both and kept concentrating.

The crushing force of the rising pod finally abated and the pod shuddered and came to a complete stop.

Ryan was waiting for the ramp to drop down again, but instead a new light source from above flooded the inside of the pod. Ryan looked up and saw that the roof had split and opened up like a flower head.

Looking down at them was another huge man wearing the same kind of armour as the one who had carried Ryan's suitcases. The suitcases were passed with ease between the two giants and then the Admiral scaled the ladder and out the top of the pod followed by her companion and Ryan assumed he had to follow and climbed the ladder.

To him that trip seemed rather low tech for a space ship.

He climbed up into a high and wide corridor comfortably accommodating the two huge Ontarians. Along the corridor more giants were climbing out of the other drop pods that had been on the surface. Each giant then sealed the roof of the pods by a hatch on the floor.

Ryan breathed deeply and felt some energy return to him. It tasted very sterile, yet full of vitality. The temperature of the space felt wonderful ,like he didn't know where his skin ended and the air began.

"Admiral?" the giant who had received them said.

"To the bridge," the she ordered.

The Admiral and Ontarian giants strode off down the corridor, Ryan, not knowing what to do, followed them. The Aliens seemed to be ignoring him, if not they had simply forgotten that he was still there.

He followed them left, right, up and down corridors that looked unfinished, since the machinery and wires were exposed on the walls. Some sort of fibre optic wires ran though the bulkheads, which pulsed with light in a variety of different colours. Ryan was about to ask a question about them then they left the maze of corridors and stepped into a very large room.

The room was circular and had two levels. The first level was crescent shaped and the second level was beneath it. Fixed into the farthest wall was a giant view screen. Ryan could see that the ship was still hovering over the Yorkshire moors and on the horizon was York itself lit up like a Christmas tree.

He thought of his grandparents directly beneath him, watching, waiting for the ship with their grandson on board to depart.

Then he smiled a massive broad smile. Despite the enormity of what was happening to him, realised something…he was on a space ship, with aliens. He thought this was amazing and unreal. No other human had experienced this.

The Admiral strode across the room and took her place in a chair in the centre of the first level and strapped herself in.

The two giant Ontarians flanked the entrance to the room standing resolutely still like Buckingham Palace guards, holding his suitcases.

Ryan saw that there were various other chairs in the room symmetrically placed next to pillars jutting out of the walls or floor. Sitting next to the pillars were other people that, Ryan was shocked to see, had wires going from the pillars and into their heads. But as strange as this was, Ryan was not actually feeling freaked out, instead he was uncomfortable.

The various other Ontarians in the room were giving him disturbing looks. Some scowled, others stared. Whispers passed through the room and some even pointed without even trying to hide the fact they were doing so. Ryan suddenly realised how out of place he was. His human clothes and bag slung over his back, made him stand out amongst the aliens with their scaly uniforms and advanced technology.

Every Ontarian sitting at a console had bony plates extending up their necks protecting the lower half of their skull just like Admiral Tarms. Then there were half a dozen, giant armoured Ontarians, all their faces hidden behind helmets, standing like sentinels around the room. To Ryan it seemed like he was seeing two different types of aliens, the thinner ones like the Admiral, and the muscle-bound ones like his suitcase carriers. *Could they all be Ontarians or are there more aliens out there*? Ryan thought to himself, *the Admiral had not mentioned other aliens, just Ontarians.*

"Ahem," the Admiral said and the crew members of the space ship turned from staring at Ryan and went back to their business. Then suddenly the Admiral started speaking in a language Ryan did not understand, but it sounded like a cat hissing and talking at the same time.

"Sharker sick sui," the Admiral said.

Through the view screen Ryan watched the city below disappear. The ship was heading upwards, climbing higher into the atmosphere. As the ship rose the sky outside turned completely black revealing the majesty of planet Earth below. It was a viewpoint only witnessed by astronauts. It was exactly like those pictures he had seen from space shuttles and satellites. The whole Earth was before him, continents and oceans, and to think he was only fifteen and seeing all of this.

It was truly an amazing sight and Ryan took it all in.

The distance between him and his home and his grandparents suddenly became apparent to him. He panicked, and was about to say 'take me back' but the view shifted again and Ryan saw the moon closer than he had ever seen it before. He swallowed as the sight calmed him down and dulled his anxiety, the entire experience was so exhilarating.

He felt himself go on tiptoes, he looked down and saw his feet float off the ground; the ship was in zero gravity. "Whoa," he said loudly as he floated in mid-air spinning around and feeling queasy. Everyone in the room turned towards him.

"You should have sat down," the Admiral said shaking her head and pointing towards a vacant seat with straps to Ryan's left.

The Ontarians sitting down were all strapped in and secured to their chairs. The giant Ontarians however were not floating, for some reason they remained stuck firm to the floor.

"Finish el brak," the Admiral ordered.

Ryan fell flat on his face as the gravity came back on.

Mocking laughter echoed around the room as the seated crew members found amusement at Ryan sprawled on the floor rolling around in pain. He picked himself up glared at any who laughed at him, it did not help. Ryan did notice that the armoured Ontarians were not laughing, instead they remained quiet and stoic.

"Ghrouhg," the Admiral said and silence suddenly reigned.

"Artificial gravity," the Admiral stated from her chair. "Three element blocks on the underside of the ship have huge masses replicating gravity," she explained.

Ryan did not understand a word of that, but just nodded as if he did, he felt that now was not the best time to appear stupid.

"Take a seat," the Admiral ordered.

Ryan sat down in the chair the Admiral had indicated earlier and strapped himself in.

"Ion engines ignite," the Admiral said as soon as Ryan had buckled himself in.

Why these aliens could not give him fair warning perplexed Ryan as suddenly the whole space ship rocketed forward like a bullet from a gun. Rapid acceleration shoved him into his seat and almost crushed his entire body. The G-force on his chest felt like his rib cage might shatter, then gradually the sensation eased as the ship stopped accelerating and Ryan could breathe normally again.

"What was that?" he asked.

The Admiral did not turn around to answer, "This ship is propelled by Ion engines. Some of your own space vessels use them, however ours are more powerful. The more energy you pump into them the faster they will go.

Our fusion reactor just released a burst of energy into them to accelerate the ship. It's a standard propulsion design fitted to all Ontarian vessels."

Ryan again pretended to understand what was going on.

"So how long is it going to take us to get to this planet of yours," he asked.

"Six standard Earth weeks."

"Six weeks," Ryan burst out. He was expecting at most a few hours.

"Can't this ship go any faster?" he asked.

"We're not just taking you to our home Ryan, we have work to do before returning to Ontaria," the Admiral replied, "Threngst, take Ryan to his quarters and set him up with the language teacher and subsequent material," the Admiral ordered. "Tell him where the Medical Bay is, Ryan you need to visit it once before we reach Ontaria."

"This way," a low but firm voice said from behind Ryan.

He un-strapped himself and looked up at one of the giant Ontarians who was carrying both his suitcases.

The big man exited the room and Ryan followed. He stopped just before the entrance to the corridor at the rear of the room when he noticed a plaque on the wall. It was gold and at the top was one word in a bold dominating font - DUODECIM. Ryan realised this was the name of the ship he was on. Underneath Duodecim was another set of words he recognised, *Tarms Anrib Intelligen*. Ryan guessed this ship belonged to the Admiral.

Ryan followed Threngst down the maze of corridors meeting other Ontarians, some like the big guy and others like the Admiral.

"So, tell me why there are two different types of Ontarians on this ship?" Ryan asked.

"You know nothing about the tribes?" Threngst said to Ryan.

"Tribes?" Ryan replied, "The Admiral never said anything to me about them."

"Your father never told you?"

"I was too young to remember him when he was around," Ryan responded.

Threngst did not say anything and then kept walking and Ryan followed.

"Hang on, what are the tribes?" Ryan asked.

"It's the basis of Ontarian society," Threngst said, "It separates out the powers of the Ontarian race."

"How?" Ryan sasked.

"The Ontarian race is separated into twelve tribes, each members of a particular tribe possesses certain powers. You I believe are a member of the Swift tribe who harness the power of Speed."

Ryan absorbed this new information, finally he had uncovered the reason for his speed, and it was a power, a superpower. "So there are others who can go as fast as I?"

"Many and any Ontarian who develops Speed is a member of the Swift tribe."

"Well, what can the other tribes do?"

Threngst who stopped and bent right down to Ryan face, "We don't do anything, they are gifts to be used wisely and appropriately," he said firmly.

"Sorry," Ryan said.

Threngst straightened up and continued walking. "My tribe is the called the Frayan tribe and we have the power of strength."

Ryan could understand this as Threngst carried his two suitcases like they were nothing.

"Which tribe and which gift does the Admiral possess?" Ryan asked.

"She is of the Intelligen tribe they have the gift of great feats of mental aptitude."

"What gifts do the other tribes have?" Ryan asked, his eyes shining with the possibility of witnessing new superpowers.

"The gifts of the Ontarians are numerous," Threngst said, "You will learn more about them later, no doubt. Now here is your quarters."

Threngst indicated a circular doorway. He brushed his palm over the door's surface and it slid open.

Ryan peered inside at a room no bigger than the bathroom in his grandparent's house. A single shelf jutted out of the wall, which must have been the bed, while the rest of the room had a simple sink and chair molded from the wall.

Threngst set his suitcases down inside.

"Much of the ship is off limits. The artificial gravity may upset your specific biology, the Swift tribe rarely travel in ships, and their unique physiology can't handle the strain of space for long. The upper levels of the ship are not fully under the sway of the artificial gravity, weightlessness can occur. You also have to learn our language," Threngst said. "Only those Ontarians assigned to Earth patrol ships learn English and other such languages of your world. Other Ontarians don't, you will need to be able to communicate with our people when you reach the homeworld."

"Earth patrol ships? You Ontarians watch over Earth?"

"Of course," Threngst replied.

"How do I learn this language?" he asked.

"The Information Library will show you how, third level, second section of the Duodecim," Threngst said.

Ryan was about to ask another question, but Threngst left, marching off down the corridor. "Thank you," he shouted out sarcastically, then stepped into his room and the door closed sealing him in. He stood alone in his room on an alien ship heading across the solar system., surprised he was not going insane. He searched through his rucksack for his *iPod* and took it out. The battery was low so he took out his adapter, but realised there was no plug socket.

"Awe man, I can't believe this," he said to himself.

He lay down on his shelf. He found that imbedded in it was a foam mattress which provided some comfort. He opened one of his suitcases and took out a towel he had packed and used it for a pillow.

Trying not to think about his grandparents and his current predicament, he placed his head phones on and let the battery drain as he listened to the music.

Chapter 11

The next day when Ryan woke up, his brain hit him with the reality that he was travelling on a space ship heading across the solar system.

He almost freaked out.

The truth hit him very hard and he only calmed down when he decided he did not want to let down the human race by acting all childish in front of these aliens.

As he lay in bed constantly checking his watch, he thought about what was going on at home right at that moment. He wondered what his grandparents were doing and how his former friends were reacting to his disappearance and absence from school.

He rummaged through his cases and changed his clothes. He had forgotten his toothbrush so he just rinsed his mouth out with water from the tap in his room.

The water tasted different, not unpleasant, but certainly not like Earth water. He wondered if he should even drink it. He often heard that drinking the water from a foreign country was a risk, this water was from an alien planet, goodness knows what's in it.

It was also the first sign that he was now living a different life. Something that was normal and everyday had changed already.

He stayed in his room for most of the day not really wanting to see the rest of the ship. He wasn't looking forward to the other changes to his life he knew would be coming his way, he felt better staying in his room, reading his magazines and books, little pieces of the home he had left behind.

They made him feel better.

Before lunch he went to the Medical Bay. It was a long room filled with beds, some fit for Frayans to rest on, they were much larger and had heavy-duty supports underneath. Inside were a number of Ontarians, mostly from the Intelligen tribe. One or two however were pretty much human-looking, except their blood vessels were dark against their skin like they had had them tattooed there. Ryan could see dark blood pulse just under the surface. Their finger nails also looked incredibly sharp.

Before he could ask about them an Intelligen stepped forward. "You're the Half Human, right?" he asked.

"Yes," Ryan replied.

The man was eying his left arm with a hungry expression.

He then shook his head and said, "Step this way, I will administer some injections that will help you acclimatize to Ontaria.

Ryan was led to a table where needles rested.

"Can't I just take pills?" Ryan asked.

"No," the Intelligen said, and after cleaning Ryan's right arm, started making the injections one after the other. There were five in all.

The man then took an empty syringe and cleaned Ryan's left arm as he rubbed his right to relieve the pain.

"What are you doing?" he asked.

"Taking blood," the man said and dug the needle in and extracted a small vial of red liquid.

"There we go, you may leave," the man said eyeing the blood sample with a curious expression on his face.

"What, no sweet?" Ryan said and chuckled.

He stopped when the man didn't join in.

"Get out, this bay is for people undergoing healing," the Intelligen replied.

Ryan left, appalled by the bedside manner.

In the afternoon he decided to go look for the Information Library Threngst had told him about, so he could learn the Ontarian language. Ryan had already learned some Spanish as required by the national curriculum at high school. He had been very good at it; hopefully it meant he might have an affinity with languages.

He wondered what learning Ontarian would involve. He knew it was an important thing to learn, so resigned himself to their education. The Admiral had said his arrival on this new planet was not going to be easy for the other Ontarians to accept, he did not want to look like an idiot by being unable to understand them.

Finding the Information Library took the better part of an hour and he saw some strange things on the way. He came across a gym where Threngst and the other members of the Frayan tribe were power lifting.

There were no weights in the gym. Instead, they lifted bars attached to the floor by huge pistons which struggled against the Frayan's strength.

When Ryan tried to enter the room the Frayan tribe members kept him out saying the gravity was ten times that on the planet Earth. If he had walked in his own hair would have become too heavy to lift.

He also came across the cafeteria and had a hard time accepting the food that was on offer. There was bread, meat and veg but none he recognized.

Ryan sat at a table on his own, using his hands to eat the food as it seemed like Ontarians did not use cutlery. He had a sudden craving for chocolate, crisps and steak, but those things were now millions of miles away.

The worse thing about the cafeteria was not the food, but the looks. He did not think he looked that different from the other Ontarians, other than being a child. However, the ship's crew members all stared at him. It made him feel like a wild animal at the zoo, like a lion. To them he was a creature you never normally see in real life, so when you get the chance to see it face to face you looked at it carefully. The Ontarians did not seem to think it was rude to stare and even when Ryan scowled back they did not turn away.

He decided that he would only go to the cafeteria when it seemed as if the rest of the crew were off performing their duties. That meant he was not there at designated meal times and so missed the best food. Living off the leftovers was better than being an object of interest.

Finally, he found the library and had actually passed it many times before, as it was not what he expected it to be, and had ignored it during his travels.

The room was small with just one Ontarian, a member of the Intelligen tribe, sitting in a comfortable chair next to a pillar with a wire leading from the pillar that plugged into his head. The walls and ceiling were toiling and shifting with some sort of moving-matter.

"Hi, is this the information library?" Ryan asked.

"Yes, why are you speaking English?" the Ontarian answered. He was thin and hunched over. Like all Ontarians, his hair moved around of its own accord.

"Why does your hair move like that?" he asked, ignoring the Ontarian's question.

The Ontarian frowned and scoffed at him. Then he leaned towards Ryan and the man's eyes darted towards his hair. "Ah, so you're the Half Ontarian," the man said.

"Half human," Ryan replied.

"Your hair doesn't move, does it? That's odd, you would think that being Half Ontarian would allow it to?"

"So why does yours?"

"Ontarian hair is a separate living organism we live in a symbiotic relationship with it."

"What does it do?" Ryan said.

"It lives as long as an Ontarian lives and provides us with an extra sense, one humans do not possess."

"What is this sense?"

"I don't have time to give you a biology lesson, what are you here for?"

"To learn your language," Ryan answered.

"Of course," the man responded.

"How do I learn? Where are the books?" Ryan replied looking around the room.

"They're all up here," the man replied tapping his head.

Ryan wondered if this man was messing him around, "I don't understand."

"Not completely surprising. The Intelligen tribe have the ability to store vast quantities of information in our superior brains. Our brains are so powerful they effectively run the ship just as your human computers do."

"No computers at all?"

"Yes, we have simple hardware and software, but our minds are far more efficient and advanced. Teaching you how our language works however won't be easy even for me, and you won't be fluent by the time we reach Ontaria. You're part human after all, it's going to take some time to teach you."

"Thanks for the encouragement," Ryan answered

•

Ryan spent the next week learning the basics of the Ontarian language and by the thirteenth day in space he had learned conversational Ontarian.

The words would form from the stuff on the walls, which was sort like programmable matter, taking on form at the Intelligen's will. Words and script would take shape for Ryan to read and absorb. The studying had been intense and Ryan, ever eager to prove himself, had learnt diligently.

He also learnt other things from the Intelligen who taught him. He freely gave away facts and Ryan had many questions.

"So, tell me about the tribes," he had asked one day.

"In Ontarian," the man ordered sitting in his chair comfortably with his fingers brought together in front of him.

It took two minutes for Ryan to string the new sentence together.

The Intelligen answered in English. "The tribes are the corner stones of Ontarian civilisation. They all intermingle on a daily basis performing the various functions of society."

"I'm more interested in the powers," Ryan asked.

"They are considered Gifts," the man responded.

"Fine, gifts," Ryan corrected himself.

"You've witnessed strength, intelligence and speed so far."

"I also saw one guy with bony dreadlocks and another who looked so tired he was probably going to collapse."

"Ah Sense and Multitasking," the Intelligen said. "Some Ontarians have the ability of heightened senses, while others what you would call telekinesis."

"Do any Ontarians have two powers?" Ryan asked.

"No, that is impossible," the man said.

"What about the government?" Ryan asked. "Law and order."

"Unlike planet Earth there are no countries and the Tribal council makes planet wide decisions for all the tribes. Specific tribes handle functions like the military, justice, economy. Other tribes look after the planet ensuring that our civilisation carefully manages our homeworld."

"Do I have to go to school?"

"School?" the man asked, "No of course not."

Score, Ryan thought.

The matter on the wall extended and changed colour to produce an image of planet Ontaria itself.

"This is your new homeworld," the man said.

"This image is coming from your head isn't it?" Ryan said.

The man nodded.

"What if you think of something else, will it appear?" Ryan asked.

"I have much better control over my thoughts than a human mind."

Ryan didn't care about geography, "Show me a Tredicim, I was attacked by one of them," Ryan said.

The man frowned at him, as if word Tredicim was a dirty word, maybe it was, and they were a terrorist group. Nobody on Earth like using the names of terrorist groups, as if in some way it validated their existence.

"Let's get back to your lessons," he said.

Ryan sighed.

There was one area of the ship Ryan visited as often as possible. On the top level of the ship gravity was so weak that Ryan could float around, there was also a large viewing window and he spent a couple of hours there before language lessons to just float in the air watching the stars.

Whatever route the Duodecim was taking to Ontaria it was going close to the sun to get there. Half way into the journey it was large in the viewing window and Ryan watched it shoot flares into space.

It was beautiful and it was a shame to watch the sun grow smaller every day.

On the last day of his trip through space he received a summons to come to the bridge of the Duodecim, the only time during the whole journey the crew of the ship had asked for him.

As soon as he reached the control centre for the entire vessel, he knew he had reached their destination.

After six weeks, Ryan was looking at a something no human had ever seen up close.

Another planet.

Chapter 12

The planet grew larger in the view screen as the Duodecim approached the bright blue orb. Ontaria was, in Ryan's opinion, very similar to Earth. It was round for one thing, had the usual blue, green and brown landscapes. It had a northern polar region and blue seas. There were some differences though. Strange colours laced the various cloud formations that wrapped around the planet. Reds, purples and greens, he could not explain what might be causing them. The planet had three moons and one of them had lights across its surface. These people had colonised their own natural satellite. Mountain ranges across the planet also appeared to reach much higher into the atmosphere than even Everest.

The Duodecim flew towards the planet's sunward facing side. Ryan saw one huge continent with deserts, mountains, green plains and forests. A giant hurricane was forming over a large ocean on the right side of its surface. On the dark side of the planet that was visible there was very little evidence of civilisation, only sporadic lights indicating homes and cities. What really caught Ryan's attention was an area close to the southern pole, a large island ringed with black mountains and looked extremely barren.

What was weird about it was that his eyes seemed to have trouble fixing on it. His vision seemed to slide off that area of the planet. It was like a blur, a smudge on the view screen. His eyes began to water as he stared at it for too long, and he turned away from it to view the activity in the bridge. He caught snippets of information as the crew talked to one another.

"Be glad to settle grafag for dron shore leave," one of the Intelligen said to another. Ryan still could not speak all the words of the Ontarian language so he only understood some of that.

"The Tredicim terrorists have struck the Prison again, trying to free their brethren," one of them said.

"I thought ho now we would jed got them all. There can't be that many kerp," he heard.

Ryan did not know what they were talking about. He had felt glad to have left all of Earth's problems behind, he was disappointed that he was going to have to get used to a completely new set of problems that this planet was experiencing

As he looked down on the alien planet and its shape and geography became clearer and clearer, he felt a sense of awe he had never felt before. He also felt special, he was one of only four humans to know about this place.

Threngst was standing nearby and Ryan turned to him. "How do you stop humans from finding out about this planet?" he asked.

"We destroy their deep space satellites, or constantly bombard their telescopes with false images and signals," Threngst replied.

"You can't do that to us," Ryan commented.

"It's not 'us' anymore Ryan, you're an Ontarian now, it's 'them'. Prepare for decent into the atmosphere," the Admiral commanded.

Ryan took the cue and found a seat and strapped himself in. The Frayans on the bridge remained standing.

"Control, this is the Duodecim requesting atmospheric entry on vector 243-761," the Admiral said aloud.

Booming through speakers set in the walls a voice replied to the Admiral's question, "Duodecim this is Control, vector safe for entry, clearance granted."

"Helm set the course," the Admiral commanded. "De-activate artificial gravity," she said.

Ryan felt himself become lighter and he floated in his seat despite the straps, so he tightened them to make sure he was secure.

"Reduce the thrust of the ion engines," the Admiral said and her crew made the adjustments.

"Entry check," the Admiral ordered.

"Heat panels look fine," a crew member said.

"Air brakes activated," another added.

"Fusion drive normal."

The various crew members around the room continued this status check. Ryan wished they would hurry up and just fly down onto the planet.

"Initiate entry," the Admiral ordered.

"Finally," Ryan said.

The Admiral did not appreciate this and turned around in her chair to look at Ryan. "Re-entering the atmosphere of a planet is a delicate task boy, unlike your race we do not rush things," and she turned back to the view screen.

Ryan avoided the glares of the rest of the crew who had not liked his outburst either.

Gradually the Duodecim moved closer to the planet and then the view screen erupted in fire.

Ryan's jaw fell open and was about to shout in alarm, when he remembered that when human vessels entered the atmosphere they created immense friction that made it look like flames were pouring off the vessel. He closed his mouth and relaxed, trying not to look scared at what was happening.

The ship rumbled and vibrated as the friction increased.

Eventually it stopped and the ship settled.

Soon enough the ship pierced the clouds and Ryan saw his first Ontarian city. It was huge and dotted with large spires taller than any man-made skyscraper. Wide roads and streets gave the impression of a planned-out metropolis, carefully constructed in the shape of a giant star.

"Wow," he said.

Ryan saw that the ship was heading for a huge open area on the outskirts of the city. The landing zone had a control tower looking over it.

He gripped the arms of his chair tightly as the ship slowed down, maneuvering itself for the landing. He felt uneasy. Nobody in the bridge seemed to be doing anything. The members of the crew attached to their pillars through wires plugged into their heads, were not pressing buttons or levers, just thinking commands and actions. Ryan would have preferred them to be using a steering wheel or at least look like they were controlling the massive ship.

He did not feel better until the vessel finally touched down and one last jolt rippled through the ship. The engines roared and the ship slowed down as it coasted along the runway. The ship turned off onto another highway heading for a wide-open space to park.

When the ship came to a stop the engines whined as they powered down. The Admiral was the first to stand, getting up and walking towards Ryan.

"Follow me," the Admiral ordered.

Ryan un-strapped himself and followed the Admiral out of the bridge. They strolled down various corridors until they reached the exit, stopping at Ryan's room along the way so he could grab his rucksack. As they reached the base of the ship, natural light blinded him for a second, and then his vision returned to him. He was staring out across the landing zone, a large circular, concrete, man-made, or Ontarian-made runway. In the distance he saw the city they had passed over. The buildings were very similar, towering spires that looked like stalagmites. The sun reflected off the glass of the buildings in a spectacular fashion.

The skyscrapers in this city looked far older than those on Earth; they seemed centuries old instead of just a few decades like his former home planet's buildings

As Ryan admired the landscape before him, and tried to comprehend what had just happened to him. He had just travelled across the solar system and was about to set foot on an alien world.

His mind had a hard time processing this information.

Ryan had once visited Italy with his grandparents. They had flown in a plane for two hours, travelled a thousand miles and ended up in a place where people still spoke English.

With the internet, instant communication and fast travel Earth felt like such a small place and Ryan understood that that attitude had followed him to another world. The tremendous distance he had just journeyed did not hit him.

Something occurred to him and he took the deepest breath he had ever had. The air smelled of fuel evaporating into the air and dust thrown up in the ship's wake. He slumped as he failed to distinguish anything different about it. As he stepped off the ramp and onto the surface of this world, taking a step that even Neil Armstrong had never taken, he felt heat radiating from what was probably tarmac, which was as familiar as stepping off a plane at a sunny Mediterranean island.

He noticed an object heading straight for them across the landing zone at tremendous speed. It came to a dead stop at the bottom of the ramp managing to decelerate from a mere five metres. Ryan saw that it was a man. He had never seen someone run as fast as he could before, it took him a second to put two and two together, and figure out he was watching a member of his Tribe display their powers at a higher level than himself.

He was jealous.

The Admiral greeted the man with a warm smile. He was a short but stout man with red hair flowing around the top of his head unnaturally, like everyone else he had met from Ontario.

Ryan wished he had hair like that, He ran his fingers through his locks wondering if he could excite it to move.

The man also had the same bony plates as the Admiral except they didn't run up the back of his head. They covered the same places as on Ryan's arms and legs, they were bigger than his though.

"Is this him?" the man asked the Admiral.

"Yes, this is the Half Human," the Admiral replied.

The man appraised Ryan and did not like what he saw.

"You will go with Chiqu Swift," the Admiral ordered. "Your possessions will be delivered to your new home. He is your uncle, your father's brother, obviously," she said.

"My uncle?" Ryan replied and he looked the man up and down then looked him in the eye.

"Follow me," the man said, meeting his gaze and he sprinted off at probably a hundred miles an hour.

Ryan looked up at the Admiral.

"Remember Ryan, this is your home now, you will adapt to live with us," she said.

"I'll try," Ryan replied.

He stared after his uncle, already some distance away, and sped after him. He liked the fact he did not have to hide his powers on this planet and he accelerated to a comfortable and high speed to make the most of it. He also felt great, there was no more pain or aching in his limbs, the change in planet had benefited him greatly.

Turning his attention forward once again he noticed that the shape of his uncle was rushing up very quickly, too late did he realise that his uncle had actually stopped running and was waiting for him to catch up.

Ryan decelerated as fast as he could, but it did not help as he clipped his uncle and went tumbling to the floor.

He picked himself up and dusted his hands off and brushed his clothes down. When he looked up his uncle was nursing the arm Ryan had clipped and he looked very angry.

"What happened?" he demanded.

"I tried to stop, but I didn't have time to slow down," Ryan explained.

His uncle looked confused at that remark. "Slow down! Slow down?" then a look of realisation appeared on his face. "You need a greater distance to decelerate, don't you?" he stated.

"Yes of course," Ryan replied.

"Well keep your eye on me in future. True Swifters need not decelerate," his uncle said. "Now come on."

Ryan followed his uncle through some automatic doors into the building they had stopped next to, an airport terminal of some sort. Inside were a number of Ontarians. Members of the Frayan tribe and Intelligen tribe were walking around going about their business. The Frayans, all in identical armour, strolled around head and shoulders above everyone, carrying heavy looking crates with ease owing to their strength. The Intelligens were all in groups exchanging information quickly and passing details between little computers. Ryan still did not have the language down so most of the chatter he heard was incomprehensible to him.

As he was walking next to his uncle a question formed in his mind and he wondered how best to address him, "Uncle Chiqu?" he said in English.

"You will no longer speak that language," his uncle immediately replied, "You will talk in our language because you are on our planet."

Ryan did not like that idea, he was struggling with the Ontarian language and would prefer good old English.

"What do I do here, a guy on the ship said I didn't have to go to school?" Ryan asked in broken Ontarian.

"We'll get to that, first we have another stop to make," his uncle replied.

His uncle led him through the building. He saw signs everywhere written in the Ontarian language. It was all illegible to him. As he looked around he noticed something else that he had not spotted straight away.

Every Ontarian he passed did double takes when they saw him. As he walked through the crowds of people everyone seemed to become aware of his existence and a wave of attention turned towards him, until eventually all eyes were on him.

Ryan looked back at them, determined not to turn away or stare at the ground.

He finally stopped and, looking around at everyone, then said very loudly, "WHAT?"

People continued to stare probably because he did not know the Ontarian word for *What*. As he looked into their eyes trying to stare them down, his gaze settled on two Ontarians who seemed unique in the crowd. They had no bony plates, however their hair was entwined with crystals also growing from their scalp. One was a girl probably his age and the other a taller man who occasionally lent down and whispered something to her. She stared at him more intently than anyone else. She had a plain face, but eyes that seemed to have depth, which bore into him.

Nice eyes, Ryan thought and the corner of the girl's mouth turned up slightly. *Plain face though*, Ryan added and she suddenly scowled at him.

He ignored her, obviously she thought his appearance was funny then remembered she was supposed to hate him, just like everyone else in this terminal.

No one turned away or answered his original statement so he just kept on walking.

He suffered under the downright rude stares until him and his uncle ended up outside.

There was a road leading past the building, heading out from the terminal and away from the city.

There were no cars on the road.

But there were people.

They all sped by, running at different speeds. Faster ones whizzed around slower ones complaining at their slow pace.

"Stay behind me and keep track of the turns I make," his uncle said, "How fast can you run?"

"One hundred fifty miles comfortably," Ryan replied.

"Human miles?" his uncle asked in a rhetorical manner and he did not look happy at the pace Ryan could manage, "It will take us an hour to get there," he added in irritation.

Ryan scowled at his uncle.

He sighed, "Let's go," he said, "keep up," and he sped off joining the other members of the Swift tribe speeding down the road.

This was the strangest experience of Ryan's life. He did not know how fast he was going, but was struggling to keep up with his uncle. He dared not look around lest he lose track of his relative. The other Ontarians speeding down the road gave him funny looks as they passed him by.

It shocked Ryan when another child shot past him. He must have been ten years old and yet he blasted past and disappeared down another street.

He kept an eye on his uncle's back who was actually chatting to another Ontarian as they ran down the road. The wind rushed by and Ryan's shirt flapped about as they continued down the road. His uncle veered to the left down another single carriageway and Ryan noticed that the landscape was changing. They were now far from the city and the road passed through fields that stretched for miles into the distance. It was not as packed as the wider one they had just left; fewer Ontarians were sprinting down it.

Ryan and his uncle took many turns and went down many roads. They were heading for another built up area, a town by the looks of it with a large complex in the middle. It was the strangest building Ryan had ever seen. From a central hub were twelve adjacent structures that branched off the core, all uniquely designed. What made Ryan curious and worried was that high walls and guard towers surrounded the building. *Was it a military base?* He thought. As his uncle led him through the town he slowed down and must have been going thirty or forty miles an hour. The roads seemed exclusively designed for the Swift tribe because all the other Ontarians strolled along paths and crossed the roads using bridges. He also saw no cars.

Ryan had so many questions about this new world. He still had trouble getting to grips with the fact he was **on** another planet.

It had grass, it was filling the gaps between building and roads, however the turf was much greener.

Insects flew through the air. The wind was cool on his face. The clouds looked…normal.

His uncle led him towards the distinctly shaped building he had seen from the outskirts of town. They stopped in front of a huge door flanked by members of the Frayan tribe, who wore slightly different coloured armour.

His uncle chatted to them and they grabbed huge handles on the doors and opened them. As they parted Ryan saw they were a half a metre thick. They must had weighed a few tons. He had a new found respect for the strength of the Frayans. "Let's go," His uncle said.

"What is this place?" Ryan asked.

"A prison," His uncle replied.

"A PRISON!" Ryan burst out. "You're locking me up?"

"You stupid boy, you're here to see one of the inmates."

"Wh-who?"

"Your father, who else?"

Chapter 13

Ryan and his uncle passed through the giant doors of the prison and into a courtyard intersected by two fences. One was a simple wire fence, the other thick metal poles and slats of thick steel. They provided them with a tunnel of sorts that led towards another set of doors a hundred yards away.

On either side of the wire fence prisoners were enjoying some free time out in the open air. Those on the left had the same bony plates on their arms as him. They were all wearing trousers and shirts with extra flaps between the sleeves and sides like little parachutes. Around their feet were large weights and they strolled around their part of the courtyard very slowly.

Ryan recognised them as belonging to his tribe, but they were not running very fast, no doubt thanks to all their extra clothing.

To his right, where the fence could keep out an elephant, he saw giant Frayans walking around. They still wore armour although it was much bulkier and possibly heavier, restricting their movements, preventing them from applying their massive strength.

Ryan could not see any other Ontarians belonging to other tribes.

He stopped looking at the prisoners when they started to take an interest in him as he strolled down the tunnel. He quickened his pace towards the doors at the far end.

Suddenly prisoners from his tribe's side of the wire tunnel grabbed the fence and started shouting at him.

"Go back home half-scum," one shouted.

"You're a disgrace to your tribe," said another.

The shouting and screaming intensified.

Ryan had never seen so much hatred and anger aimed directly at him before. He turned towards his uncle expecting some support to come from his family, but the man was not even acknowledging him or the prisoners.

The braying and mocking continued, the Frayan prisoners joined in.

"SHUT UP! SHUT UP! ALL OF YOU," Ryan shouted back at them.

The prisoners kicked the fence and shook it in response to his outburst.

Finally, the near riot attracted the attention of the prison staff and Frayans appeared in the Swifter's courtyard.

The prisoners tried to run, however they could only move at normal human speeds thanks to their clothing.

The Frayans, whose strength dominated the smaller Swifts, quickly quelled the riot. Frayan guards also appeared on the other side with their own tribe members, and to Ryan's shock they started beating down the prisoners, with giant maces.

Ryan ran down the tunnel catching up with his uncle who he glared at for not leaping to his defense. His uncle did not meet his gaze. "What do you expect me to do?" he said as they strolled on together.

Two Frayans in guard uniforms complete with armour were waiting for him and his uncle and they opened another set of heavy doors for them to pass through.

Ryan found himself in a waiting area. The decor was very plain, just what he expected from a prison, with dull grey colours splashed on the walls and there was little in the way of decoration of any kind. There was a crescent shaped desk in the centre of the room and behind that, shelves filled with files, managed by several Ontarians.

These Ontarians were very different from any Ryan had seen so far. Their clothes virtually hung off very small, frail frames and they had tired faces with drooping eyelids and gaunt pale looks. They hovered around flying through the air like cherubs. They had no bony plates on their bodies, but like all Ontarians their hair did move around of its own accord, although in their case it was like flowing water.

At one end of the desk was an Intelligen linked with a wire protruding from his head to a pole sticking out the floor. He stared off into the distance with a vacant expression on his face.

As Ryan's uncle led him up to the desk, one of the new Ontarians came floating over then dropped down next to them, he looked half-dead.

"Visiting?" he said in barely a whisper.

"Yes," Ryan's uncle replied, "Edeps Swift."

What happened next caused Ryan to recoil in surprise as suddenly a file leapt from the shelf behind him and settled itself down in front of them on the desk.

It then opened itself up and the sullen faced Ontarian starting making notes inside with a floating pen.

"They are members of the Motus tribe," Ryan heard his uncle say.

"What?" Ryan replied, watching as the pen gracefully wrote on the pages of the file control by some unseen force.

"Their tribe manages our society, their ability to move objects through their minds makes them perfect multitaskers, bureaucrats and organisers."

"Oh," Ryan said, and he remembered he had seen these powers before, when had been pursued in Whitby. One of the men chasing him had had the same tired look and the ability to move objects without touching them.

"Guard," the Motus whispered.

Someone obviously heard him as a Frayan stepped out from behind the shelf and beckoned Ryan to follow him.

Ryan moved to go with him, his uncle did not.

"Aren't you coming?" he asked.

"I have said all I need to my brother," his uncle replied coldly.

Ryan followed the Frayan guard down a corridor and then down another one and another one leading deeper into the prison complex. They reached a large circular room roofed by a dome and branching off it were twelve other corridors and Ryan could see that they were all constructed differently. He walked down one that zig-zagged every five metres and it had humps, square ones, which disrupted the floor. At some places it even narrowed to the width of the average Frayan. "This is a poorly designed corridor," he commented.

"It's designed to work against the abilities of the Swift tribe, they can't run as fast are they normally can in a structure of this kind," the Frayan guard answered.

Ryan noticed that all the cell doors were open and empty, no doubt they were all in the courtyard he had passed by. One of these cells at the very end had its door closed. As he approached he felt a little sick to his stomach, his palms started to sweat.

He had not met the man in this cell since he was a toddler, barely remembered him. Now though, he wanted to meet him, he might be the only person who would treat him nicely. Then he backed off a little, he might be like those criminals on TV, fierce and brutal. Ryan was certainly curious to find out more about the man whom his grandparents had just said he 'was no longer around'. But he certainly did not want to do it in prison, he was slightly ashamed because of his incarceration. Ryan was the son of a criminal and the entire stigma that came with it.

The guard pulled out a key for the door, unlocked it and slung it open, revealing a cell slightly smaller than Ryan's old bedroom.

"Hello Ryan," said the prisoner who was standing almost to attention in the centre of the room. His prison uniform, made out of one piece of material with no stitches, was neatly ironed and pristine and his prison shoes complete with weights were brightly polished. He was clean-shaven, with a few cuts around his chin and his short red hair was actually neatly combed and refused to move around.

Ryan did not see a lot of himself in the man before him.

"Hello?" he replied.

"It's so good to see you after so many years," the man said and he stepped forward gesturing him to shake hands. "A traditional human welcome, I still think."

Ryan did not move.

"I am your father," the man stated.

"But I don't know you," Ryan replied.

The hand dropped down. "But I know you though," the man replied. He went back into his small room and started rummaging around in his meagre personnel belongings. Ryan looked into the cell and saw quite a few odd objects littering the man's bed and a small desk jutting out of the wall. There were report cards from his old primary school, letters addressed to his father pinned on the wall, a few geography and Spanish textbooks that Ryan once used at school, as well as some chocolates from Earth. Ryan found himself staring at one object in particular, a picture of his mother smiling sweetly into the camera. It was pinned right next to the bed. Ryan smiled at her, recalling sweet memories of them alone visiting a carnival, a preschool and trips in the park. There was also a picture of him from two years ago next to that one.

"See," the prisoner said returning to the door. He held out a number of photographs each showing Ryan at a different stage of his life from a little boy, to teenager, to present day. "Your grandparents made sure I got these."

"My grandparents?" Ryan said

"Yes, they were allowed to correspond with me; do you have anything from them at the moment?" He asked.

"Yes, they did give me something actually," and Ryan fished the letter out of his bag and handed it to the man who took it and opened it immediately. Inside was another picture of Ryan and piece of paper filled with writing. "Tisk, tisk," he said shaking his head and reading the letter.

"You're doing very poorly in your maths exams, it's good to see that your history marks have improved though."

"What?" Ryan exclaimed, "that's in there?"

"Oh yes, do you think your own father wouldn't be interested in your school grades." Then he said, "Me Alegra ver que tu espanol es tan Bueno come siempre," in Spanish.

"You speak Spanish?" Ryan asked.

"Of course, I wanted to be able to bond with you the next time we met, plus this is a language only you and I speak, which could be fun, a secret code."

"Well, I never thought you cared," Ryan said.

The prisoner looked at him with his cold grey eyes that stared deep into Ryan's icy blue ones, "Of course I cared."

"Then why did you abandon me?"

"I didn't abandon you, I was arrested," he answered.

"What for?" Ryan replied.

He sighed, "One of our race's highest laws, enacted when we first discovered the human race, is not to divulge our existence to humanity, and certainly not to marry a human," he said. "When your mother died the Ontarian authority discovered our union and arrested me. They then sentenced me for my crimes. I've been here ever since."

"How did you meet mum? How did you get to Earth?" Ryan asked.

"Well, that is an interesting tale..." Edeps began.

Chapter 14

17 Years ago, on planet Earth

Edeps Swift trudged along in the dark. His feet splashed in muddy puddles and his trousers kept getting caught in the local plant life, heather he believed it was called, and it grew everywhere on the alien landscape before him.

He walked slowly and could have been moving a lot faster, but he was injured. Blood flowed from a wound in his right shoulder, it also took a lot of energy for him to concentrate on running as fast as he could and the pain was preventing that. In his left hand he held a small metal box which he kept tight to his body, he glanced down every five seconds to make sure it was still there.

Behind him his crashed ship was on fire illuminating what he knew to be the Yorkshire Moors, in the country of England, something his ship's computer had told him right before the crash.

Suddenly a humming noise filled the air and it passed over him heading for the wreckage of his space ship.

He really did have to pick up the pace, so he started running at normal human speeds, leaping over bushes and through long grass desperate to get away.

He stopped when suddenly he met something he did not expect a wide stone path with white lines painted on it. He heard another strange sound, like a roaring animal and he looked to the left spotting two lights moving towards him, it was a local inhabitant's vehicle.

Suddenly something careered into him from behind and he landed in the prickly plant life.

The lights grew nearer, bathing the area around him in yellow light. Before he could even pick himself up something grabbed him around the waist and threw him back into the road where he struck something hard.

There was a screeching noise and then he blacked out.

•

Emma Barns was stunned, she had just hit something! She sat in her seat hands still clasped firmly to the steering wheel of her Mini. The knuckles on her hands were white and she was shaking.

Was it a sheep or a person? She thought to herself with the latter option filling her with dread.

She unbuckled her belt and got out the car, her breath immediately condensing in the air. She went around to the front of her car and her gut tightened, hanging down beside her left headlight was an arm, an arm with blood flowing down its sleeve.

"Oh, my goodness," she said and she immediately went over to the person slouched next to her car.

"Are you alright" she asked. She was a little taken aback by the weird clothing he wore. She bent down next to his side and saw the wound in his arm, she felt his pulse and she almost leapt back in surprise when she felt it rapidly pulsing through her fingertips, far faster than she had ever known, faster than in people she knew to be having heart attacks.

She was about to go back to the driver side for her phone then suddenly the man stirred.

*"**Ow**," he said. Emma did not understand what he had said, it was in language she did not recognise.*

"Don't try to talk or move I'm a doctor."

He started to get up.

"No don't move," she repeated and she put her hands on his arm and immediately recoiled when she felt something she did not expect. She reached down and felt plates, bony plates on his forearms. She had never seen anything like it before.

The man then grabbed her by the wrist.

"Run," he said in slightly slurred English.

"I'm not going anywhere you need medical help. What are these?" she asked pointing at the bone plates.

"You wouldn't understand," he replied groggily.

Emma then heard deep breathing coming from behind her. She looked over her shoulder, however she could not see anything in the darkness, but there was a foul smell in the air. Then stepping into the glow cast by her car's lights a foot appeared.

Certainly not a normal foot, it ended in three black clumps.

Her eyes looked past the foot up a dark, green leg and she saw a black shadow and peering down at her were two white, gleaming eyes.

Edeps was just coming around.

They had caught up to him, they were using his power like they always did, and it was the only way they could have got to him so fast.

The human female who had come to his aid was staring over her shoulder seeing something in the darkness.

As his eyes grew accustomed to the light he saw it too, a Tredicim, one he recognised, standing over him and the human.

He had failed.

*"**Give me the key or you and the human will die**," it said to him in his people's own language.*

*"**Never! Your tribe is sealed away you will not rule us again**." Edeps replied.*

*"**We will rule again, once my kind is free. We were born to rule lest you forget**," Trettan replied.*

Edeps mind raced, he had to do something, the future of his people rested on him.

●

Emma could not understand what was being said. The man next to her and the creature that stood before them both were conversing in a language she did not understand, it was very sharply spoken, like a cat hissing and trying to speak at the same time.

Suddenly something dropped into her lap, she did not look down though, as the white eyes glowing in the dark darted towards her, in fact they seemed to brighten once the object came to rest on her legs.

"Take care of it," the man said to her in plain English and he stood up.

"What are you going to do?" she asked.

If she had not been shocked enough tonight, to her horror the man ran away. It was not that he deserted her that surprised Emma, but the fact that he ran at an unbelievable speed accelerating away from her like a cheetah chasing a gazelle, becoming a blur.

●

Edeps sprinted down the road, he knew he could only be going fifty miles an hour, it was enough though to get him a fair distance from Trettan, he was going to need a run up for what he was about to do.

*"**You save your own skin, very wise**," Trettan jeered, as he ran down the stone path out of the light created by the human vehicle.*

He came to halt, looked back and saw Trettan bent down over the human his clawed hand reaching into the light to grab the box he had given her, the object that kept his people safe.

Edeps was not running away, not with so much at stake.

"Nothing like a good run up," he said to himself then he sped back towards the Human.

Despite the pain racking his body he concentrated in order to build up his speed. He had once clocked himself at four hundred miles an hour, on a good day and on flat ground. Right now he was injured and tired, but he gave it his all.

In one second he had covered the two hundred metre distance that separated him from Trettan and at that speed it would hurt.

He slammed into Trettan's side, shoulder barging him just before he got his hands on the metal box.

Trettan growled in anger and started to get up.

Edeps grabbed the box from the human, "Let's go!" he said to her grabbing one of her arms and pulling her to her feet and then he placed her over her shoulder and sped away.

•

Emma gasped as the man she had seen dash away from her leaving her at the whim of the creature, appeared out of nowhere to knock the big green monster away from her moments before the clawed hand was inches from her face.

Then suddenly the man yanked her off her feet, and without warning bundled her over his shoulder, fireman style.

"Hey," she protested.

But she did not say anything when she realised that she was moving very fast. The headlights of her car got smaller and smaller and smaller.

Emma looked around, the man was carrying her at probably forty miles an hour down the road, as she was jostled by his running her glasses came free and fell to the road.

"My glasses," she shouted out.

"I wouldn't worry about them," the man said.

"Stop, stop," she yelled, the cold wind rushed past her face and she kept getting jolted in her stomach.

"Cannot do that, we need to get out of here," he replied.

"How are you doing this?"

"You wouldn't understand," was the reply.

"Stop," she yelled again.

The man seemingly obeyed as suddenly without even decelerating he skidded to a halt. She had not prepared for it and the force of coming to a complete stop so quickly, knocked the wind out of her as her body continued on into his. She felt crushed as if she was in a crowd of people trying to get of the underground.

He took her off her shoulder and let her stand on her own two feet.

They had reached a main road, and a street light shone above them illuminating the marked tarmac in an orange glow.

"Thank you," she said sarcastically, brushing her hair back.

The strange man was not looking at her, she followed his gaze and what she saw was horrifying. Two powerful legs ending in three clumps, which supported a huge heavily muscled body much like a human, it was seven feet tall at least. It had two arms and its head, most horrifying of all, was triangular and vicious. Tentacles protruded from the back of its skull moving around as if excited. The white eyes glowed.

It spoke in the hissing language.

The man next to her replied.

"What's going on?" she asked.

The object the man had given her earlier was thrust back into her hands.

Then a fight began between the two of them and she could only watch in amazement. It was like a Kung Fu movie in fast forward.

Eventually the man grabbed an over extended punch, spun rapidly on the spot and threw the beast. It landed roughly a metre away from her with a thud and it rolled a little. There was a tinkling sound and small metal circles like links in a necklace scattered everywhere. A locket rolled away from the beast ending up where the tarmac met the rough heather of the moors.

The creature growled and reached out and picked up the locket, putting it in a pocket. It tried to stand and it stumbled a bit with the effort. Although she and seen nothing like this beast before, Emma knew the creature had a fractured leg, she had seen enough to recognise the symptoms.

The man shouted something. Before she could react the creature grabbed her and took the object from her hands.

She felt the creature's breath on the back of her neck as it held her in front of itself like a shield.

•

*"**Release her Trettan**," the Edeps said.*

"**No, she's my hostage, I have the key,**" *Trettan replied then he started fumbling with the box and opened it up.*

The human suddenly shouted, "Help me," *in her own language.*

"**What's this**?" *Trettan said and he held the open box out showing Edeps that it was empty.* "**Where is the key**?" *he asked.* **"Give me what I need to free my family!"**

"Help me," *the human female said again.*

"I will," *Edeps replied in English.*

"**What?**" *Trettan said,, then he shook his head and repeated,* "**Where's the key**?" *and brandished the box. Edeps eyes fell on it, he had tried bluffing the Tredicim and now Trettan had found the truth, if he did not take him down then his ruse would make containing the Tredicim much harder.*

"**I will never tell you**," *Edeps said.*

"**Then she dies**," *Trettan said clutching the human tighter making to crush her.*

"**No Wait**," *Edeps said.*

"**Where is the key, tell me**," *Trettan said.*

"**I will**," *Edeps said in his own language and while patting a pocket on his jacket.*

Trettan's yellow eyes glanced at the pocket and he smiled "**very clever using this diversion**," *Trettan said chucking the box to one side and holding out his hand for the key.*

"When I say so, duck," *he said to the human female in her language and slowly reaching for the pocket.*

She managed to nod back.

"**Do not speak her language again**," *Trettan said, thankfully unable to comprehend.*

"Duck," *Edeps suddenly said, and the female obeyed.*

Drawing on his last reserves of energy Edeps accelerated hard and fast, just as Trettan looked down at the human and then back up as Edeps came straight for him, flying over the female's head with his elbow extended out which struck Trettan right on his nose. The soft flesh there gave away and Trettan's head flew backwards as the blow landed.

Edeps pushed the human away then ran fast in a circle back towards Trettan and kicked him on his leg at the knee joint, which buckled under the blow. His enemy roared in pain, however Edeps was not finished and leapt upward with another kick that struck Trettan under his jaw jolting his head back again.

The pain and blow was too much and Trettan fell forward onto his face and twitched a little trying to move his limbs.

The human, who had not moved since ducking, sat up from her prone position on the road and looked back at Trettan then swayed uncontrollably.

"Th – Tha - Thank you," she managed to say.

"You're welcome," Edeps replied. He strolled over to Trettan pulled a circular device from his pocket and placed it on Trettan's chest. The Tredicim stopped moving, finally restrained.

Edeps looked around for the box and saw it at the female's feet. He crouched down and picked it up. He could now do what he supposed to, hide it on this planet to convince the other Tredicim that the key to their tribe's release was on Earth. He took the red crystal from his pocket and placed it in the box. He then stood up meeting the fear filled gaze of the human female. It was his first good look her and for a human she was strikingly beautiful.

She looked back at him her mouth open, her eyes wide trying to comprehend what had just happened to her. He could understand her reaction it is not every day a human met a member of his race.

He racked his brain trying to remember a traditional human greeting, and then it came to him. He reached out with a hand, "My name is Edeps," he said.

For a few seconds the human did not respond then finally she took his hand they shook. "Emma," she replied.

"Nice to meet you," Edeps said and smiled warmly.

She looked back at him with a dazzling smile.

There was an awkward silence, but they did not care and just stared into each other's eyes under the soft light from the streetlamp above them.

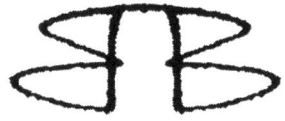

Chapter 15

Ryan absorbed this story.

No one had ever spoken about his mother like that before. His grandparents had loved her, and talked about her with pride. Not the kind of affection this man now spoke with.

"How did she die?" Ryan asked.

"I don't want talk about that...it's too painful," he muttered, staring back at the picture of Ryan's mother on the wall. "I wish she was still alive, then she could have taken care of you. She was a doctor, maybe she could even find a way to ensure you could have stayed on Earth," he mused.

"What's going to happen to me, everyone on this planet seems to hate me?" Ryan asked.

"I assume you came here with your uncle?"

"Yes."

"Then you'll probably be living with his family and some other relatives of yours," he said.

"Grandparents?"

"No, your grandparents on my side of the family belong to a different tribe they don't live with your uncle," he said.

"How can they live with a different tribe surly they must be like us, members of the, erm Swift tribe?"

"That not how it works Ryan, when a child is born on this planet, they are observed to see what tribe's abilities they develop, when they display said abilities, they are placed with that tribe. In most cases a child will be born with the same powers as their parents, but on rare occasions they develop another tribe's power and end up being placed far from their parents."

"Sounds a little sad," Ryan said.

The man chuckled, "Not on this planet Ryan, here the tribes do what they have to, and each fulfils its own purpose."

"So, what's my purpose?"

"Let's not talk about that right now, I haven't seen you for ten years. I want to know more about you and I guess you want to know more about me."

"Yes…I guess do," Ryan replied, cautiously.

"I understand you like rugby?" he asked.

"Yes, it's my favorite sport," Ryan answered, smiling a little as they discussed a familiar subject.

"And you won a cup recently."

"Yeah, thanks to me," Ryan boasted with a big, fat grin.

"I thought your grandparents would have told you to limit your abilities."

Ryan's smile faded, "They said I shouldn't hide what I could do, and it wasn't like I was cheating."

"No, I agree, but it's a little unfair don't you think," the man said.

"I suppose," Ryan replied looking away. He had not expected to get a scolding.

"Time's up." The Frayan who had led Ryan to this cell, strolled up to him and indicated for him to go back down the corridor.

Ryan shrugged his shoulders, "Bye…" he said.

"Bye son, you'll do fine and come and visit whenever you can," and he held out his hand again.

Ryan looked at this prisoner and his pleading expression, but he was not ready yet. "Sorry erm, sir, I have to go." Ryan then turned around and went back down the corridor, he heard the guard lock the door behind him.

He did not look back.

Chapter 16

Ryan sped down a seemingly unending road. After miles and miles of running his mind had wandered and he was thinking about the chat he had had with the prisoner.

His conversation with him had not gone like he expected it to go.

He had not thought for one moment that his dad would be in jail, it had been a shock to him and he wondered what kind of relationship he would have with him now. Ryan did not like the idea of going back to a prison just to talk with him, he didn't want to see the snarling faces of those prisoners again.

He tried not to think about it, one way or another it was going to be a while before he returned there, it was an issue he did not have to deal with right away.

Instead, there was a new problem to face; he was now heading towards another place that would no doubt hold its own surprises. He was hoping that his Ontarian family would receive him better than most Ontarians had so far. The sounds of those taunts and the hatred towards him from those prisoners, was something he could not shake.

His uncle was speeding ahead of him leading the way. It was now late in the day and getting dark and they had both been running for ages. Ryan did not feel tired at all; he assumed that this planet's environment had cured the medical problems he had been having on Earth. He had not coughed at all ever since boarding the Duodecim or landing on planet Ontaria.

His uncle turned off onto a dirt road without tarmac and Ryan took the opportunity to look around the landscape squinting in the dim light to make out the details. He saw huge fields and a view that was very flat in all directions. There appeared to be no civilisation for miles just, random houses dotted around the area. A mountain range bordering the horizon was the only significant feature on the plains.

The farmland he ran across reminded him of the Yorkshire moors. The air smelled of something he couldn't place. Then it occurred to him that it was a plant or crop he had never smelt before, that no human had ever smelt before.

To his left the sun was setting, to his right were two of the three moons. He stopped when and thought, *three moons.* He couldn't believe it. They were different sizes and bathed the landscape in more light than the Moon alone could.

This view every evening was something he could get used to.

Ryan then put all his efforts into catching up to his uncle and running alongside him. They were heading towards a cluster of houses right at the end of the dirt path. The dwellings were of various sizes and all the same design, shaped like caterpillar cocoons with one end that was bulbous then tapered to a point at the other. At both ends of each structure were two triangular arches and on the larger buildings there were two extra arches extending from the centre, Ryan assumed they were decorative as they did not seem to have a function.

Doors and windows punctuated the buildings at various points. Lights were on all across the compound.

His uncle started to slow down and Ryan slowed with him they continued to decelerate until they stopped in a stone courtyard surrounded by smaller cocoon like buildings. When Ryan saw them up close there was something about them that did not seem right. The buildings appeared to have no foundations because they sat on the ground instead of rising out of it as most buildings do.

The courtyard was quiet except for some sort of cricket making noise all around them.

"Are you ok Chiqu, you were going quite slow as you came towards the house?"

Standing in the doorway to one of the buildings was a middle-aged woman, with long flowing brown hair moving around like all Ontarian hair. She was quite thin, had sharp, angular facial features and green eyes.

"Because of him," Ryan's uncle said, motioning to Ryan. The women looked at him and nodded her head in understanding.

"Edeps' son?" she asked.

"Yes, he needs to decelerate before stopping," Chiqu said.

"His cases arrived, big bulky things, they'll take up all the space in his room," she said.

"Is dinner ready?" Ryan's uncle asked.

"We've been waiting for you," the woman said and then she finally turned to Ryan, "I am your aunt, my name is Nar," and she disappeared inside the house after that curt introduction.

"Come on Ryan, meet your family," his uncle muttered.

•

Ryan walked down narrow halls inside the largest building. He heard shouting and laughter from somewhere inside of the maze of corridors. The sounds got louder and Ryan slowed down. There were butterflies in his stomach and his skin felt clammy and cold. He was about to meet quite a few Ontarians and he was not sure how they were going react to seeing him.

He stood up straight and put on a smile, something he felt would make him seem confident. He stepped out into a large room, a dining room that had two wooden tables lined with chairs and to one side a kitchen with cookers and cupboards all molded from the floor and walls.

What bothered Ryan was the silence that fell when he entered the room. What bothered him more were the stares.

On one table were seated the adults and on the other, children of various ages. The adults did not seem too interested in his appearance in fact they took one look then turned back to their conversations. The children however were different.

"That's him," one of them whispered.

"Uncle Edeps' human son."

"What kind of hair colour is that?" another said.

Ryan instinctively combed his fingers through his hair and he suddenly realised that no Ontarian he had met so far had black hair, *great*, he thought, *another thing to help me stand out*.

"Take a seat at that table, we are eating in a moment," his aunt ordered.

Ryan, avoiding the gazes of the children took a seat at the very end of the table facing a girl. He noticed out of the corner of his eye that she was staring at him. He did not meet her gaze.

"Check out his bones," another kid said who looked about ten. "Did they hurt?" he asked Ryan.

"Hurt?" Ryan said.

"When they grew?" the kid said.

"Silence Deeskly," his aunt said and she strolled off into the kitchen collecting the evening meal.

In huge bowls the food was shared around. Most of it was vegetables that came in a variety of shapes and sizes Ryan had never seen before. He looked down the table for some meat and saw something that looked like it had once been alive. Unlike chicken or beef though, it was purple.

Once all the dishes had been placed in the middle of the table everyone turned to his aunt Nar.

"Let us Rai," she said.

Everyone, apart from Ryan, closed their eyes and his aunt began to say what was unmistakably - a prayer. Ryan was surprised to hear one from these aliens and he wondered what god they believed in. Then as he listened to the words she used, he understood that they might not actually be praying to their own god, but the God. He waited for the amen, but it did not happen, his aunt ended on a thank you and no one echoed her sentiment, they just opened their eyes.

Then children on Ryan's table started helping themselves to the food, taking more of their favorites and less of what they did not like. Ryan cautiously helped himself to food, choosing by what he liked the look of and anything that was similar to stuff he had eaten while on the Duodecim.

"What are we doing after dinner?" someone said from down the table and the conversation between the children started from where they had left off before Ryan had entered the room.

"I say we go to the mountain range, the Frayans are starting their celebrations for their Patriarch, we could see their strength games," Deeskly said.

"No, you don't, tribes do not mix during the celebrations," Ryan's aunt called out from the adult table.

"Mum," the boy replied in a whiney tone.

"No," said Ryan's Uncle, "your mother is right, the tribes to not celebrate the arrival of the Patriarchs together."

"We're just going to watch not interfere," said a girl, older than Deeskly probably the same age as Ryan. She had dark red hair and a thin face. Her bony plates were developed more than Ryan's and he wondered if something was wrong with him if his were not like that.

Ryan debated with himself whether or not to ask what they were talking about. He was not sure if wanted to break the ice with them or not. He sensed coldness from the adults behind him. Somehow he had fallen out of their favour and he did not want to risk making a bad impression with potential friends on his table.

"So, you're from Earth are you?" someone said from opposite him.

Ryan had kept his head down ever since taking his seat, and looked up into eyes of the girl opposite him. She had curly brown hair, but it did not flow around her head instead it stayed still, vibrating on occasion then settling down again.

"Yes," he replied. "It's where I've come…"

"Alright, alright I didn't want a life story," she said and went back to eating.

Ryan bit his lip and looked down at his plate again. No one was using knives or forks so he picked up a fat, pink fruit. It was hot and was soft to touch. He bit into it and it burst in front of his face like a balloon, covering his lips, nose and cheeks in goo.

The kids on the table roared with laughter and pointed at him. "Crush it before you bite into it Human," one of the kids shouted down the table at him.

"Half human," another kid commented.

"Half of nothing," the girl with the red hair said.

Ryan turned his head to face her and scowl, but it was not a good time to be hostile, so he looked away hoping to be ignored again, however it was too late.

"What you don't like that?"

"My mother was human," Ryan muttered under his breath.

"What?" the girl demanded.

"He said his mother was human," the little boy called Deeskly replied for him.

"Yeah, we know," the red-haired girl said. "We all know about what Uncle Edeps did," she added. "What's Earth like? Is it true your planet is separated into hundreds of countries?"

"Yes," Ryan replied in a tone that made it clear there were to be no follow up questions.

"Hah," the girl said with a sneer. "How fast can you run?" the red-haired girl added.

Ryan did not want to say, he felt that no matter what he said he would turn it into a side comment.

"What's-the-matter-don't-understand-me? Don't-speak-our-language-just yet, do-you?" the girl said loudly and slowly.

"I speak it fine," he responded.

"Then how fast can you run?"

"One hundred and seventy," he exaggerated.

"Is that all? Deeskly can do that and he's twelve," the girl said.

"Nur," a voice behind Ryan said, it was his uncle, "tidy up and clean the dishes."

"Make the human do it," Nur replied.

"He needs to settle in, do as I say. Ryan, follow me."

Ryan looked back at the children; Nur was in a huff and the others were concentrating on polishing off their meals. It did not seem as if he had made a good first impression.

He got up off his chair and followed his uncle. He was led back to the courtyard and into another building. His Uncle stopped at the doorway to a small room, which reminded Ryan off the room he had occupied while on the Duodecim. "Tomorrow you will start work and see how the Swift Tribe contributes to Ontarian society, you will wear different clothes, not your ones from planet Earth. Consider yourself an Ontarian now," his uncle said then left.

Ryan stepped into his room and lay down on his bed.

His mind felt heavy, he felt like he was being crushed. Beyond his own skin it was like there was nothing at all…just him. He let tears flow from his eyes and down his cheeks. He was all alone and he had nothing except his suitcases that took up half his room, which only reminded him of the comfortable, familiar room he had had on Earth.

He closed his eyes and tried to fall asleep wondering if he would ever consider himself an Ontarian.

Chapter 17

In the morning, pounding on his door woke him from a terrible night's sleep. The loud thumping boomed within the confines of his small room like the bass on a speaker system.

He sat up with one eye open and the other firmly shut.

"Wha...?" he muttered.

The knocking continued.

"I'M UP, I'M UP," he shouted in English.

"What did you say?" someone replied in Ontarian.

"I'm up," Ryan repeated in the right language.

"Be in the courtyard in ten minutes, you missed breakfast."

Ryan shot up out of bed when he heard those words. He scrambled out from under his sheets and to his door, which he had to slide open. He poked his head out of his room and saw his uncle already strolling away down the corridor. "Is there anything left?" Ryan asked.

"No, you'll need those clothes," he stated without looking over his shoulder.

Ryan looked down at his feet and caught sight of some trousers, t-shirt and some shoes. Like all Ontarian clothes, they were seamless, without a crease anywhere on them, they were scaly, like lizard's skin. The trousers were silver and the t-shirt was dark yellow.

Ryan bent down and picked up the shoes. They were some sort of leather and had thick, very thick rubber on the soles. Despite the thickness of the rubber on the soles, they bent and contorted very easily like a flimsy sandal. He tried one of them on; they were an exact fit, perfectly matching his own feet.

He went back into his room and closed the door. He opened his rucksack and pulled out a pack of sweets that he had almost finished. When he was on board the Duodecim they had taken away the taste of the food he had not liked. Now they were going to be his breakfast. He put on his new clothes and ate the sweets, finishing them all off.

After putting both his shoes on, he closed his suitcases and sealed his bag then left his room. It took him a few minutes to find the exit to the building.

Finally, he stepped outside and he squinted as the early morning light shone right in his face. It was cold despite the blazing sun, since it had not had the chance to warm up the world yet, plus there was a slight breeze that wafted through the courtyard.

The adults were already very busy, moving around sacks, transferring them from the courtyard into a nearby building.

The kids were chatting away, stretching and joking. Ryan wondered what he was going to be doing this morning, were they going to some sort of school? Practice their super speed? *What is this day going to be like?*

The kids looked at him as he entered the courtyard. He heard whispers regarding his absence from breakfast. He stayed away from them, moved out of earshot and leaned against the wall of one of the buildings. He felt around for some pockets in his trousers but found none.

His clothes felt very odd. Apart from the lack of seams they had the habit of suddenly clinging to his legs and his chest when he turned or walked. When he attempted to detach them from his body they just snapped back and clung to his skin like a wet shower curtain. Only when he stood still did it not matter and the clothes flapped around in the breeze.

Without a jumper he shivered slightly and crossed his arms in reflex.

Ryan noticed he was not the last to enter the courtyard as coming out of the building was the girl he had sat opposite last night. Unlike the other girls in the courtyard, she had put far more effort into her appearance. Her hair was also not moving around, it merely shuddered every so often.

She saw Ryan standing alone looking back at her; she wandered over and appraised him.

"Your hair's a mess," she said.

Ryan's gaze looked upward at his fringe and felt his hair, was all over the place. Although it was bothering him that his hair was in a mess, he shrugged so as to appear as if it did not matter to him. "It's a human style," he explained.

"Why doesn't it move around?" she asked.

"It can't move," Ryan said, "What about yours?"

"I like it to stay still, especially when it's not been cut," she responded. "What's your name again?"

"Ryan," Ryan replied, "Yours?"

"Reesa," she said.

Ryan looked over at the other children some were taking sneak peaks at him over their shoulders, he did not understand what they expected to see.

To distract himself from their stares he asked Reesa, "So are you my cousin or something?"

"I'm not related to anyone here on the farm," she replied.

"You're not?" Ryan said.

"My parents are of the Motus Tribe, but I was born with the abilities of the Swift Tribe so I was sent here," she answered.

"How did that happen?" Ryan asked.

"It's rare, but one of my great grandparents was a Swifter, so I suppose it had something to do with it."

"Why not stay with them?" he asked.

"I'm a Swifter, I have to learn to do what Swifters do. Your uncle is a friend of my parents so I came here.

Ryan stood up straight, frowning, "I'm sorry did you just say Farm?"

•

Reesa explained the situation, and Ryan could not believe what he was hearing.

He was going to be a farmer.

There was no school for him to attend just the crops in the fields.

After a brief introduction from Reesa about the farm, he stood in the courtyard listening to his uncle Chiqu describe the morning's activities that were to be completed before lunch.

The yellow shirt he was wearing marked him out as someone who would tend a group of fields on the outskirts of his family's territory. He was so disappointed at the prospect of spending the best years of his youth working in the mud and growing food. Worse still Reesa had told him that he would never, ever, do anything else.

He learned that all the tribes on Ontaria used their powers to further Ontarian society. His tribe, the Swifters, farmed huge tracks of land and headed animals that would eventually end up feeding the whole of their society. They also distributed it to the cities.

Ryan would give anything at this point to be back at school doing maths, rather than mucking about in the dirt. Reesa told him that it was the best use of their speed since with it they could look after huge acres of land with a small amount of people.

When his uncle had finished talking, he turned to the building where the sacks had been loaded. Ryan saw him point at it and then suddenly, with a tremendously loud groaning sound, the building lifted up off the ground on six legs the width of tree trunks.

Ryan backed away and he heard laughter, without even looking around he knew some of the children were mocking his reaction. The building started to move away from him heading out down the dirt path Ryan had used the evening before to reach the small cluster of buildings.

The ground shook as each leg moved to carry the enormous bulk of the building down the path. Ryan looked around wondering if any of the other buildings were going to start moving.

"Let's go," His uncle called out and the courtyard emptied of adults and then children as they sped away. Reesa smiled at him finding amusement at Ryan's surprised expression, and then set off and Ryan followed.

For an hour Ryan ran down roads and paths that cut through huge fields. He had a hard time keeping up as he followed his uncle leading a group of other yellow shirted Swift tribe members. He always lost ground on the corners; since he had to slow down in order to take them, he would always lose the group. Either Reesa or some other disgruntled child would come back for him.

The shoes he was wearing handled his super speed very well, able to grip the surface of the roads and paths without pain or discomfort. He also figured out why his clothes were so clingy when he moved, it was to prevent drag as he ran.

Eventually they reached the fields that Ryan's group was going to be working on. They stretched for miles lined with paths for high-speed access.

"Nur take Ryan and unlock the water veins," Ryan's uncle said.

Ryan looked at the girl called Nur who was the red-haired girl from last night. He scowled when she met his gaze. Without a word she sped off down a path in between two fields.

"Follow her," His uncle ordered.

Ryan obeyed and followed Nur who was not bothering to wait for him to catch up. When Ryan finally reached her, Nur was bent over a concrete platform with a metal ring in its centre. Nur was currently turning the ring like a screw head and the ground beneath them groaned as water was pumped from somewhere underneath them. After about five turns the ring was about a foot out of the platform and the groaning had turned to a roar. On the final turn at the corners of the concrete platform nozzles sprang out.

"What is that?" Ryan asked.

"Part of the irrigation system, go and find the others there are about fifty of them scattered among the fields," Nur ordered.

"Where are they?" Ryan asked.

"Why don't you look?" Nur said then got up and sped away to continue her work.

Ryan looked around then sped off in the other direction. He ran for a mile before he spotted another concrete platform and copied what he saw Nur do, turning the metal device bringing it out of the concrete and with one final twist the nozzles sprang out of its top.

He searched for more and found fifteen. After forty minutes he went searching for his cousin and saw her running between two fields and moved to intercept.

They met up and she asked, "How many did you get?"

"Fifteen," Ryan replied.

"I got the other thirty five," Nur boasted then she ran off.

Ryan sighed then followed her, they were heading straight for a small group of people waiting in the shadow of the buildings that had walked all the way from Ryan's new home to the fields.

Ryan kept an eye on Nur as he followed her, he did not know the system of paths and he did not want to become lost again. Ryan sped up and acted as if these kinds of speeds were not making him exhausted. Nur looked behind her and saw Him hot on her trail; an evil smile crossed her face and suddenly she darted left without warning.

Ryan was not ready for the turn and tried to follow, suddenly he became aware that his feet were snagging on something and he tripped up at very high speed. He must have tumbled for twenty feet coming to rest in the dirt and remains of some crops.

"WHAT HAVE YOU DONE," someone shouted.

Ryan looked up and saw that he had accidentally run into a field and his speed and fall had cut a deep scar in the plants that ran in neat rows.

His uncle was strolling through the field to where Ryan lay and he grabbed by the arm and hauled him to his feet. "DON'T RUN AT SUCH SPEEDS IF YOU CAN'T HANDLE THEM," he shouted and dragged Ryan out of the field back to a path, where he could do no damage, then let go of him.

Ryan caught sight of Nur smirking and pointing with some of the other children.

He never felt more embarrassed in his life.

•

Ryan spent the rest of the day looking after the land belonging to his paternal family, and he had to admit it wasn't all bad. The water veins Ryan had spent time opening with Nur, were part of a huge irrigation system, which when switched on in the bright sunshine, created miniature rainbows. He watched it from a rise in the middle of the farm. Such colour and light was something he had not seen before.

After an area of thousands of aches was drenched, Ryan went to work with his cousins. The sacks his uncle had loaded in the walking buildings were full of seeds, which Ryan had to plant in a ploughed, unsown field nearby.

He also had to pick some vegetables, at high speed. His cousins zipped down row after row of crops stopping for seconds at a time to pluck and then move on. Ryan was seriously falling behind since he could not come to a dead stop at super speed. When he tried, he would skid past rows of crops he was supposed to pick. This meant that he could only gather food at a rate half that of the others.

After spending the whole morning working on the fields his uncle called everyone together and they ate lunch. Like last night, the adults split from the children, as they ate sitting in the shadows of the walking buildings.

The children were all in a circle, one Ryan was not allowed inside. He sat with his back to them all, letting them know he did not care if they ignored him. He stared out across the fields that basked in the bright sunshine. He could see other Swift Tribe members in the distance still working. Ryan found it hard to believe this was what he was going to be doing for the rest of his life. The only good thing about it was that he was outside running, which gave him a little boost. Moreover, he had an epiphany, he was seeing new places, new things no human had ever seen. There was so much to see and with his speed, surely, he could range far and wide and explore?

That afternoon they left the fields, the entire group speeding across the landscape into another wide-open area of grassland. Ryan noticed that this area was un-touched by the hands of man...or Ontarian.

"Yellows find the herd," Ryan's uncle said.

He trailed behind his fellow yellow farmers who ran up a hill and when they came to the top they stopped and Ryan's eyes boggles at the sight he saw. When he had heard the word herd, he knew they were going after some animals, but he expected to see cows, not the beasts that stood before him.

They were all grey with mouths as large as cement mixers, but they did not have teeth, instead they closed their jaws around huge tuffs of grass and literally sucked them out of the ground. They had huge shoulders and small hindquarters, like bulldogs. The whole herd was making a tremendous noise, each one sounded like a vacuum cleaner with a sock stuck in it. At a rough guess there were at least ten thousand of them.

"Found the herd," someone said to Ryan's left. After a minute Ryan's uncle, Nur and Reesa and the rest of their group joined them.

"We need to move the herd to the next field so they can continue to graze," Ryan's uncle said.

"Yellows track the herd on the east side, we'll track them on the south." His uncle gathered the group together and showed them a map, "Move the herd in this direction," Ryan heard him say to those adults.

"Reesa what are those things?" he asked

"Flavadores," she replied, "our principal source of meat," she added.

The group split up again and Ryan followed the yellows as they swept up behind the herd. The animals started moving away from them, leaping across the plain like frogs. Ryan felt like a sheep dog, what with this constant running back and forth keeping the Flavadores in line.

Ryan felt the rumbling of thousands of Flavadores even at a hundred miles an hour. One of the adults directed him to sweep backwards since a group of the animals started lagging behind.

He ran back and circled round to face the small group of Flavadores that had broken away from the main herd.

One particularly huge Flavadore refused to move as Ryan chased away the others that surrounded it. "Come on beast move, join your friends," Ryan said. And he started shooing the animal to get it to move.

"Thrummmmm," the animal bellowed and charged at Ryan.

"Whoa," Ryan said.

It did not occur to him to run; his first reaction was to hold up his hands to block the animal as it leapt. The air shimmered in front of him and he felt all the energy drain from his body. The animal hit an invisible wall that Ryan had somehow conjured in front of him and fell to the ground.

Ryan let his hands droop and he breathed in deeply, his body ached. He felt sick, like he had just done the most punishing session at the gym.

The Flavadore struggled up onto its feet and opened its mouth to bellow at him, spraying him with its drool. It stepped forward towards him and Ryan did the only thing he could and swung a hand weakly and to his surprise he battered the creature aside like an elephant could cast a lion aside.

The animal hit the ground, and rolled in the dirt. Ryan advanced on the animal and it yelped and followed its fellow Flavadores.

"Wow," Ryan said examining his hands. He stood there panting slower and slower as the weakness left him and his energy returned.

"Come on Human," someone chided him and he snapped out of its thoughts. He then followed the herd continuing the round up, wondering how he had just fended off something as large as a rhino.

•

The day finally ended after the herd moved into a new area where they were free to graze. As the afternoon gave way to the evening and the sun drifted towards the horizon Ryan was bringing up the rear of his group of tribe members heading back home.

The group reached the cluster of houses just as it was getting dark. Ryan's clothes were soaked with sweat, he was panting and slouching like an old man. He went straight to his room and collapsed onto his bed.

"So how did you like your first day," Reesa asked him from his bedroom door.

"Tiring," came his muffled response from his face buried in the mattress.

"You'll get used to it," she said and left him to lie on his bed.

"Not likely," he said to himself.

Chapter 18

Later that night Ryan was sitting alone in his room.

He had just had dinner with the rest of the family and he was angry at all of them, his uncle, Nur, Reesa, cousins, aunt all of them. He had tried to strike up conversations, but found himself snubbed by everyone. In the end he had just sat silently scowling at his dinner plate.

He did not understand his uncle or his aunt; they did nothing to help him integrate with those around him. It was like they had just forgotten he was there. He wished he was back on Earth even if that meant dying, at least there he had family who liked him.

His gaze drifted to his forearms where his new bony plates were, he rubbed one of them with his fingertips. He then slumped where he sat and bowed his head, knowing they would never go away. He looked around his room trying to think of something to do that would elevate this sadness. A bulge under his clothes in his suitcase caught his attention.

Underneath was his rugby ball, *I could chuck that around*, he thought, *but who with*? *Wait I don't need anyone else.*

He smiled, picked up the ball remembering its weight and rough imitation leather surface; it was good to hold it again.

He received odd looks from those adults he passed in the corridors on his way outside, but he did not care. When he stepped into the courtyard the sun was setting on the horizon leaving a red sky behind it, basking the fields of crops in a warm glow. The air was cool and dry and a slight breeze made it even chillier. He passed by Nur and a few of the other children his age. He did not look at them just walked on towards the road.

Everything was quiet on the farm, no one zipping about, it was just him on the path. Over his shoulder he heard some snide comments and laughter, which he knew was about him. The anger he felt towards them made throw the ball as hard as he could giving a huge amount of spin.

The ball arced gracefully in the air and Ryan used all his speed to race down the track in order to catch it. He ran backwards after he had gone far enough and saw it plummeting to Ontaria and caught it.

He looked back down the track and saw the children all looking at him, as well as some of the adults. *Wait till they see this*, he thought.

On Earth he had never managed to throw a rugby ball as it should be thrown. He could not use his speed as much as he wanted to, his grandparents said he could not take that risk. He didn't need to do that here though. After a quick glance to make sure everyone was watching, Ryan accelerated further down the track and then launched the ball twisting his wrists in the final moment of the throw to produce beautiful spin.

He chased it and only just kept up with its speed, the gyroscopic effect of it twisting in the air kept it flying for hundreds of yards. Then it began to descend and Ryan dived for the catch and rolled along the floor as if making that winning try in the rugby world cup.

For the next twenty minutes he kept on throwing and catching, always keeping the farm building in view. On one easy throw he managed to speed well ahead of the ball and waited for it to reach him. Nur ran across the path of the ball and intercepted it.

Ryan opened his mouth to object but stopped himself; he was not going to make a scene.

Nur did not say anything at first, she had obviously expected Ryan to whine and asked for his ball back, he wasn't going to play that game. Though it was one he realised he had played before, but not from this side, he had always been the person like Nur, waiting for his victim to whine. For a second, he zoned out as he felt a stab of shame.

"I said what is this?" Nur repeated, smiling as she did so, just as the group of children ran up to join them, Reesa was with them.

"We call it a Rugby ball," Ryan answered.

"Rugby?"

"A game on my other planet," Ryan responded.

"I can see how it works and I can see that you can throw far. Do you think you could catch a pass from me, from someone who can throw it much faster?"

Ryan saw what was going on here, it seemed as though Nur was giving him a chance, but in fact was hoping to properly embarrass him. Ryan knew though that throwing a rugby ball was about technique, not power.

"I'll catch anything you throw," he boasted.

Nur's smile disappeared.

"Then catch this," she said and accelerated to top speed down the nearest available track. Ryan accelerated with her, but could not keep up and lagged behind noticeably.

Then Nur threw the ball and just as Ryan expected, it tumbled through the air without precision or poise. He ran past Nur after the ball and easily made the catch. Despite all Nur's speed she had put into the throw, without a good spin, it was worthless.

He turned around and tossed the ball with one hand. Then he ran back to Nur.

"You'd be no good at rugby," Ryan said within earshot of the others.

He did not get the response he was hoping for. None of the children looked pleased with him or impressed that he had beaten Nur.

Instead, they ran off, as did Nur who shoulder barged him as she went.

"Hey," Ryan called out.

He got nothing but scowls from the other children.

"What?" he said raising his hands in exasperation.

He wondered where they were going, *what do they do for fun around here*? He thought to himself.

Ryan stowed his ball behind a building then tracked them across the farmlands. They left the flat featureless plains ascending into some hills bordering his tribe's territory.

Eventually they crested a hill and as Ryan reached the summit he ducked down, and crept up to the edge. On the far side was a racetrack carved out of the earth. It was mostly made of straight sections of track, but had a few corners. The strangest thing about the corners was that they went very wide on their outer edges severely straightening out each corner.

His excitement grew when he saw several Ontarians step out onto the track. They all placed helmets on their head to and lined up on the starting line.

Surrounding the track were giant steps where other young Ontarians were gathered, cheering for their favourite racers.

The race started and the competitors sped off around the track as fast as a Formula 1 driver could race. Ryan watched the race with interest marveling at how fast they were. He wondered if he would ever be able to run as quick as they could one day.

As he watched the race he noticed something was off about the way they were racing. The racers always took the outside line to every corner and

Ryan wondered why? If one of them took the inside line of the track then they could come out in front if they accelerated quickly enough.

Then he understood why none of the others bothered. They were so concerned with going fast that the thought of slowing down never crossed their minds. By taking the wide line on every corner they sacrificed a lot less speed.

The crowd cheered as the racers crossed the line.

Ryan remembered those cheers; he had been on the receiving end of them before.

The winning racer took off his helmet and one particular group of spectators cheered louder than the rest. Ryan saw that they were wearing similar coloured and tailored clothes to the winning racer. He concluded that they must be from another farm, supporting their champion.

A new set of racers stepped up to the starting line, Nur was among them.

In his mind his thoughts battled between wanting Nur to win for his family's farm, and for her to lose in order for her to be embarrassed.

The race began and Nur got off to a good start sticking to third place for most of the lap until a competitor outpaced her on the last straight, finishing up in fourth place.

There were cheers for the winners and when Nur took off her helmet there were jeers and mocking laughter.

"You're all as fast as the humans," one group of youths called out and there was more laughter.

Ryan felt anger at the children from other farms, they were dissing his family, and he could not have that.

•

The next race was about to begin and Ryan had already slipped on a helmet he had procured and waited on the line.

"Who are you?" someone said to him.

Ryan tried to think of something clever to say, "The one who's going to win," he blurted out, regretting his choice of words, they didn't sound particularly cool.

"He's wearing the clothing of Nur's family," one of the other racers pointed out.

"Where the Human is living," the first racer commented.

"A slow family," another said to general laughter.

Ryan was going to say something in response, but the race was about to kick off so he bit his tongue.

Everyone lined up.

He gathered his strength and knelt down in the stance a PE teacher at school had taught him when starting a race.

"What are you doing?" one of the racers asked.

Ryan felt his cheeks go red, luckily, they were underneath the helmet so it was un-noticed. Of course, they do not this sort of thing on Ontaria.

"Forget him," a racer said.

Then the race began.

He pushed with all his might from his 'human' starting position and accelerated ahead of the pack. The track was flat and consisted of dry dirt. Dust flew up in his wake as he sped along its length. He was in the lead, but not for long as the other racers caught him up and ran level with him.

Then came the first corner, a left turn.

Predictably the other racers took the wide line Ryan however slowed down and hugged the bend in the track as close as he could, trying to maintain balance. He made it round and accelerated out of the corner, ahead of the other racers who despite their speed had not completed the turn.

Ryan was only a few metres ahead and he heard the other racers catching up once again behind him.

Cheers followed him around the track, spectators were side stepping at top speed alongside him to watch.

The next corner was a hairpin bend to the right and Ryan repeated his tactic taking an inside line and decreasing his speed to make sure he did not go careering off the track. The other racers took the wide line without slowing, but it did not matter the sharper the bend the more distance they had to travel and Ryan was already shooting off down the straight as they were halfway through.

On the next corner Ryan once again took the inside line and this time he was followed by another racer who had noticed his success.

But he did not slow down, he continued into the corner at high speed and on the way out. He couldn't turn properly and so skidded in the dry soil of the track. He lost his footing and tumbled off the track rolling in the dust.

Ryan was thrilled, people were cheering for him again and he was in the lead ahead of the pack.

The last turn came and Ryan continued his tactic and was alone this time. Then he became concerned.

After the last turn was a long straight section of track and it went on far enough for the other racers to catch him.

He made his way around the corner then pushed his legs for all they were worth. They screamed in pain and he felt the beginnings of a stitch form across his stomach.

It was not enough.

Halfway down the last straight the other racers had caught up with him his lead was gone. Three quarters down the straight, a couple of them had past him. With ten metres to go, he knew it was all over. Then he did what every rugby player knew they had to do when they were running for the try line and were not going to make it.

He dived.

It was not a normal dive though it had power to it, more power than he had ever put into a leap like that. He soared through the air flying past the front runner arcing just above the finishing line then he came down and crashed back onto the ground a few metres beyond it.

The crowd of Ontarian youths roared their approval.

They gathered around him.

Ryan felt he did not have to hide anymore, he had their adoration…*at last*. He took the helmet off and raised his arms yelling, "Yeah," into the night.

Big mistake!

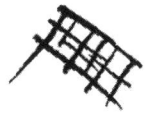

Chapter 19

The cheering stopped immediately.

Ryan's smile shrank and disappeared, his arms, that he held in the air in celebration, drooped. There was a palpable sense of both confusion and disappointment that hit him, as cheerful faces s crunched up in anger

"What's wrong with his hair?" he heard someone shout.

"What the hell is he doing here?" he heard Nur exclaim loudly.

"That's the half-human?" one of the racers said, stepping forward with his fists clenched, echoing Nur's earlier statement.

"What's the problem?" Ryan asked.

"You're the problem," one of the other racers said.

"You cheated," another added.

"That's a lie," Ryan retorted, "I beat you fair and square."

"Fair and Square?" a few repeated, not understanding Ryan's idiom.

"Humans are not faster than us."

"This one is," Ryan said pointing at himself.

Suddenly the children from Ryan's farm were right next to him.

"We're going," Reesa said forcefully.

Nur grabbed Ryan's arm. "NOW," she added.

Ryan shook him off. "WHY I WON, WHAT'S THE PROBLEM?" he shouted out.

In moments every other child who had been watching or participating in the races took up positions around Ryan and the rest of his family group. "Nur get your dirty cousin out of here," a racer said, he was as tall as Nur with dark blue hair, cut short so it barely moved around.

Ryan was about to answer that insult, but Nur spoke up first. "Shut your hole Saft, I'll take care of him," Nur said.

"Protecting the human are we Nur?" Saft commented.

Nur ran forwards and pushed Saft to the ground.

"I'm not protecting anyone, but when you insult him, you insult my family," Nur said.

Saft was back on his feet in less than a second and engaged Nur in a fight.

Ryan was fascinated as he watched the two of them duke it out at high speed. They even seemed to be performing some sort of marital art. Then he realised that he should be the one confronting Saft not Nur, it made him seem weak. Then Saft dodged a punch to the face from Nur and responded himself with a punch to Nur's stomach. Nur doubled over and Saft kicked away at her legs and she fell to the floor.

"Weak, just like the humans," Saft said.

Nur stood up, but she was unsteady on her feet. "Still trying to protect him," Saft said and he rushed forward to strike another blow to Nur.

Ryan, who could fight his own battles, stepped in front of Nur and blocked Saft's punch. He raised his arm bending it at the elbow forming an L shape, stopping the punch from Saft from connecting. The boy screamed in pain and cradled his arm, backing away from Ryan. The other racers and spectators did not move, just looked at him in surprise.

"What is your arm made of?" Saft replied rubbing his own limb.

"Bone," Ryan replied.

"Solid bone," Reesa added.

"You mean you all have hollow bones?" Ryan replied.

"Less weight more speed," Reesa explained.

"Get out of here," Saft said waving his good arm at them.

Everyone, apart from those Ontarians belonging to Ryan's family group, shouted, "LEAVE!"

Before he could respond, Nur and Reesa grabbed him and dragged him away at high speed. Ryan's legs trailed behind him as him and the rest of his family ran from the racetrack and stands back towards the crops and farmland beyond. When they far enough away, they dropped him to the ground. "What the hell did you think you were doing?" Nur yelled at him.

"Winning," Ryan shot back and scrambling to his feet.

"You're not fast enough," Nur replied.

"I'm the only one from our family who actually won a race tonight," Ryan sneered.

Then he discovered that Swifters weren't just fast runners as Nur's fist arched through the air like a swing ball and hit him in the face,

Nur screamed in pain at striking Ryan's skull made of far denser bone than a normal person. She stumbled away.

Ryan went into a brief spin, even slipping into unconscious as the hit jarred his brain. He stumbled backwards and dropped to the floor. He grabbed his head and managed to get his head clear. "You want to fight," and he stood up on weak legs raising his fists.

"You have no idea do you," Nur roared, "You think this is about you," she cried out. Nur breathed deeply trying to steady the pain in her hand, holding it in front of her face.

"What do you mean?" he said.

"Our family lost land when your father chose the human over us. I was six years old when I watched our farm carved up for neighboring families. Every week I try to restore some of our family honour, my father's honour and you came along thinking you could match us."

"I did match you, I won," Ryan said.

"Doesn't matter, they think you cheated, now we're the family that cheats," she said.

"Nur, we need to get you home, that hand will need ice." Reesa said.

"Let him find his own way home, he's embarrassed us enough," Nur said and she led the rest of the family away down one of the roads, throwing up so much dust that Ryan's eyes were filled with it. He tried to run after them but his coughing, spluttering, and dust-filled eyes made him fall to the ground again.

Ryan looked up from the dirt, spitting sand from his mouth. "Hey," he called out to them, but they were already gone. He stood up. He was angry, he should have been accepted not rejected by everyone. He had won the race, maybe in an unorthodox manner, but without cheating though.

"I HATE THIS PLANET," he shouted into the night.

Everything was going wrong for him, everything he tried to do to integrate did not work.

And worse...

...as he looked around the fields and roads, and it occurred to him that he did not have a clue where he was.

Chapter 20

Ryan ran about the land his family possessed for an hour. He was still trying to find his way home.

It felt like the early morning when he finally saw it, the family farmstead illuminated by dull lights.

He walked the rest of the way, too tried to keep running.

When he reached the courtyard, he hesitated at the door to the residential area. Maybe it was not a good idea to maybe wake everyone up and incur more wrath.

Ryan sat down in the courtyard. He signed and kept his eyes down and wiped them of the tears that started to flow.

He slumped and stared off into the night, not even the sight of three moons lifted his spirits.

Why are my family treating me this way, he thought to himself.

He looked up into the sky and saw the moons and stars, the entire Milky Way in front of him clearly visible without light pollution. "Just like Yorkshire," he said.

He then sniffed. It was not, nothing like it.

Yorkshire, his real family and food he liked were far away.

He suddenly heard something behind him, the patter of tiny feet.

His eyes widened and a shiver went down his spine, wondering what creature was approaching him. He knew it could not be a fox or a rabbit. Did Ontaria have giant spiders?

He turned slowly and saw of all things a dog.

It was panting and had a big tongue flopping out of its mouth. It was about the size of a sheep dog and had grey fur.

Ryan smiled, and lent over to hold out his hand.

The dog blinked and wandered over and licked his palm, then snuggled closer.

"I didn't know there were dogs here," Ryan said to the dog.

He rubbed its neck and did not find a collar, he wondered if it was a stray or maybe Ontarians did not need to register their dogs.

He sat there and patted the dog on the head and it sat next to him panting hard and looking out over the farm.

He felt better for a while. Bill had had a dog, a little Chihuahua called Arnie. This dog reminded him of Arnie a little bit, of the walks in the park with him when Bill was still his friend.

It then clicked in his head, this place, this farm was not for him, he wanted to go home, he wished he could run there, but he could not, his home was far away.

Then it occurred to him there was a way to get back there.

Ryan stood up and petted the dog one last time. "Thank you," he said to it and it licked his hand one last time and trotted off.

•

The next day Ryan navigated the early morning wakeup call and breakfast on autopilot. He blocked out everyone, every curse or insult or indifference by the adults.

When everyone assembled in the courtyard to receive the daily instructions. Ryan was there, alone in the corner waiting to do his part.

His uncle gave out instructions and ignored Ryan.

Then everyone started running in different directions to do their jobs.

Ryan was in his uncle's group and was the last to leave the courtyard. "Keep up," his uncle said to him before the rest of the Swifters ran off.

Ryan did not follow, instead he stood there alone in the courtyard the dust of the recently departed floating around him.

He took one last look at the farm then started running.

But not to where he had been instructed.

He ran for the highway; his uncle had brought him down. Then he followed it in the direction he thought he had come from. This led him to another road and he tried to remember which direction it was from here.

He took a guess and started running again. His guess was correct as he saw the city, which had a spaceport.

He headed towards it and to his great relief the Duodecim was still parked on the runway.

The spaceport was just as busy as it was the other day.

Ryan stood out, not just because he was half-human, but because he was still wearing farm clothes. He received odd stares and ignored them all.

Eventually he found what he was looking for, a gate leading out onto the runway. He assumed that Admiral Tarms would be by her ship.

There was virtually no security as far as he could see, no check in or anything like that. Ontarian culture seemed to be more streamlined or even more trustworthy.

He wondered how they did it.

"It's because of us," someone said behind him.

Ryan froze, wondering if he had just entered a restricted area of the spaceport. That, coupled with the fact he was the Half Human, probably meant deep trouble for him.

"Turn around, you're not in trouble," the voice said.

He slumped in defeat and turned to face what he assumed was a cop, but instead found himself looking into the face of a young girl probably the same age as him. He also recognized her, she had been staring at him when his uncle had led him through the space port on his first day. She wore a one piece jumpsuit, and embedded in it were crystals that glowed in time with the pink crystals in her hair, which jutted from her skull like a crown.

"Yeah that's right it's me," she said. "Come on you need to leave this area."

"I'm just looking for the Admiral," Ryan said holding up his hands.

"Do you really think that an Admiral will see you?" she asked.

"She brought me here, she can take me back, I'm fairly certain I don't have to be here if I don't want to be."

"So now you think that we'll put a ship into space for you, just so you can go back to your other planet?" the girl asked.

Ryan opened his mouth to speak, but instead she raised a hand.

"Don't bother, I know you do want those things, you want to go back to Earth, that you're fed up with Ontaria already."

"How do you know..?" he began.

"My name is Laveria Astral," she replied.

"I don't know who you are, are you famous or something?" Ryan asked.

She rolled her eyes, "My name, my surname," she said.

Ryan opened his mouth to speak again.

"I'm a member of the Astral Tribe," she clarified.

She spoke again before Ryan even had time to form his next question in his mind.

"You don't know about us, have you not done any reading on our cultures or the tribes, no, you haven't. Look I'm from the Astral tribe we have the power to see into the minds of others and affect them."

"You, you can mind read?" Ryan asked.

"Yes and by the way I am not plain looking."

Ryan did not immediately clock what that meant until he thought back to his first encounter with this girl. "Oh," he said.

"Indeed," she said with a false smile. "You have to go, run back to your farm and live your life."

"I don't want to, I want my life on Earth again," Ryan said.

"Thinking only of yourself I see," she replied.

"Look I didn't ask to come to this world I was forced. I'm sure I could have continued to live on Earth if I wanted," Ryan said.

"Not with their atmosphere, the toxins in their air or even the radiation. You would die there. Our tech could give you a few months there at best."

"Better than dying here, where I have nothing, where I am nothing, where no one wants to even get to know me."

"So that's it, one day and you're done?"

"It's not the life I wanted," he said.

"When people get what they want, it's usually at the expense of others," she said.

"Look I..." He stopped and thought, *what am I doing, telling my life story to this complete stranger*. Then something she had said finally sunk in.

"You can read my mind, are you controlling me right now?" he asked.

"Of course not, but I am making you comfortable to tell me the truth," she answered.

"What is it your tribe does for Ontaria?" he asked.

"We smooth out the rough edges, we grease the wheels, we open people's minds. You thought to yourself earlier how easy it was for you to pass into places, how there was no security. Well, it is easy when people like us know what people are thinking. We don't wonder why people are in the areas they are, we already know."

"We are one of the smallest tribes on Ontaria, but we are everywhere, taking away rudeness, getting people to speak the truth, letting them see what they normally wouldn't see. To give them everything they need to make choices."

Ryan backed off, he was not sure if he wanted someone in his head, even though it had felt good to talk a few minutes ago.

"It does feel good doesn't it, better than bottling all up inside," Laveria said.

Ryan huffed, "Listen I'm more human than Ontarian, those people on the farm, supposedly my family - don't care for me, just because I'm different. We have a word for that on my homeworld. Do I deserve to put up with that for the rest of my life? No, I do not. They have no reason to hate me, they do not love me and I can tell they never will. I want to be back with my grandparents, who love me and I love them."

Laveria breathed deeply and closed her eyes, "I can feel that love, I can feel your pain," she said. "Now feel your family's," and she grabbed him by the temple and forehead.

Suddenly he felt a rush of memories flooding into his mind, seen through the eyes of many people, every so often they would pause and he would witness something played out in sharper detail,

He saw his uncle standing before some sort of official government Intelligen, who handed him a tablet. When uncle Chiqu read it he said, "Half of our land?" he said in dismay.

The man replied, "This was your brother's farm, technically it's half his land, fair price for his crime," the Intelligen replied.

The he saw the farm, except there were many more buildings making up the courtyard. Then he saw some were getting up and leaving the area. His uncle Chiqu and his aunt Nar watched the farm be reduced to a few scattered buildings. He witnessed them comforting each other as their farm strolled off before their very eyes.

He felt pain and sadness, he had a sense of his uncle and aunt toiling away for respect or dignity.

He saw two brothers his dad and Chiqu arguing, with Edeps trying to explain and his uncle hearing none of it. *"It's not the fact you were in love it's that you told us nothing, you didn't involve us at all, and now everything has changed."*

Then he saw his uncle and then saw through his eyes as he watched the Duodicim land, thinking, *how do I do this, what will this boy be like?* Then as the ramp opened and Chiqu saw two figures emerge, one he recognised and one he did not. As Chiqu ran towards the ship Ryan slipped into focus and his uncle remembered his brother, this boy's father. The broken brotherhood, the farm and what he had lost and coldness came over him.

Then he was seeing through Nur's eyes. They darted from Ryan to her father, noted his frustration and sadness, and then fixating on Ryan thinking it was all because of him that her dad was sad.

Then Laveria released her grip on him and Ryan's brain assimilated the new memories and processed them.

He blinked once then looked at Laveria.

"They don't hate me," he said.

"No Ryan they don't, to them you are a reminder of the past," Laveria said.

"How could you show me that?"

"You are not the first Ontarian to be given the gift of seeing through the eyes of another, to understand their pain. To have the One Beyond open their Mind. They should not feel hatred to you, but they cannot help it. Like humans we are complicated creatures, but unlike your other half, we can allow others to feel the pain of the past and better understand it, my tribe doesn't allow Ontarians to silence themselves or bottle up the feelings inside, we bring them out."

"Who is the One Beyond," he asked.

"Who do you think?" she replied.

"So, you're like the priests as well?" he asked.

"Kind of, only we don't dress funny," she replied.

Ryan looked at the Duodicim, it was still an option, only now he felt he owed an apology to his family.

"Tell me more about what they went through," he asked.

"Your family can tell you more if you ask them, if you see where they are coming from yourself."

Ryan stared back at her.

"Go, run along home," she said.

Ryan wanted to say thank you, but the words could not come out, they were clouded amongst his own feelings of guilt, not to mention the giant epiphany he had just had.

"You're welcome," Laveria said.

•

It was lunch time before Ryan returned to the farm.

Everyone was in the courtyard eating lunch, relaxing, resting or getting stuff ready for the next shift.

He skidded to a halt at the edge of the courtyard and all eyes were on him for a second, before they turned to his uncle, who had his back to him.

His uncle looked over his shoulder, did a double take then rounded on Ryan.

He immediately strode forward clicking a finger and pointing to an area just beyond the courtyard and Ryan followed him as his uncle marched over there. He heard the man breathe intensely through his nose, and saw that his fists clenched as both of them met at the spot his uncle had indicated.

"Where did you go?" his uncle seethed through gritted teeth once they appeared to be out of ear shot of the others. "Do have any idea how worried we were?" and he raised his voice slightly.

Ryan saw out the corner of his eyes everyone in the courtyard staring at him. Nur was smiling while she chewed her food.

He kept his head down, wondering if he should lie, but the memories he had seen were still rattling around his head.

He wanted to bottle everything up inside and just take his punishment. *What was the point though?* he thought. He needed to be honest with his family, now that he knew the truth.

He breathed in, sniffed and looked his uncle in the eye.

"I tried to go see Admiral Tarms, I hoped she would take me back to Earth," and he wiped his teary eyes. "I'm sorry uncle, I just wanted to go home so much," he blurted out and hung his head.

His uncle looked away for a bit, the plates on his arms rose and fell slightly. "We were looking for you, we thought you were lost," he managed to say.

"I was at the space port," Ryan explained.

"Did you see the Admiral?" he inquired.

"No, I didn't, I was stopped by a member of the Astral tribe."

"The Astral tribe?" his uncle said. Chiku turned on the spot rubbing the back of his head with one hand as he processed this.

The courtyard was silent as everyone tried to listen in.

His uncle then stood still and let the hand drop to his side.

"I don't know how it feels to be you Ryan, no one else is half human half Ontarian, but that doesn't mean that you get to do this sort of thing," he said.

"I know, I was only thinking of myself," he admitted.

"And what have you learned?" his uncle said.

Ryan paused, squaring away in his head the fact that this family of his had suffered and he was not making it any easier for them. "That I owe you and everyone else here better than to run off like that. I have much to learn and I am prepared to learn."

Chiqu huffed.

"Everyone expects me to shout and scream at you, that's what I should do, it's what I want to do. This is my farm..." he began.

Ryan opened his mouth to speak.

"...It would have been your father's, if he hadn't sought Sanctuary somewhere else. I understand what it is like to get a life you did not expect."

136

He sighed deeply.

"I'll give you a pass today, but this doesn't happen again."

Ryan nodded meekly.

"I'll do better too," he added then his uncle patted him on the back and gestured for him to go back to the courtyard.

Nur looked confused, but when she looked at her father, and saw his pained face soften with a smile, she stared off into the distance deep in thought.

Reesa was next to her, sat really close and she watched the whole thing with the detached interest of a non-family member. The others were whispering to one another.

His aunt yelled, "Get some food, Ryan," which sounded like an order so Ryan came and took some of the bread like stuff he liked, and stood a way from the others, red in the face, however he felt better about himself.

Chapter 21

Trettan was scouting out the Half Human's current location. He noted that the farmhouses this family used were scuffed, with rusted joints, and smiled.

He was concerned with the flat land surrounding the farm though, as that would mean that the superior speed of the Swift tribe members might compromise the operation.

He moved through tall crops along the hills and ridges surrounding the property, always when possible avoiding casting a silhouette against the sky. He noticed that five hundred yards out from the farm were some unattended channels that separated two fields for irrigation purposes.

We will encourage the children to seek safety in this area, no doubt the Half Human would join them there, *Trettan thought.*

He smiled, everything was going to plan, just one more push and everything he wanted for him and his people would come to pass.

•

Ryan lay alone in his room, his mind racing with the memories Laveria had shared with him and what he now knew.

Despite the anger and frustration of the last couple of days he realised that he had to make some kind of effort. That he had to at least try to fit in here properly.

A loud humming noise interrupted his thoughts. The walls of his room and indeed the whole building vibrated as the source of the sound seemed to pass over the house. Ryan did not care about it and he turned over to get comfortable.

The next noise certainly grabbed his attention when he heard an explosion. He sat up and looked around. There were no windows in his room and so he saw nothing, but he heard screams and shouting. He got off his bed and put his shoes on, he got the feeling he was going to have to run very fast.

When he stepped out of his room his cousins and fellow tribe members were already rushing out of theirs, slipping on jackets and their shoes.

"What's going on, what was that?" Deeskly cried out standing in the middle of the corridor shouting at any adult that went past.

"BACK TO YOUR ROOMS," Ryan's aunt barked out strolling down the hall, bellowing orders at the other children.

"Mum what going on?" Deeskly shouted again.

"Not now," she replied, "rooms!"

Suddenly the whole building started to shake. Ryan realised this was not like the last time it had shook, it was moving, rising.

For one moment everything went forty five degrees as one side of the building raised itself on its legs. From every room was the sound of things like furniture or plates crashing into one another. Then everything levelled out as the other side rose as well.

"Evacuate," his aunt ordered, and there was riot as everyone still in the building clamoured for the exits.

Ryan struggled down the corridor, as with every footfall of the building, it would rise and dip. He finally made it to the exit and looked down at the ground that was at least ten feet below him, he did not want to jump, but someone shoved him in the back. He landed awkwardly and rolled on the ground and found himself in a situation more chaotic than the one inside the house.

All the buildings were beginning to move and the adults were shouting pointing their hands at them commanding them to stop. Ryan spotted that they had some sort of remote controls and were frantically pushing buttons to try to stop the buildings from getting up and about. The ground shook as a dozen or so structures started to move, they did not seem to be going anywhere just wandering aimlessly around. Adding to the problems they were facing was that it was getting dark. The sun was skimming the horizon and the only light was coming from those on the buildings themselves, which were moving around erratically. It was like being at a destruction derby at night with only the car headlights to illuminate the 'race'.

"Nur get all the children to the irrigation channels," Ryan's uncle shouted out

"Yes dad," Nur replied who had just come out of the building behind Ryan.

"Deeskly, Reesa, Hamour, Liolet and the rest of you get going to the Rayner Ridge," Nur shouted out, even pushing some of the little kids, "Follow Hamour," she shouted at them.

"You too," she said to Ryan who followed the group of children fleeing the area.

The ridge was only a couple of hundred yards away and it offered a terrifying view of what was happening back at the home site.

Ryan watched as the buildings circled around the courtyard tearing through nearby fields, bumping into one another and falling to the ground.

"What's happening?" Reesa asked.

"I saw the control tower on the way out, it's been destroyed," Deeskly said.

Ryan gazed towards the outskirts of the home site where there was a fire, its black smoke rising into the air from a tangled mess of metal.

"Are we being attacked?" Ryan said.

"By whom?" Nur asked.

Screams and shouts and the sounds of pounding buildings were everywhere. Ryan then recognised a noise he had heard before, the humming sound that had first passed over the house before this chaos had begun.

Three shapes hovered above them. To Ryan, squinting in the in the dim light, they looked like giant wasps.

He then saw three more black shapes descended from the hovering objects, which landed in amongst the children. Nur reacted first.

"TREDICIM," she shouted, "RUN."

"Come on Ryan," someone said next to him, pulling on his arm.

Ryan pulled his gaze away from the creatures and followed Reesa and they both sprinted away from the ridge.

"Where are we going to go?" Ryan shouted as they ran.

"Back to the home site, there are no Tredicim there," Reesa responded.

"What can they do?" he asked.

"Do?"

"We can run fast, the Frayans have super strength what do they do?" Ryan asked again.

"They can use the powers of the other tribes."

Ryan suddenly skidded to a halt when a Tredicim appeared out of the darkness to block their path.

Ryan and Reesa turned around to run the other way, but two creatures surrounded them. "What do you want?" Reesa said.

"The Half Human," one of the creatures said in a voice that sounded like a roar.

"Why?" Ryan said.

"Not your concern."

The trio advanced on Ryan ignoring Reesa.

"Run Ryan," she shouted and then she was pushed aside.

Ryan sprinted for a gap in the advancing creatures, but they were just as fast as him and blocked his path. Ryan could not slowdown in time and slammed into one of the creature's sides, rebounding off it and rolling to the ground.

"You can't escape," one of them said to him.

The creature then looked away from him like it was sensing something else in the air. Then bounding out of nowhere came Ryan's uncle and some of the other adults.

The Tredicim roared at their adversaries. The three black creatures immediately started to attack and Ryan was amazed as everyone fought at super speed.

One of them broke away from group and started speaking into a gauntlet on his arm, and then Swift tribe members overcame him.

Ryan got up and while avoiding the fight going on around him he made his way to Reesa who was just picking herself up.

"Let's get away from here?" Ryan said, helping her up.

"Move," she cried out and pushed him to one side.

A gigantic foot stamped down in the place they were standing just moments ago. The ground shook and dirt flew all over Ryan and Reesa.

Strolling into the fray came the buildings from the home site. They towered over everyone, Tredicim and Swift tribe members alike. One of the creatures pointed at Ryan and Reesa, and one of the buildings, a small shed, advanced on them both.

They did not have time to get up and run away as the building's foot rose off the ground and slammed down on the pair of them.

Ryan foolishly, but instinctively, raised his hands and closed his eyes.

When he opened them he almost fell over in surprise. The building was actually struggling as it tried to bring its foot down. Ryan's hands, raised above his head like he was trying to block out the sun, were somehow enough to hold back the building. He felt the cold metal of the foot as his palms rested against it. He did not quite understand how he was doing it, but he found it was actually quite easy to do, like holding back a small child that was trying to punch you with an outstretched arm.

Ryan pushed back and then the building fell onto its side, its legs flailed around, like an upside down turtle.

"How did you do that?" Reesa said.

He looked down at his hands as if they held the answer to the whole thing. "I don't know," he replied.

Another building came in from his right and this time swiped a foot at him like a bear swiping at a salmon in a river.

Ryan, brimming with confidence, grabbed the arm and once again held the whole building back on his own.

"You have Frayan strength," Reesa spluttered.

He looked up at the building whose mechanical limbs were whining in an attempt to pull away from him. Ryan decided to test out this Frayan strength. He pulled at the leg and tore it out of its socket. The metal and plastic snapped, wires sparked, as they were torn free. Ryan then swung the leg like a cricket bat and knocked the shed aside, denting its walls.

Another building tried its luck and tried to belly flop on him. It was a smallish shed and Ryan got underneath it and raised his hands catching it like a ballerina catching another dancer.

He then threw the building at another one and the two building crashed into a heap of legs, metal and foodstuffs.

Nur was suddenly by his and Reesa's side.

"How are you doing this?" she asked.

"I don't know," Ryan replied.

Another building came striding towards them, larger than the first.

"Girls, launch me at that thing," Ryan said.

Both girls looked at him.

"You what?" Nur asked.

"Throw me using your super speed," he said.

"You sure?" Reesa asked.

Ryan was bouncing on the spot he licked his lips as he looked up at the building coming towards him. "Yeah," he said with a broad smile.

Nur shrugged at Reesa and they grabbed his arms and rushed forward accelerating as fast as them could just a few dozen metres.

They launched him forward and Ryan, drunk on power, yelled in joy and fear as he stuck the building on its barn doors caving them in.

The building went flying backwards and Ryan bounced off the building to fly backwards where he landed, cracking the dry ground around him. It was exhilarating.

Suddenly one of the Tredicim was by his side and grabbed his arms.

Ryan felt a jolt of anger rush through him, at being touched by a stranger, especially one that had tried to attack him on Earth. Muscle memory kicked in from years of taekwondo training and he wrenched the Tredicim's arm aside, ducked a crude punch, then lashed out with a kick sending the Tredicim flying.

"Ha, HAH!" Ryan called out and he bounced on his feet and held up his hands. "Come on then," he said to those around him "Pick on my family would you." Swifters and Tredicim nearby looked on in shock, the battle had paused as everyone took a moment to process a Swifter knocking aside a building like a toy.

The lead Tredicim stepped forward to look at the down building, "This changes everything," he said, "retreat," he bellowed.

A roar washed over the area as the Tredicim bellowed into the air, immediately the other buildings shut down and collapsed into the ground. The Tredicim disengaged from their fights with Ryan's Uncle and the other adults and sped away disappearing into the night.

"Don't follow," Ryan's uncle called out, "see to the wounded."

Seconds later the humming noise passed over them and zoomed off.

Ryan was still looking at his hands and the building he had pushed over.

Nur and Reesa rushed to his side and he embraced them in a celebratory hug, just like he would do with his teammates on Earth.

"Well done, did you see that, that's team work," he yelled as Nur and Reesa let him clap them on the shoulders.

Then they smiled and yelled and hollered too.

Eventually their revelry dimmed and Ryan was suddenly aware his uncle was standing over him. His expression made Ryan uncomfortable, because for the first time his uncle looked worried.

Chapter 22

The entire area looked like a war zone.

The moving buildings had done a lot damage having torn up the home site as they blundered around uncontrollably, stepping on equipment and trampling the courtyard until it looked like several meteors had struck it. In the fields of crops surrounding the farm there were long gashes and upturned crops. Pillars of smoke rose from shouldering fires, giving the air an ashy smell.

All the adults were busy tidying, rushing around at high-speed carrying the wounded and removing wreckage. Other Ontarians had joined the Swift Tribe; a number of Frayans had arrived in some floating cars. They were busy lifting the buildings and returning them to their proper places, no one wanted them to move of their own accord for now. Ryan was sitting in a nearby field with the children, told to clear the area lest the Tredicim return. He watched the Frayans in groups of three lift up entire buildings like humans would lift a sofa, the ground shook when they placed them back down.

Everyone was then in for a real treat as a ship flew down to hover above the site. Ryan recognised it instantly, it was the Duodicim, which parked itself in mid-air. When it was stationary, drop pods descended from it, dispersing more Frayans and Intelligen who set about trying to fix the building's walking mechanisms.

He was also very sure that he saw an Ontarian from another Tribe. This one had no plates on his arms or legs, but he had dreadlock looking things made of bone protruding from his skull, which realigned themselves to produce something like radar dishes around his ears. His eyes were huge and he seemed very alert even a small gust of wind seemed to excite him. At one point he sniffed the air and took a particular interest in Ryan, eventually he strolled off in the direction of the ridge where the battle with the Tredicim had taken place.

Ryan was surprised to see that the Admiral had also come with them, who went straight to Ryan's Uncle.

He watched the two of them talk together and for a second, they both glanced over at Ryan. In his uncle's and the Admiral's eyes Ryan could see what they were thinking. They were rattled by Ryan's ability to be as strong as the Frayans.

It had unnerved him too, now that the excitement had worn off. When Threngst had told him about different tribes and their abilities he had never said anything about someone having two of those powers. *Super speed and strength, I am turning into a comic book character!* He thought to himself.

Right now, he did not want to think about it, he had other questions and so he turned to Reesa who was sitting with him, watching the activity going on in front of them. "Reesa, who exactly are the Tredicim?" he asked.

She looked back at him as if he had just said a rude word.

"They are the Thirteenth tribe and were our rulers at one time."

"Rulers?"

"With their ability to mimic the powers of the other tribes they were deemed the strongest tribe. They were to rule us, use all the tribe's abilities for the greater good. But with their powers they also had a desire for more power. They stripped away many freedoms, passed alternate laws the Patriarchs had laid down. Very soon they made slaves of the weaker tribes. Then they decided that they didn't need the other tribes and started exterminating them, millions died, we resisted, and after a long war we defeated them."

"What happened to them?" Ryan asked.

"The remaining members of their tribe were incarcerated in a special prison. Some however escaped imprisonment and have tried to disrupt our society or free their brethren ever since," Nur answered and she shuffled over.

"But why attack us?"

"I have no idea," Nur replied.

"Nur?" a voice stammered behind them

Every one of the kids turned as one to see Saft and some of his family standing there, looking over the farm with their mouths agape. Ryan recognized that it was Saft who had spoken, and scowled at him.

"Saft," Nur said in confusion. "What are you doing here?"

The boy swallowed and his eyes bulged as he took in the devastation. He paled when he looked at a bloodied group of Ontarians receiving medical attention.

"We-we heard what happened," he blurted out.

"Well, our farm got attacked by Tredicim," Nur said and turned her back to him.

"Thanks to Ryan, the half human, some of us would be dead," Nur added over her shoulder.

Saft looked down at Ryan. He saw on the young Swifter's face a look of respect and surprise that the human could be of any use. "You fought the Tredicim?" he asked.

"I did," Ryan replied.

"You fought for Ontarians, for these Swifters?" he asked.

"Why wouldn't I, they're my family," Ryan replied curtly, and he turned away from Saft and scowled along with his cousin. Then like Nur he said over his shoulder. "You think because I'm just a half human I wouldn't fight for my home?"

"Ryan, come with us," someone said.

He looked up at his uncle and Admiral Tarms. His uncle turned to Saft and his friends. "Shouldn't you be on your own farm?"

Saft nodded, "Sorry sir," and he and his group ran off.

Ryan got up and followed his uncle and the Admiral in the direction of the home site.

He ended in the kitchen and took a seat, for some reason he felt he was in trouble and to try to lessen any punishment, he obeyed and sat down quietly.

"Why did you never say you had the strength of the Frayans?" the Admiral asked, Ryan was not sure if she said that accusingly or out of curiosity.

"I didn't know," Ryan replied.

Another figure entered the room, a Frayan wearing his customary armoured uniform with helmet; only when he spoke did Ryan recognise him. "You wanted to see me Admiral?" Threngst asked.

"During the attack last night the half human displayed strength that could only be that of Frayan," the Admiral stated.

Threngst looked at Ryan and even though he could not see his eyes Ryan knew he was wondering if they were talking about the same person.

"But sir his physical characteristics aren't compatible with the Frayan tribe," Threngst replied.

"Never-the-less, Ryan here stopped one of these buildings from crushing himself and another of the Swift tribe," his uncle said "Then toppled it over."

"But some of them weigh close to a ton," Threngst said disbelievingly.

"Please test the boy we have to be sure," the Admiral said

Threngst nodded and stepped over to Ryan, he held out his hand like he was about to wave at someone then said, "Ryan, punch my hand."

Ryan thought he had misheard what he had just said. But when the Frayan remained where he was, waiting patiently, he got up and hoping that the word punch meant the same thing on this planet as it did on Earth, he did what Threngst told him.

"As hard as you can," Threngst added as Ryan balled up his fist.

Ryan, feeling both a little stupid, and a little nervous about doing this drew back his hand then struck Threngst's palm.

Threngst had to steady himself as Ryan's blow actually caused the huge man to move backwards.

"Arrah," Ryan cried out grasping his hand then shaking it vigorously, it was like he had just punched a wall.

"It is true he has our strength, though not as strong as it should be for a Frayan his age, also the punch lost its power straight after it struck it doesn't seem to be under his control," Threngst replied.

"How is this possible?" Ryan's uncle asked Admiral Tarms.

Ryan noticed that the back of the Admiral's neck actually pulsated faster as she looked away obviously thinking of an answer.

"His great grandfather was a member of the Frayan Tribe," the Admiral then said.

"So, in his genetics would be the DNA codes for a Frayan's super strength," his uncle concluded.

"Yes, many Ontarians have DNA segments of other tribes," the Admiral added.

"But only one gift can assert itself, not two, he would require the physical body to use them as well?" Ryan's uncle said.

The three adults had turned away from Ryan at this point, discussing him like he was not there. He listened as best he could, but he had never got a feel for biology in science class.

"I think it's what humans call puberty, the final stages of a human's growth into adulthood. It triggers all sort of changes, some at the genetic level. It seems like it's activating some genes that in a full-bloodied Ontarian would be recessive, activating his non dominant traits," the Admiral explained. "We'll have to get a biologist to examine him to make sure."

"Will he display other Tribal abilities then?" his uncle asked.

"It's possible."

"But that would mean he'll have the Intelligens' intelligence as well," his uncle said.

The Admiral suddenly glared at Ryan's uncle, as if suggesting that this half human was going to be as intelligent as her was a major offense. Ryan's uncle seemed to shrink under the Admiral's withering gaze and then changed the subject.

"What will this mean for the boy?"

"He will have to be trained by the Frayans, otherwise he won't be able to control his strength and could hurt someone."

"But what will he do?" Threngst asked.

"I will discuss this with the Tribal council, most likely he will remain with the Swift tribe," the Admiral said.

Ryan who had not been a part of the conversation for some time spoke up. "What do you mean by train with the Frayans?" he said.

"You will join our tribe in the mountains and learn to use your strength and control it," Threngst said. "We can't have you walking around with super strength breaking everything."

It occurred to Ryan that as member of the Swift tribe he was a farmer, which had been a surprise. He decided that he may want to know right now, what he would be doing with the Frayans. "What jobs will I be doing with the Frayan tribe?" he asked.

"Our tribe…" Threngst began and obviously including Ryan as one of them now, "…are the builders of Ontarian society and form one third of the military,"

"Military!" Ryan exclaimed, "I'm going to be a solider?"

"No most certainly not," the Admiral responded.

Ryan was very glad to hear that, being a solider did not interest him at all, the discipline and regulations, just did not excite him in any way. Then he suddenly had a question about his super strength. How had he used it to conjure that wall that stopped that Flavadore? To him that seemed like a completely different power. He opened his mouth then closed it again, suddenly realising that telling them he already had another power, might mean he had to go train with that too. So he kept his mouth shut.

"Arrangements will be made later, Ryan go now, re-join the children undoubtedly the clean-up operation will involve them soon," Ryan's uncle said.

Ryan had more questions. He was not stupid, during that attack the Tredicim had come for him and he wanted to know why. But he had a feeling he would get no answers if he asked directly, besides he could find out another way.

He stood up and left the room and the door closed behind him. Then he made several loud steps away from the door. Then he snuck back and looked through the keyhole.

"Were any of the Tredicim captured?" his uncle asked.

"We couldn't track the ships," the Admiral answered.

"There's nothing of real value to them on the farm what could they possibly want?" Threngst asked.

"Nur told me they went straight for Ryan," his uncle said.

"To use as a hostage? To provoke Edeps?" Threngst suggested.

"They have done it before," the Admiral said, "using a family member to get him to give up information," the Admiral added.

"But the previous incident that revealed his indiscretion with the human, was before his prison sentence, how would they force his hand with Edeps in our most secure prison?" His uncle asked.

"No doubt they had a plan," the Admiral mused.

"Ryan will have to be watched," his uncle said, "closer than before."

"And Edeps moved to a more secret facility," the Admiral added. "We'll discuss this later, the Tribal Council has to be informed of these developments," the Admiral said, moving for the door. Not wanting to get caught eves-dropping Ryan sped off down the corridor and left the building just as the door slipped open and his uncle, the Admiral and Threngst stepped out.

There was only one human family member they could be referring to.

His mother.

Before learning of his heritage, the details of her death had been too awful for Ryan to even contemplate, now he needed to know what exactly had happened and how it involved his father.

Chapter 23

Two days later Ryan was at the tail end of a convoy heading towards the nearest city to the farm. He was following Deeskly, Nur, Reesa and his uncle Chiqu along a highway. His uncle led them all towards a squat glass building in the city centre, surrounded by a manicured parkland.

"Nur, Reesa and Deeskly, you will wait here at the museum while I take Ryan for his appointment," Chiqu said.

"Excellent, the Prison Key is on display right now," Deeskly said.

"Seen it," Nur said while yawning.

"The Prison Key? I thought it was what kept the Tredicim in their prison why is it on display?" Ryan asked.

"Forgetting the past breeds the future's folly," uncle Chiqu said as if he was repeating a mantra.

"What does that mean?" Ryan asked.

"Just something we learn from the Astral tribe," Reesa said. "It's under very tight security Ryan, no one's going to be able to steal it," Reesa added.

"What does it look like?" Ryan asked.

"Check out the banner," Nur said nodding over her shoulder towards the building.

Hanging above the museum's entrance was a banner, displaying a beautiful piece of red crystal of unbelievable angles and edges.

"And that's the key that keeps them in?" Ryan asked.

"It's impossible to fake," Deeskly replied.

"And my dad was the one who used it to end the civil war?"

Nur nodded.

"Let's go Ryan," Chiqu said dismissively, and he shot off before Ryan could ask another question. He followed his uncle through the streets of the city alongside other Swift Tribe members. It was weird for him not seeing any cars, traffic lights or anything like that, even stranger that it all worked and there was no chaos.

They reached a building that in Ryan's eyes looked like a bunker. It was one level and virtually featureless. "This is a research building, inside is the biologist. He will examine you," his uncle said. "When you're done, return to the museum, do you remember where it was?"

"I do, thanks uncle," Ryan replied

"If anyone can figure it out it's this Intelligen, hopefully you'll turn out to be ok," his uncle replied, before speeding off.

The doors to the building were automatic and parted to let Ryan enter.

The inside of the building was in an extreme state of disrepair. Lights were flickering on and off at random and it had dusty floors and machinery spread throughout the corridors that were not being used.

His uncle had said one Intelligen scientist worked here, but the building was big enough to accommodate dozens. Ryan sped through the corridors at high speed trying to find them.

Eventually he heard noise, glass breaking and what sounded like Ontarian cursing. He zeroed in on the sound and found himself at the door to a laboratory. This room was neat, tidy and high tech, with clean futuristic machinery, futuristic to a human anyway, covering almost every wall. A large screen probably one hundred inches across dominated one wall displaying 'scientific information', Ryan didn't have a clue as to its meaning.

With his back to him was the scientist he was here to meet. Like all Intelligen his head bulged at the back, however this Intelligen had tied his hair down in a ponytail and it just flicked about like the tail of a snake between his shoulder blades.

Ryan cleared his throat.

As the man turned Ryan was expecting the customary frown of most Ontarians who were not pleased to see him.

The scientist turned on his heels quickly, surprised by Ryan's entrance and his fists were clenched and his teeth were gritted.

His eyes appraised Ryan's feet legs then torso, which he looked confused by, then his gaze reached Ryan's head and something appeared to click in his mind when he saw the static and uniquely coloured hair Ryan had.

Ryan steeled himself for the casual indifference he was about to face.

However, the man smiled broadly and opened his arms wide as if greeting his oldest friend in the world.

"RYAN," he called out and stepped forward grabbing his hand and shaking it warmly. No Ontarian other than his father had ever performed that human greeting with him before now.

"Err hello," Ryan muttered.

"Oh of course you won't remember me," the scientist said in a booming voice. "The last time I saw you, you were only two years old," he added.

"You've met me before?" Ryan said.

"Oh yes, your father asked me to examine you when you were young, to make sure that you were healthy," he said.

"I've been to this planet before?" Ryan exclaimed.

The scientist let go of his hand and made a grand gesture with his hands, "Oh no I went to planet Earth and secretly performed the examination, I was surprised at how healthy you were, the first Human Ontarian hybrid," he said.

"I don't understand, how did you get to Earth and examine me? It's not like crossing the street," Ryan asked.

The scientist smirked at his question, "Edeps Swift, your father, was stationed on Earth, and of course against all reason he fathered a child with an Earth woman. He arranged for me to come to your planet on a scientific expedition. I was keen to visit Earth and went gladly. I travelled across space and landed on your other homeworld without incident. In my spare time away from the prying eyes of humans and the other Ontarians, he took me to you and I examined you."

Ryan felt disarmed by this scientist's manner; he did not seem at all bothered by Ryan's half human heritage.

"My goodness, I haven't introduced myself, I'm Sensatus Intelligen, pleasure to meet you after so many years," he said. "I was sorry to hear of your mother's death. I only knew her for a short while, but she was a lovely human being," he added.

"You knew my mother?" Ryan said, pleased to find an Ontarian who spoke highly of her.

"A little, a doctor I believe, my how she doted on you when you were younger," he added. "Anyway, you've come for another an examination, one authorised by the Tribal Council this time. I hear you've displayed strength on par with the Frayans."

"Yeah I didn't notice it the first time it happened, a big Flavadore came at me and I simply pushed it away, then two days ago I held a building up, a whole building," Ryan explained, purposefully omitting the part where he conjured a wall in thin air first.

Sensatus beckoned him into the room, "It has never been heard of for an Ontarian to display the abilities of two tribes before, of course human growth cycles might be affecting your Ontarian Genetics," he explained. "Please lie on the table," he said pointing to the piece of furniture that sat in the centre of the room.

Ryan obliged and as soon as he was flat on his back probes and sensors erupted out from underneath him and began running beams of light across his body.

"Whoa," he said.

Sensatus turned away from him and looked at the giant screen on which was displayed Ryan's body as a heavily detailed x-ray.

The screen at first focused on his legs and feet.

"I see that you have all the physical attributes of a Swift tribe member. The tendons in the legs and feet give you more power and of course there's the spoiler fins," he commented.

"Spoiler fins?" Ryan said.

"Yes the plates adorning your body, when you move them correctly they provide down-force and more grip," the scientist responded.

"I didn't know that," Ryan said.

"It has to be taught, I not surprised no one has bothered, I bet your family aren't pleased you're here on planet Ontaria," he remarked.

Ryan opened his mouth to say things were getting better, but the scientist started talking again.

"It does appear as though your body has also developed minor physical traits of the Frayan tribe. Your bones are denser than they should be even for a human, as are your muscles, which probably slows you down. The added weight is not good for speed. However, you lack the height and necessary haemoglobin count to sustain the strength of normal Frayans," the scientist said. "You're unique Ryan, truly a one of kind, that makes you special, don't let anyone else tell you otherwise," he said reassuringly.

"I don't feel special, back on Earth I was popular and had friends, now I have none of those things," Ryan said.

"Oh, don't worry my friend, I bet you're slightly more popular now," Sensatus commented.

"Yeah right," Ryan said.

"No seriously, technically you were born into one tribe now it's two, many Ontarians would love to experience that," Sensatus said.

"I'd think they would be jealous," Ryan retorted.

The probes and sensors retreated from his body and Sensatus sat on the edge of the bed. "On Earth did you ever dream about having superpowers?"

"I run at super speeds," Ryan replied, "I was a living breathing superpower."

"You never wanted to be super strong or move things with your mind?" Sensatus prodded.

"Strength would have been cool I suppose, no one would be able to touch me, I would feel safer," he replied.

"It may surprise you, but even a race of super-powered beings dream of other superpowers. I myself wish I could swim without effort in the sea, going to unfathomable depths exploring one of the last wildernesses on the planet." At the mention of the sea the old scientist looked away with a dreamy expression on his face. "You see to an Ontarian, to experience the powers of another tribe would be like gaining more freedom, they'll start looking up to you more, want to know what it is like, maybe hope they will experience it too. I think you'll have all sort of Ontarians clambering to speak to you now, you'll be popular again," he said.

Ryan looked away and smiled again. He felt goosebumps rise on his skin as he imagined a crowd of Swifters gathered around him. Of him being the centre of attention once again. Everyone cheering for him, listening to him, taking his side in arguments.

"I imagine that your human friends liked you for being fast. You must have been powerful, different, but in a good way. Maybe you can recapture those feeling again? To have a power everyone wants that maybe they can get if they just hang out with you. That will make things better for you right?" the scientist suggested.

"Yeah," Ryan said, "I would have friends again just like Barry and Bill…"

Ryan trailed off when he remembered that the last time they had seen him they had rejected him. They had been his friends for years and then ditched him when he revealed his plates, plates that were totally natural for an Ontarian to have.

"Friends like that aren't friends," Ryan replied, his fists clenching. "When they knew what I was they rejected me. Suddenly having a friend with these…" and he motioned towards his plates, "…was too much. Being the buddy of the school sports star was fine, but a freak, no."

Ryan stared into space for a minute. "I don't think I would like friends who stayed around me only for my power. Popularity isn't friendship, which why they severed our relationship so easily."

"Oh," Sensatus said with a red face, and then he got off the bed and stared at the screen again.

Ryan rubbed his plates and they trembled under his touch. He stretched out his arm and consciously flipped them up and down and smiled. These were going to make him faster, make running, which he loved so much, more wonderful.

He dropped his arms and breathed deeply and let out a chilled and relaxed breath.

"What do you mean, more freedom?" Ryan asked, changing the subject.

"Have you not heard of the *Privileges of Power*, a fundamental tenant of Ontarian society?" Sensatus said, turning back to him.

Ryan shook his head and starting thinking that maybe he should be in school learning all about this stuff.

"You may have not realised, but being a Swift tribe member and being fast gives you the enormous privilege of having access to the whole world. Have you not noticed that the cities have layouts built around Swifter's speed? Have you ever seen another tribe member cross a road without first giving way to the Swifters on it?"

"No, I haven't," Ryan said, he had seen all non-Swifters cross bridges to get across a road, as if to prevent anything from slowing down a Swifter.

"That's the privilege of being a Swifter being allowed to run without hindrance on our roads. The other tribes have other privileges too, the Frayans may fight anywhere they want and their incredible strength has dictated how we built our world. It's why everything has to be as durable as possible otherwise a Frayan would break it easily. The other tribes sacrifice perhaps more efficient constructions to help them. Motus members get the privilege of food and drink required to sustain their powers, a little less for the rest of the tribes, however it's necessary. Intelligen may study and know anything to our heart's content, there are no secrets in my tribe. You have the freedom of a Swifter, now as a Frayan you have their freedoms too."

He let Ryan absorb these facts. Ryan was surprised to learn that this society worked in this fashion, ascribing different freedoms to match different tribe's abilities. Yet the different Ontarians longed to be like the other tribes and experience their joys and privileges too.

"What if, I don't know, some Ontarians asked for those other freedoms?" Ryan queried.

Sensatus smiled. "An Ontarian might dream of such things but never demand them. Since the days of the Patriarchs we have all worked together, making sacrifices to prevent war and maintain peace. Maybe one day we might all have such freedoms, but for the moment our varying powers mean we must restrain ourselves."

"I've never asked anyone who the Patriarchs are?"

"Ancient Ontarians who were the best the tribes had to offer, they came together and gave us the laws we live by, giving each tribe an important place in our culture and cementing each privilege they possess. We used to war against each other all the time, each tribe fighting for their rights. In the end we gave each other new rights and freedoms and sacrificed others to be friendly, cooperative and safe."

Ryan nodded, agreeing to this goal, this Ontarian philosophy.

"They taught that keeping their ways would one day produce the permanent solution to our differences and the gaining of true freedom, where sacrifices will not be made, where contentment will reign between all Ontarians."

"What does that mean?" Ryan asked.

Sensatus shrugged, "While I look forward to knowing I have to leave that for the Astral tribe to figure out."

"Couldn't you figure it out, aren't Intelligen very smart?"

"We are, however I don't have their powers, I could never figure it out."

Ryan watched the old scientist sigh and stare off into the middle distance. "Well, the only thing that's left now is the blood sample," the scientist said.

"Blood sample?" Ryan asked.

A few minutes later he was nursing a needle injection on his right arm.

"There," said Sensatus, "I'm sure if I examine this I can find out what's causing your multiple abilities and to determine if any more are going to present themselves in you," he said, holding the blood sample to the light.

Ryan looked as the scientist gazed almost adoringly at his blood, like a boy with a brand new book. "I hope you enjoy it," Ryan said, bitterly as the sharp stabbing pain lingered.

"Sorry, we may be more technically advanced than humans but we still use syringes," Sensatus said.

"So, what are the powers of the Tredicim?" he asked.

"They have no powers essentially. Their bodies can mimic the powers of another Ontarian if in close proximity. If they consume the blood of another tribe their body can shift to match their powers in a stronger fashion, literally changing its physical structure, in many ways they are like the Shifter tribe. It was why they were deemed to be our leaders since they could oversee all the tribes and become one with them by drinking their blood, cleanly of course."

"They could have all the powers of all the tribes?" Ryan asked astounded that these Tredicim could have such power.

"No, they can only assimilate one power at a time and it wears off after a while. For example, if they drank a Frayans blood they would be as strong as a Frayan then the second they drank Swifter blood they would become Swifters," the scientist explained. "It only has to be one drop of blood it's like a trigger that causes change in the Tredicim's body."

"When I was on Earth three of them attacked me but they looked like humans, not what I saw a few days ago," Ryan commented.

"Strangely enough if they drink human blood they can become clones of that human."

"Huh, but they were using other powers of the other tribes?" Ryan said.

"The addition of human blood into the mix doesn't have the same effect as two Ontarian sets of blood, while in a human form the Tredicim can use another tribe's power, but not two Ontarian powers."

"Good to know," Ryan said, "I'm glad those things can't be too powerful."

"Indeed, well thank you Ryan, it was pleasure to see you again after so many years, you can pop in any time if you have questions or medical problems. I'm probably the only scientist on the planet that knows a lot about your unique physiology."

"I will," Ryan said getting off the medical bed. He liked this scientist and was glad to know he liked him, which is why he had one more question for him, difficult question but one Ryan needed answering.

"Do you know how my mother died?" he asked.

Sensatus looked uncomfortable with the question.

Then he smiled. "Something you should ask your father not me. Now off with you, I have work to do," he said shooing Ryan away.

•

Ryan ran back to the museum and appreciated the speeds he could run, and the space for him to do it in this city. In York, Manchester or London cars would be filling the streets, sometimes clogged with pedestrians trying to cross. Both parties slowed one another down and only worked together because of laws and policemen and traffic wardens. Here on Ontaria the other tribes had given a gift to the Swifters who returned the compliment with other privileges as well, there was a mutual respect.

He found the museum and went inside to find Uncle Chiqu, Reesa, Nur and Deeskly.

He saw virtually no exhibits on display as he wandered around, which Ryan thought was strange. Instead Intelligen stood next to pillars attached to their skulls and next to them floating balls of matter hovered off the ground.

Ryan went to the nearest Intelligen. As he walked closer the Intelligen frowned at his black hair. Since there was no exhibit or posters denoting a subject, Ryan just asked, "What can you tell me?"

The man's frown disappeared as he focused on his job.

The swirling ball of matter formed itself into an island with a dome on it, with pylons around the circumference broadcasting into the dome. It looked a bit like the O2 centre in London.

"The Shield Prison, within which the Tredicim army are forever imprisoned," he answered.

Ryan stared at the dome, which his father had helped to set up.

"How do they survive in there? Are they all dead by now?" Ryan asked.

"Tredicim require only food and water, which is sent in through special gaps in the shield, only those on the outside can open," the man answered.

The floating matter then showed exactly that. A missile of some sorts streaking towards the dome, which then opened a small gap allowing the missile to pass through, closing quickly. "They will stay there till the last one dies, then the dome can be dropped."

"How many are in there?"

"Roughly 300,000," The man said.

"What about the Tredicim civilians?" Ryan asked.

The man looked bemused.

"The children, old people etc," Ryan clarified.

"There are no civilian Tredicim, all became soldiers in their war against the tribes."

Ryan stared once more at the dome, "What about the fortress?"

The matter transformed into a representation of the building within. The building was on top of steeply sloped hill and had high sheer walls built in a star shape. There was a single doorway in the wall with a paved road leading from it that extended a short distance from the fortress walls before disappearing into ash fields. Spikes jutted out the roof, adorned with weapons that towered over the battlefield around the fortress. As the model rotated to Ryan it looked like the maw of a creature buried in the sand, with teeth barred to the heavens.

"You'll like this, half human," the man began. "The fortress is the only such building on Ontaria, a one of a kind, its walls laced with the rarest metals we were able to gather across the solar system. Built in secret over the course of a year in the crater of a super volcano. Its design is based on two human fortresses. The Mehrangarh Fort in the human nation of India and Bastion Forts of Europe, a continent on Earth."

Ryan looked at the man, with one eyebrow raised.

"Yes that's right, you see Ontarians had never built a fortress before, there is no point having static defences of such magnitude when a variety of powers can be used against it. Yet we needed one that could last for a few days and Humans were the only ones with experience building them. We combined aspects of both to create this. Plus, our own technology to keep any tribal powers being used by the Tredicim from breaking inside."

"It was a trap, correct?" Ryan asked.

"Indeed, we built the fortress, loaded it with automatic weapons and intricate defences then it was leaked to the Tredicim that the tribes had nearly created a biological weapon, one capable of infecting only them and it was being developed in that fort. We hoped that the Tredicim would assault the fort with a majority of their army desperate to stop development of the weapon. We would trap that portion of the army giving the tribes the advantage against their remaining forces outside."

"What happened?"

"The Tredicim sent a tiny portion of their army at first, then as that small force failed to crack open the fortress, they had to send more troops into battle. Eventually 80% of their forces were committed, more than we could have hoped. Then an Ontarian activated both shield bubbles from within the fortress and escaped before it trapped him inside."

Ryan watched as what the man said played out on the model, the door to the fortress opened, several figures, his father included, ran from the building, which sealed behind him. Then a shield bubble erupted from within and covered the whole fortress. Then a second shield burst outwards like the shockwave of an explosion, encompassing the first shield then the whole prison.

"Why not just use an automated system to activate the shield?" Ryan asked.

"The Tredicim would have detected such a device in their assault and wondered why the fortress was uninhabited. Making them realise that the fortress was a decoy. The Ontarians inside were there for several days, making sure the ruse convinced them. After activating the fortress' shields, they ran to the crater's edge. Before the large one encompassed them as well as the army inside. Edeps Swift then used the Prison Key to password protect the whole system.

"Prison key?"

"It's on display in another room, the Ontarians inside the fort used it as a key to maintain the shield. The system cannot be hacked, you need the crystal to shut down the system, if you wanted to free them."

"What do these pylons do?"

"They deliver energy to the fortress to power both shields. They require a lot of power, more than the fortress could provide on its own, by transmitting power through the shields we can keep them there indefinitely."

"Is there any way for them to get out?" Ryan asked.

"The Tredicim possess no weapons capable of breaching the shield protecting the fortress or the around the crater. Most Ontarian shields will fail if damaged significantly, but the ones sealing their prison are very powerful. So, they cannot get to the shield generator, which keeps them trapped and they cannot get out of the dome to destroy the pylons that power both shields. The pylons around the outside are all linked to independent power generating networks, so they cannot be shut down simultaneously. It's like locking yourself in a safe with the only key."

"You said only 80% of their army was inside, can't the remains of their army just destroy those pylons?"

"They would need a fleet of ships and an army as big as the one in the crater to defeat the defences around the pylons. And there are twenty of them. Most of their remaining forces were captured after the dome was created."

"What would happen if they escaped?" Like global warming or nuclear war, the Tredicim sounded like the only disaster that could befall Ontaria.

"Their army would erupt with a fury they displayed seventeen years ago, the civil war would begin again."

"Surely we're ready to repel that army?" Ryan said. "Plus, they have been trapped for years, do you know what they are doing under there?"

"We are prepared as we can be, and no we don't know what they are doing. But they can't dig their way out, the volcano might erupt if they try, when the shield opens when we deliver supplies we get quick sensor readings, as far as we can tell they have built some sort of town or city."

Ryan did not need to hear anymore, he turned to leave and resume his hunt for his family.

"One minute please," the Intelligen said.

"Yes?" Ryan asked.

"I have questions about Earth," he said.

Ryan paused; he remembered the frown the guy had given him earlier, yes he had answered his questions, but that was his job. Then Ryan remembered what Sensatus had said, *no knowledge was forbidden in their tribe*. "Ask away," Ryan said.

He spent a few minutes fielding questions on America, Chocolate and TV, before the Intelligen was done with him. He actually did not mind giving what knowledge he could, he was basically the only expert on humanity on this planet. Eventually he found his uncle, cousins and Reesa, standing by a larger ball of matter that two Intelligens were manipulating.

It formed the shape of a destroyed city.

"What is this?" Ryan asked.

"The Destruction of the city of Esparda," Reesa answered.

"What happened to it?" Ryan asked.

"The Tredicim destroyed it during the war," she replied.

The floating city reverted to its former glory then it started to move through a sort of replay, as an army invaded and destroyed buildings and chillingly, people.

"Why did they do this?" Ryan asked in horror as the tiny figures of people tried to avoid the bombardment.

"It was the opening salvo of the war," Nur replied standing next to Reesa. "The Tredicim decided to eliminate the city to prove what they were capable of, to threaten the other tribes into submission."

Ryan looked around the room holding these floating exhibits.

One was of a mass grave formed in 3D from the floating matter. Another was an execution, others of a speech a Tredicim appeared to be giving to a large crowd.

Once Ryan had gone on a school trip to the Imperial War Museum in Manchester. Some of the exhibits had been haunting. In every way they had tried to show the horrors of war. Ryan had joked with his friends about the wars while on the coach. After touring the museum, they had gone away quiet. Ryan wondered if he could be that brave, and make those kinds of sacrifices. These Ontarian exhibits brought the death and destruction to life of their recent civil war in a different way. It seemed more real in this technologically advanced state.

Then he remembered that his father had ended all of this. "Is there something about my father in here?" he asked. "Didn't he end the war? Surely there is an exhibit that explains what he did."

His uncle gritted his teeth, then led Ryan to an exhibit he had missed. It was one of only a few that was not formless until an Intelligen manipulated it. It looked like a plinth, only the statue that should have been on top was gone. The remains of its feet were still there on top, weathered by time and the elements, around the feet where broken bits of stone that if put together might form a person. Ryan noticed however that the statue had not been broken at the feet, as the tops were smooth. They had been carved that way originally. An inscription on the front, transcribed over the Ontarian word for hero, said 'No one is above the law.'

"My dad," Ryan asked pointing at the poor excuse of a monument to a man who had ended a war.

"Your father was a hero Ryan, but no hero is above the law," his uncle said. "No one is special on Ontaria, for our abilities are gifts. Not to be used to climb above one another, not since the time of the Patriarchs.

"We used to be a warlike and violent race, pitting our differences against one another for power and control. That all ended centuries ago and we have to guard this new future we've created, with laws to guard our hearts and souls.

"Your father failed to guard that law," his uncle added.

Ryan stared at the inscription. He knew what specific law his father had broken, forming a relationship with his mother.

His mother's death had revealed that crime and led to this dilapidated stone carving, sitting in a museum, silently reminding everyone of one man's failure.

More than ever he wanted to know what had killed her, and how this hero was to blame.

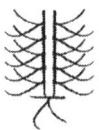

Chapter 24

Ryan knew his father had all the details; however, he would not see or speak to him for a couple of weeks, but some interesting things happened to him while he waited.

After another day of toiling in the fields and moving the herds of Flavadores to another grazing area, Ryan stepped out of the main house with his rugby ball once again.

The house had been re-positioned and was in its proper place as were all the other buildings. The sun was low on the horizon, there was probably only two hours of light left. Ryan took a moment to stare at the dazzling array of colours in the sky as the light faded.

Ryan headed for an empty space to play with his rugby ball.

He would be on his own though. The other children were playing their own games. Behind the house and other buildings was a field put aside especially for speed related activities. The children were playing a game Ryan had learnt the rules of by watching. The grass field was marked with five circles. The idea was that half the children would be trying to tag the others, who were safe if they were in the circles. If another child entered your circle you had to leave it and if they were tagged, they swapped places. It was a great use of the children's speed as they darted around the marked-out pitch evading each other at fifty miles an hour and trying to stop dead in the circles without braking too early or too late. The pitch they were using was huge, almost three times bigger than a standard rugby field.

Ryan watched for a little while then decided to play with his rugby ball. Although he had no one to play with it did not matter, not with his speed and strength if he concentrated. Using an empty part of the field, he would throw the ball.

Thankfully it took his mind off things.

After making a spectacular catch and being lost in the moment, Ryan celebrated with his hands in the air, jumping up and down. "Ryan Barnes wins the six nations with a spectacular catch and try," he said mostly to himself.

"What game are you playing?" someone said.

Ryan spun on his heels to see Nur, Reesa and the other children looking at him, or more accurately the rugby ball in his hand.

He blushed with embarrassment then answered, "Still rugby."

"What's that?" Deeskly asked pointing at the ball.

"A rugby ball," Ryan answered.

"Ball?" Nur said with a puzzled expression.

"You've never heard of a ball?" Ryan said.

"What's it made off?" Reesa asked.

"Leather."

More puzzled expressions, "Like the skin of a cow," Ryan elaborated.

Still puzzled expressions.

"Like the skin of a Flavadore," Ryan tried, trying to speak their language.

"How do you play this rugby?" Nur asked.

Ryan laid down the basics.

"We don't have any posts?" Nur said.

"What, you want to play?" Ryan said surprised that Nur was even interested.

"It looks fun and we've never played it and besides we've never had a ball before," Nur said.

"Never played games that used anything other than our speed," Reesa pointed out.

Ryan spluttered for a moment. "Yeah great, err, in that case let's play, we'll make do without the posts."

For hours, well into the evening right up to dinner Ryan played rugby with the children. Using a much larger pitch to accommodate the super speeds the children had lots of fun learning how to play. Ryan was amazed at how tough they were even at high speeds. Collisions did not faze any of them, which he chalked up to the bony plates that grew on their bodies. Ryan himself was careful not to use his new found super strength in case it did any damage. Everything went smoothly.

In the days after when all the farming chores were done, Ryan played rugby with everyone else, watched sometimes by the adults who were finding an interest in the game themselves. This passed the time for Ryan who had been waiting as patiently as he could for the day that he would visit his father in the prison once again.

Also, he noticed that the daily grind was getting easier. Some of the kids actually helped him with his side of the chores.

After a particularly energetic game, Ryan and the others sat on the grass in the middle of the field. They were all tired, Ryan especially since he had to push himself harder to keep up with the others. "I am still so surprised that you guys have never played with a ball before."

"The idea that you would take the skin of a beast and make into something that can be thrown is so bizarre," Nur said twirling the rugby ball in her hands.

"Nowadays the balls are synthetic," Ryan said.

"But throwing something for entertainment, it's weird," Reesa said.

"Humans like to use all the physical aspects of their bodies in sport, not just running or jumping," Ryan replied.

"You have more games like this?" Reesa said.

"A lot more," Ryan replied, "In fact on Earth a few months ago there was a huge sporting event on called the Olympics, the best athletes competed."

"What's the main event?" Nur asked.

"Well, everyone watches the 100 metres," Ryan said.

"100 metres?" Nur said.

"The fastest athletes run 100 metres as fast as possible, millions watch it and it's all over in about ten seconds," Ryan said.

"Two if it was one of us," Nur commented. Everyone laughed, even Ryan who was pleased to be fitting in.

The day finally came for him to visit his dad again and his uncle took him there when the time came. When he reached the prison, he went through the now familiar routine of walking through security gates, talking to the telekinetic Ontarian who moved folders and files around with his mind, and then following the guard to the appropriate cell.

His father was waiting for him as the guard opened the door to his cell again. It was a little tidier than the last time Ryan had visited. In ten years this was the second time Ryan had ever seen his father and he did not feel any closer to him than he did before. He was still a stranger.

"Ryan," his father said beaming at him. "How are you fitting in?" he asked in Ontarian.

"Fine I guess," Ryan replied in English.

"No, no, in Ontarian. I know you must be homesick, but you have to learn the language," his father scolded him playfully. "So, tell me what is having super strength like?"

"You know about that?"

"Of course," his father replied.

Ryan shrugged, "It's kind of hard to describe, and everything feels fragile when I touch it, like I could break something if I didn't concentrate."

"Well, I hear your visiting the Frayans so that they will teach you how to use your strength and focus it," his father said.

"What will I be doing?"

"The Frayans effectively build Ontarian civilisation, they demolish and construct, clear roads. They also form one third of the military and police because their strength is an over powering force against the other tribe's abilities." His father looked at Ryan as if wondering why he had asked. "I assume you never thought you would be a farmer, eh?"

"No never, why don't I go to school, learn stuff like geography or science?" Ryan asked.

"It's not like that here, your tribe has to do what's it was tasked to do, it keeps our society functioning."

"Why is it like this, why can't I do something other than farming?"

His father sighed, "It about history, for thousands of years the various tribes warred with each other over our differences. In the end we had to learn to use our powers for everyone's benefit, it stopped the wars and our society progressed like never before."

"Oh," Ryan said. He now felt that the conversation had moved far enough for him to ask the question he had been waiting to ask for weeks "How did my mother die?" he blurted out.

His father's bubbly smile vanished from his face and he turned away.

"I don't like to talk about it," his father said then tried to change the subject. "If you're interested in Ontarian history we do have libraries compiled by the Intelligen..."

"But I do want to talk about it. I want to know," Ryan interrupted. He had derived a conclusion, from what he had overheard from the Admiral and his uncle, and what his father had said to him at their last meeting. It was clear how she died. *"When your mother died the Ontarian authority discovered our marriage and arrested me,"* his father had said. "*Using a family member to get him to give up information"* the Admiral had said. And finally what his uncle had mentioned, "*But the previous incident that revealed his indiscretion with the human was before his prison sentence, how they would force his hand with Edeps in our most secure prison".* It all meant one thing and although Ryan knew it would hurt to hear it, his desire to know the absolute truth had made him ask.

His father looked into his eyes and seemed to recognise that Ryan knew the answer to his question. "It's not like you think," he replied.

"That's what they all say, but I bet that it's not true," Ryan shot back angrily, "it's exactly what I think, you let her die."

"There... there was more at stake than her life," his father replied raising his voice.

"Tell me what happened," Ryan ordered, coldly.

Edeps turned away and stared at the rear wall of his cell and made some awkward movements, like nervous ticks. After a pause and after he had gathered himself together, he turned back to face Ryan. "I was once tasked to keep something safe from the Tredicim, something that would have secured their release from the prison where they are now kept. They kidnapped your mother when you were five and demanded I tell them where I had hidden what they needed. You could not imagine what I went through in the short time they gave me to come to a decision. I should have told the Ontarian authority, but I could not bring myself to do so. I had to make a choice, weigh the lives of millions of Ontarians against my own wife."

"You let her die!" Ryan said.

"No choice, I had no choice she would have wanted it this way," he said consoling himself more that Ryan. "I knew your mother Ryan, longer than you did, she was a doctor, she saved lives and she wouldn't have wanted me to sacrifice my people even to save hers," his father practically spat back.

Ryan stepped back as if he had received a slap in the face. "Surely you could have saved her, lied to stall for time, figured out a way. I'm pretty sure you owed it to mum over the rest of Ontario who locked you up."

"But you've met them, you've met those Ontarians. Do millions deserve to die so your mother lives?" Edeps said.

"They wouldn't have died, so you give them the key, so what. I've seen that fortress, that bubble, they are not getting in, even with it."

"I could not take that chance."

"Don't you care that she's dead, that you gave her up for the people who put you in jail, who kept you away from your son?"

"We all make sacrifices...for our tribes."

Ryan shook his head, he could not bear to hear what his so-called father had to say anymore, he stepped back and nodded to the guard to close the door.

"Where are you going?" his father called out to him with a hint of desperation in his voice and moving forward. The guard pushed Edeps back into the room and shut the door, inserting the key and locking it.

Ryan stared at the cell door. The guard stepped back and gave him space, even shuffling a bit and looking away from him. He heard his father's hands slide down the door, then the sound of his bed's mattress sinking.

Ryan's lip wobbled. his father had let his mother die, he didn't want to speak to him again. He then heard sniffing, then he bent down and looked through the key hole.

His father had his head in his hands and was sobbing.

Ryan straightened up, then rubbed his eyes and walked down the corridor heading for the exit.

Chapter 25

Ryan arrived back at the farm late in the afternoon. He stood in the courtyard alone, no one was returning from the fields yet.

He had had plenty of time to think on the run home. He found it hard to believe that his own father had let his mother die. But then again this was exactly the image he had grown up with of his father, someone who abandoned his family - abandoned his son.

"You're back," someone said.

Ryan looked up from his feet to meet the stern gaze of his aunt standing in the doorway of one of the buildings.

Ryan just nodded and looked away.

"How is Edeps?" she asked.

Ryan was certainly surprised she asked this question, and he looked back at her, "Fine," he said.

"Not what you thought?"

"Pardon?" Ryan replied.

"Your father?" she prompted.

"No, he's not."

"Considering that you never really known the man before a month ago perhaps it was wrong to have any expectations," she said.

"What's that supposed to mean?"

"Don't judge him too harshly," she said, "You have no idea what he went through," she added then disappeared into the house.

•

One week after seeing his father Ryan once again found himself following his uncle to an unknown destination. Early in the morning before the daily toil in the fields, they had set out for a local Frayan settlement. It seemed to Ryan that while the various tribes lived peacefully together, they still kept themselves very separate from one another.

Since the entire region belonged to the Swift tribe and was used for farming and herding huge animals, Ryan could not see any form of settlement that might belong to the Frayans.

After an hour of running the roads pulled away from the fields and plains and led into the mountains. Twenty minutes later the road ended at a sheer rock face and embedded in the cold grey stone was a huge ornate door. Frayans depicted on it held huge hammers and stood as sentinels guarding the mountain.

Ryan and his uncle stopped a fair distance from the door. "Now Ryan," his uncle began, "the Frayans live differently to us, and right now they are celebrating the arrival of their Patriarch. Every month of the year a tribe celebrates the arrival of theirs. While you'll here you'll have to put up with the celebrations the Frayans put on, you will not be used to what goes on here."

Ryan smiled and laughed inwardly at his uncle's comment, was there anything on this planet that he was used to?

At that moment Ryan heard a rumbling sound and turned away from his uncle to see the massive doors to the mountain slowly open. As Ryan expected Frayans pushed them open. These Frayans wore the traditional garb of every other Frayan minus the helmet and Ryan realised this was the first time he had seen one of them without it. They all appeared remarkably similar, with features that looked like someone had chiseled them out of stone. Their hair, though it looked as stiff as whiskers, moved around like all Ontarian hair.

Strolling out of the mountain as the door opened came another Frayan without his helmet, but wearing armour Ryan recognised. He had always wondered what he looked like without it.

"Threngst," Ryan's uncle greeted him.

Threngst face was like the other Frayans, strong sharp features as solid as a hunk of stone. He had dark green hair trimmed too short to tell if it was moving around or not. He had bright blue eyes and a thin beard around his mouth.

"Chiqu, I understand Ryan will be staying with us one week," the big man said, looking down on Ryan and his uncle.

"Yes, just teach him to control his new powers; his place is with the Swift tribe," his uncle said.

"Follow me Ryan," Threngst ordered and started walking through the giant doors and back into the mountain.

Ryan turned to his uncle who was already running out of the mountain range creating a dust cloud in his wake and leaving Ryan to enter another new world all over again.

When the huge doors closed Ryan followed Threngst down a tunnel lit rather primitively with torches mounted in the walls. To Ryan this indicated that the Frayans lived under ground something he didn't look forward to, considering that he was already freezing cold and the torches offered very little light or warmth.

"You will be staying with my family while you are here," said Threngst as he led Ryan down the tunnel. "Down here you must wear different garments and be warned, these tunnels and caves aren't the perfect place to run at high speeds. There are tight corners, some could collapse as they haven't been inhabited for a while."

Ryan nodded, but did not look at Threngst, his attention focused on the end of the tunnel which he could tell opened into a vast cavern. As they moved out of the tunnel Ryan saw a spectacular monument before him. The tunnel opened into a cavern shaped like a theatre. On the far wall four tunnels branched off this cavern deeper into the mountains. Standing astride of these tunnel entrances was a giant statue that must have been as tall as Big Ben. Ryan could tell this was of someone of great importance. The stone of the statue was perfect without defect, scratch or bump. It was of a Frayan wearing a helmet with a crown set in it, the armour had a depiction of a waterfall on its chest and the figure had one of its hands reaching above its head as if holding up the ceiling while the other held a huge metal, not stone, hammer.

"Our Patriarch, guarding the mountain," Threngst said as Ryan stared upwards at the statue admiring its size and grandeur.

He led Ryan into the tunnel on the far left of the cavern passing by one of the feet of the statue. It could have squashed two double Decker buses.

They travelled down more tunnels continually lit with primitive torches. In fact, Ryan had trouble spotting any technology at all in the tunnels.

They came to the end of another corridor which opened again into a wide, tall cavern one that offered a view more spectacular than the statue. Ryan entered it at the very bottom, it was so huge it could have easily encompassed any skyscraper on Earth with mountains of room to spare. A waterfall cascaded down into a lake at the bottom of the cavern; the walls were pockmarked with holes, each with a light in them, which Ryan took to be houses built into the stone. Giant elevators ran up to the very top of the cavern, ferrying large groups of Frayans around. On the shores of the lake were actual buildings only a few stories high.

"Follow me," Threngst said.

He led Ryan to an elevator which was a box covered with a metal woven mesh to stop passengers from falling off. Ryan received some odd looks from some of the other Frayans who looked surprised and confused to see someone like him in their world. He was very out of place, wearing his body-hugging clothes of the Swift tribe where everyone, including children, wore some type of amour.

The elevator filled quickly as more and more Frayans stepped inside, armour clinked and clanked as the giant Ontarians made room for one another in the tightly enclosed space. Occasionally an Intelligen or Motus tribe member would enter the elevator. Ryan even spotted an Ontarian that had those dark blood vessels etched on their skin.

The elevator then started to rise with tremendous force, which almost caused Ryan to sink into his ankles it was so powerful.

Ryan looked over shoulder and through the mesh that covered the elevator, to admire the view as the elevator rose upwards. The buildings started to shrink as they climbed higher and higher, He felt a sudden sprinkle of water fall upon his face as the waterfall crashed into rocky outcroppings nearby and sent out spray.

The elevator stopped very suddenly and Ryan actually felt his feet lift off the floor for a second. Threngst did not get off so neither did Ryan. Passengers disembarked and others embarked and then the lift started going upwards again. This happened another five or six times until finally Threngst got off and Ryan followed.

More tunnels snaked their way into the mountain, Ryan saw that metal plaques on the walls of the tunnels marked out various tunnels but also houses. He could tell they were houses as they had heavy doors with numbers on them. Ryan had no idea where they were going, he still had not learnt to read Ontarian properly so the names of various tunnels meant nothing to him.

Finally, though they reached their destination and Threngst took out a key from within his armour and placed it in the lock.

Threngst was barely through the door when a young girl careered into him. Ryan stepped to one side as father and daughter shot past him. Threngst pushed back on his daughter and she struggled with him giggling all the while, until he finally picked her up and carried her into his house and she burst out laughing.

Ryan followed Threngst into his house and closed the door behind him a little embarrassed to have just witnessed what had happened. The house or rather flat he had just entered was just like the tunnels. Torches lit the rooms hewn out of the rock and in the more confined space of the flat they gave it warmth. From the front door extended a small corridor towards a room with a domed ceiling, a central living area with sofas cut from stone with thick heavy blankets spread over them for comfort.

Unlike he previous calm and stoic nature Threngst was laughing with his daughter, swinging her around the room with a big smile on his face.

A woman was in the room as well, she wore armour two but it had more joints and was thinner. Ryan wondered if it was meant to be more comfortable, like casual armour or something like that. She had a mass of green hair cascading form her head and was not tied down.

"She needs to be disciplined," her mother said, "don't encourage that behaviour."

"She has time to learn," Threngst replied.

Then out of a nearby room thundering all the way came a boy a foot taller than Ryan and wearing armour just like his dad, but only on the chest.

"Hello dad," the boy said, he then turned when he noticed Ryan out of the corner of his eye. The boy seemed to think something through for a moment as he scrutinised Ryan's appearance, then his eyes widened when he worked out what he was thinking about. "Is this the Swifter?"

"Yes, this is Ryan who will stay with us this week," Threngst replied.

"He doesn't look very strong," the boy said.

"He's not Torngs, not yet, he needs to learn how to use his strength, which is why I want you to take him to the park. Keep out of the way of the preparations for tonight, but get him to use his strength, which he must become more comfortable with."

"Let's go then," the boy called Torngs said as he started to leave the flat.

"Is this what a human looks like Farthy," the girl then said. Ryan stopped walking and looked back at her.

She was still upside down and was then righted by her father and plonked down on the ground. Ryan believed she had the disposition of a six year old, but was almost as tall as he was. She wore armour like her mother, whom she was the splitting image of, with long whisker hair tied back, but her expression was a lot more pleasant.

"Yes Lima," Threngst replied to his daughter.

"They don't look much different to us do they," she said.

"No Lima they don't."

Ryan wanted to get out of the flat as quickly as possible to avoid any conversations about him, but did not involve him.

"Wear this," the mother said with a voice almost as deep as her husbands. She held up a suit of armour just like her son's, it looked heavy.

Ryan took the armour from her and he bent over double as its weight dragged him down. He had to crouch down to fit it on and use the greater strength in his legs to lift the thing. His ankles and legs complained under the weight of the metal vest.

"Let's go," Torngs repeated.

Ryan took a cautious step forward, and after finding that he did not snap in half and his ankles didn't break, followed the boy slowly out of the flat.

"So, you're human then," Torngs said and he started walking away down the tunnels, Ryan followed struggling to keep up under the weight of the armour he wore.

"Yeah I am."

"What do they do then?" Torngs asked.

"What do you mean?"

"With their lives, do they have tribes?"

"Well, no we have countries," Ryan answered.

"What can they do?"

"Well, nothing if you're referring to strength and speed," Ryan answered realising that he was more carrying the armour than wearing it, his joints were already aching.

"Are all humans the same?" Torngs asked.

"Some look slightly different, but yeah," Ryan replied.

"Hmm," Torngs said. "This way," he said and he led Ryan around a corner and under an arch way which opened out into another cavern.

In Ryan's mind it had the appearance of a football stadium, only underground with concentric circles acting as seats dug into the rock and smoothed over. There was a type of playing pitch at the bottom of the cavern about the size of a football pitch covered not with grass but some sort of moss. Ryan was glad that this cavern was lit with proper lights not torches so everything was not dim or illuminated with flickering light.

"Let's go get some practice," Torngs said.

"Practice for what?" Ryan asked.

"The games, it's the final night of the Patriarchal celebrations which always end with the games, all the families in the local area gather in this park to participate." Torngs explained.

"What kind of games?"

"I'll show you," Torngs replied.

Torngs led Ryan down the sides of the stadium to the field at the base. Along the way Ryan saw other Frayans preparing for the celebration, putting up decorations, which were merely extravagant cave painting in Ryan's opinion. Motus tribe members floated over the stadium, doing their work. Stalls and food vendors were occupying their own miniature caves set in the sides of the park, cooking food for what was going to happen tonight. The waft of succulent, roasting meat entered Ryan's nostrils it smelled great, just like big, fat steaks, Ryan wondered if they had chips to go with it.

The field at the bottom of the cave stadium was a large oval and laid out in various places were various sports that were intended to be played tonight. The field was occupied mostly by Frayan children of various ages mucking around or practicing with the equipment.

"This is one game my family is competing in tonight," Torngs said proudly as he led Ryan over towards a stack of cannon balls piled at one end of the field.

"You do Shot Put?" Ryan asked.

"What's Shot Put?" Torngs asked.

Ryan had completely forgotten that this boy would not know a thing about the Olympic Games and it was useless to make comparisons.

"Oh nothing," Ryan replied.

"Anyway, the point of this game is to take these and throw them across the arena." Torngs picked up one of the cannon balls in one hand quite easily. Ryan did not think much of this game, it sounded pretty simple. He grabbed one of the balls and tried to pick it up, but it would not budge from the pile even when he used both hands.

"Are you sure you're strong?" Torngs asked.

"I held back a building that was trying to crush me," Ryan replied. "How do you pick it up?"

"I use my strength."

"But how do I use mine?"

"Well for some of the tribes it's a matter of concentration and willpower if you don't have that, your abilities are very weak and unpredictable. As a Swifter have you ever tapped into the well of energy within you?"

"I guess, sometimes I'm running fast entirely due to my physical body, then sometimes when I go faster, I draw more power from within."

"Well that same power can increase your strength too, give it a go," Torngs said.

Ryan bent down and grasped the cannon ball with both hands then using his legs to lift pulled and strained to raise it into the air, but it would not budge. When the end of his fingers slipped of the ball due to his effort he fell backwards.

Torngs laughed aloud as Ryan almost rolled over.

"I'm sorry but you looked so ridiculous," Torngs said as he continued to laugh.

"It didn't work," Ryan said. "I don't understand I did it before back on the farm."

"This is a really heavy object," Torngs said rolling the cannon ball he had picked up in his hand, "Lighter ones come very natural, but Frayans have to focus to lift heavier objects. Plus, you were still trying to lift with your normal strength. Try again."

Ryan, still feeling a little embarrassed and not wanting to make himself look stupid again, reluctantly stepped up to the cannon balls and grasped one. He closed his eyes, he imagined himself standing over the cannon balls, then start trying to lift one of them. In his mind he picked up the cannon ball with ease. Ryan opened his eyes and realised that he was still straining with the cannon ball.

He gave up again. "Can't do it."

"Swifters, you expect everything to happen so quickly," Torngs said. "It takes time to do something like this."

Torngs turned drew back his arm and tossed a cannon ball with all his strength. It flew down the length of the field reached its zenith and started falling back to the ground. It crashed into the field sending pieces of rock in all directions then settled into its own miniature crater.

"Wow," Ryan commented. He really wanted to be able to do that.

He grasped another cannon ball and pulled with all his might and added to that his desire to be able to lift such heavy objects confident that he could do so.

Suddenly the cannon ball came out of the pile, however he had used too much power. With the ball still clasped in his hands it swung in an arc over his head and threw him backwards, its weight pulling him with it.

He landed on his back still clutching the ball, which he now let go of and it rolled away from him.

Torngs bent down to look at him he trying hard not to burst out laughing by biting his lip. "Very-hmmmm-good," he said.

"Thanks," Ryan said.

Torngs showed Ryan all the other games around the field and after a couple of hours Ryan was starting to be able to summon his strength more quickly, but was unable to maintain it or control it. This resulted in some of the very heavy equipment almost falling on Ryan. The armour he wore was also getting lighter, easier to move in. He followed Torngs back to the house when they had finished in the field and some of the adult Frayans had kicked all the children out of there on the account that there were still decorations to be put up.

Torngs gave him a tour of the entire city for the next few hours. The giant cavernous spaces erased any feelings of claustrophobia. Underground rivers swept through the city falling in spectacular water falls. Torngs pointed out hundreds of passage ways that were now defunct. He said the entire mountain was riddled with passages with entire sections uninhabited. He even indicated a fire escape and showed Ryan how to open the door.

Ryan asked why some passages were not inhabited.

Torngs sadly said that the war had taken many soldiers and therefore Frayan lives. It would be many years before their numbers rose again.

"We try not to dwell on it," Torngs said, "And our games will help our memories," he said.

Ryan found himself looking forward to them as well, he had had never seen super strong aliens battle it out in games before.

When they arrived back in the flat Ryan was surprised to find a call for him.

He did not know there were phones on planet Ontaria.

Torngs showed him the phone and it was not what he had been expecting. It was a crystal disk attached to a wall with giant hand print etched into it.

"How do I use this?" Ryan asked.

"Just place your hand on the disk," Torngs said then strolled off to his room.

Ryan looked at the disk and saw nothing special about it, but he raised his hand and pressed it to the disk.

Instantaneously he found himself staring into the faces of Nur and Reesa. The image was distorted though; their heads were enlarged as if they were displayed on a concave surface, like a reflection in a spoon.

"Hi Ryan," Reesa said.

Ryan let go of the disk in surprise at what he saw.

Then wanting to experience the sensation again he pressed his hand down once more.

"Keep your hand on the disk," Reesa said as she reappeared.

Ryan withdrew his hand again; it was such a weird feeling, as if his mind was disconnected from his body.

He touched the disk again.

"Don't take your hand off," Reesa repeated.

Ryan saw that Reesa and Nur held out their hands towards him touching another disk wherever they were.

"What is this?" Ryan asked.

"It's an Astral Disk, it's made by another tribe for our communications," Reesa said.

"We have something to ask you," Nur said.

Ryan was surprised by this statement, but he smiled, they were finally warming up to him.

"What do you want...I mean need?" he asked.

"We want to see the Frayan celebrations," Nur stated.

"What?" Ryan replied.

"The celebrations, we want to see them, can you get us into the mountains?" Reesa said.

"How am I supposed to do that?" Ryan asked.

"Just find us an entrance and let us in," Nur said.

"This is Frayan city, you'll be spotted instantly," Ryan said.

"There must be a way inside without being seen it's a cave isn't it. Won't it be dark?" Reesa said.

Ryan was about to deny that, then he remembered the large uninhabited areas of the city. They would be a perfect place for to sneak in. Nevertheless, he still did not think it was a good idea, he didn't want to get in trouble.

Then he had an idea, a way to turn this request to his advantage, "If I can do this for you, will you do something for me?" he asked, trying to sound pleading as he spoke, as if he needed them more than they needed him.

"What is it?" Nur asked.

"I want to race with the family, with you guys, please?" Ryan said.

Nur seemed to back away for a moment as if frightened by the request.

"Look I want to win for our family, think how embarrassing it will be when the other families lose to the half human. That will shut them up."

Nur stepped forward. "You really want to race with us?" she asked.

"Yes."

Nur looked at Reesa who nodded. "Ok, when you get back, I'll show you how to run faster and you can join us."

Ryan smiled he was in their group now, they had opened their circle to him, of course he had to deliver for it to be a done deal.

"Alright, here's the plan," Ryan began.

Chapter 26

Ryan was worried that the celebrations would not be impressive, that Nur and Reesa would be let down and maybe they would back away from the deal they had made. However, Ryan was not disappointed, the celebrations were huge.

First there was the food.

Ringing the stadium was a band of shops and stalls all of which sold different kinds of meat.

Ryan was ravenous and he sampled as much as he could alongside Threngst's' family who were keen to show him around and boast about their caves, food and celebrations. This seemed to be the only time that the Frayans were keen to cut loose with their strength.

They displayed that strength openly. Considering their might, everything was very fragile in their hands, but it did not seem to matter. No one cared that seats and equipment broke, or walls ended up being demolished.

Frayans were fighting almost everywhere they went but there seemed to be no anger, just the thrill of combat. Circles of Frayans were cheering combatants on.

If this was Earth then policemen would have shown up and arrested anyone who threw a punch. Here though, fighting was natural. Ryan assumed that this was another *Privilege of Power* that Sensatus had spoken of. The Frayans wanted to use their strength, show it off, and so they were allowed to, regardless of what got smashed or destroyed. The Frayans themselves were so hardy that they did not fear themselves getting broken.

Threngst and Torngs led the family and Ryan through the food court, which was kind of like alfresco dining, a ring of seats stood in front of each restaurant which doubled as small stadiums as inside each ring was a battling group of Frayans.

Threngst and Torngs stopped walking when they spotted another father son duo on the opposite side of one ring.

Ryan was both thrilled and terrified when the two pairs suddenly charged at each other and started throwing punches.

Threngst and the other father locked their arms and tried to push each other like sumo wrestlers. Torngs and the other boy went blow for blow, blocking and punching in equal measure. Sometimes they would land a hit and their armour would dent, Ryan was sure he even felt shockwaves in the air from the punches.

He felt the colour drain from his face and he stepped back in fear. On Earth he had never been hit, not once, he was too fast. He had never been scared of a fight. Here though he was aware of how frail he was, he was not a true Frayan nor had he mastered his strength, here he could be hurt, badly.

Yet as he watched the fight he was fascinated, maybe keen to start cheering alongside the others watching this scuffle. Was this his Frayan side, the urge to fight to get involved? He suddenly remembered the recent superhero movies that were being pumped out by *Marvel* or *DC,* of the thrill he got when he saw two titans with power wail on each other. Now he was seeing it for real and it was far more exciting.

Threngst managed to lift his opponent and toss him into the nearby stall. Pots, pans and food went everywhere.

The owner did not look angry at the mess, he simply tossed Threngst's opponent out and started cleaning up.

Torngs was not fairing as well as his dad, the other son was slightly taller and looked more determined. Torngs was on his knees being punched in the face, yet he would not go down.

Eventually his opponent made one last punch, and looked at Torngs in the eye who swayed on his knees and smiled through a few missing teeth.

The boy who was winning smiled back then declared, "I can beat this warrior down, yet I cannot defeat him."

Everyone who was watching cheered. Torngs' sister went to him and lifted him up and walked him out of the ring, but not before Torngs and his opponent shared a brief moment of respect by fist bumping, which made Ryan suddenly feel nostalgic for home.

The boy then noticed Ryan for the first time.

"I've never fought a human." he said, "And this is one I know can take a hit from me."

Ryan instantly knew he was being called out for a fight, yet he certainly did not want to.

Torngs was brought to his side by his sister, "Your turn," he said. "I softened him up for you."

"I can't fight him, look what he did to you," Ryan said.

"You're part Frayan Ryan, draw that out, but don't forget you are also a Swifter."

Torngs put his hand on his shoulder and pulled Ryan into the ring.

Ryan stumbled forward and had to duck immediately as the other boy threw a punch.

He rolled along the ground and turned around as fast as he could.

"Catch him if you can Perow?" Torngs called out.

Ryan's opponent turned away from him, "I hope he will last longer than you," he shot back.

Ryan did not want to run from this fight, he didn't want to be hurt either. He needed to defend himself. His muscles tensed, he felt the strength inside him build at the prospect of a fight and he saw his opening.

He leapt forward and rugby tackled the boy before he could do anything, opting to bring him down, not punch him down. His left shoulder went into the boy's gut and Ryan wrapped his arms around his upper thighs.

Perow gasped as he was winded and gave ground.

However, he remained standing.

Then he grabbed Ryan by his waist. He lifted him up and Ryan flipped as his legs went skywards and his back faced the ground.

He knew what was coming and the fear of pain made him freeze.

Perow body slammed him.

Ryan felt the ground beneath him give away as it cracked, it was an extraordinary sensation, and he wasn't hurt that badly as he was able to roll away again feeling only the dull ache of someone who had slipped on ice and fallen on their butt.

Perow came at him again and Ryan dodged the punch, then another and another. He kept avoiding each hit and Perow started to punch himself out.

The crowd was going silent, Ryan was playing this tactically and now the crowd was trying to gauge the victor not just on strength, but skill as well.

Ryan started to get cocky, with each missed punch he started to dash around to Perow's back, putting more distance between his punches, making him work for it.

But Perow was not a dumb, tough ox. He threw back his arm for a large punch, he didn't hide it, Ryan saw it coming a mile away, like the guy had *Snap-Chatted* it beforehand, with a caption marked *For Your Face*.

Ryan dodged and made his way around his opponent, too late to realise that Perow's leg was rising up and heading for his chest.

He folded in around the foot that felt like a football had hit him, one filled with concrete. Ryan went flying out of the ring and into the same food stall Threngst had thrown Perow's dad into. The stall gave away under Ryan's strong body, like a cardboard stand rather than one of metal and wood.

He was in a daze as bits of it fell around him. Then two strong hands grabbed him and lifted him up, it was the stall owner who was wearing an apron covered in meat juices and crumbs

"Thanks for helping me up…" Ryan began.

Unceremoniously the owner chucked Ryan out of the remains of his stall.

Ryan landed back in the ring, but did not get up, he felt like the biggest boy in the rugby team had just fallen right on top of him. As he scrambled around in the sand he rolled onto his back breathless and knackered.

Perow stood over him, and raised his arms in the air. "Behold the first Frayan to catch a Swifter," he said.

The crowd cheered.

Ryan smiled, and feebly raised his fist, he had to give Perow his respect.

Perow returned the gesture, then left the ring and his dad embraced him.

After some more meat and drink Ryan felt better, and he sat down with the Threngst's family to watch the show in the centre of the arena. He wondered if he should ask for ice for his head, but guessed that Frayans rarely sought medical help, and for the sake of his dignity maybe he should not either.

Ryan could see that there were more to the Shot Put game Torngs had shown him earlier. While the aim of the game was to throw your cannon ball as far as possible, in this adult version there were a number of obstacles in the way. Five other Frayans held up what Ryan could only describe as walls on sticks which the Frayans moved back and forth. Whoever was throwing the ball had to launch it at exactly the right moment so that it avoided the walls and its journey continued through the air. It was impossible though to avoid all the walls and on more than one occasion the cannon balls shattered the stone slabs but continued on, thrown with such force that they just crumbled.

Ryan leapt into the air with the other Frayans as a spectacular throw missed the first two waving walls, but struck the third, continued on into the fourth and then embed itself into the fifth with rubble sprayed everywhere.

A klaxon boomed out over the stadium indicating a foul throw since the ball failed to land on the ground.

Half the stadium roared its approval and inside the cavern it was truly deafening, echoing off the walls all around them. No football pitch on Earth could possibly compete.

He was certainly enjoying himself and getting into the spirit of the celebrations. Ryan had also got the chance to learn some history and had a better understanding of the reason for the celebrations. He had learned that it was all in the honour of the Frayan Patriarch, a historical figure that lived hundreds of years ago. He was legendary, reputed to be the strongest Frayan ever and for one month every year the whole Frayan tribe celebrated his life, showing off their own strength in memory of him and reveling in ancient traditions, one that would about to be re-enacted right in front of him.

Ryan got up out of his seat, "I'm going to get more food," he said and the family nodded after him, unconcerned.

He watched the action all the way to the exit. The games had drawn every one out of the stalls. Ryan made his way to an area of the stalls whose numerous corridors and passages led to a deserted section of the city.

He ditched his armour in a side corridor, then kicked in his super speed.

The corridors led to a door in the mountain sealed from the inside, Ryan fiddled with the mechanism that locked the door and using all his strength, the way he had been shown, he pushed the door open.

Waiting for him was Reesa and Nur and to Ryan's surprise Deeskly.

He looked at them in confusion.

"I know, but he followed us, and he wouldn't leave," Nur said.

"Whatever let's go."

"Cheers Ryan," Nur said and the trio made their way into the mountain and Ryan closed the door.

"This is brill," Deeskly said with the biggest smile on his face.

"Follow me," Ryan said and they all ran back to the stadium.

Ryan crept out of the abandoned tunnels and was pleased to see no one about. He turned back to the others, "Ok guys, you can watch from one of the entrances to stadium, don't be seen. If you are, get into this passageway and run like hell," Ryan said.

"Don't worry Ryan, we'll stay out of sight," Nur said.

Ryan had trouble believing her, but left them alone where they should not be and went back to the family, happy that he could now race with them in the near future.

He resumed his seat with Threngst and continued to watch the games.

The arena was now clearing and at one end of it, led in by six Frayans, was a huge beast in tow walking under its own power, partially restrained by chains. It bellowed and Ryan was sure its roar vibrated his stone seat. The creature was like a lizard only it was as large as a dinosaur. Its front legs looked much more powerful than its rear quarters and it had rocks growing on its skin.

Strolling in from the other side of the arena came a Frayan wearing armour made of gold. He raised his hands like a victorious gladiator and the crowd cheered for him.

"This is a re-enactment of the battle between the Holy Patriarch and a Gorgath, or rock lizard," Threngst said to Ryan. "A family of them once burrowed into the caverns and the biggest male charged through the under city. He stood before it and fought it until it could take no more of his punches and furious attacks and led its brethren out of our city," Threngst concluded, speaking of the patriarch as if he was all powerful, holding him in awe.

Ryan watched as the creature's chains loosened and its handlers ran from the arena climbing the walls leaving it alone with the Frayan in Gold.

The Gorgath looked positively livid and sought out something to vent its anger upon and it choose the golden Frayan. The stadium shook as it ran towards him. Spectators rose steadily from their seats, eyes widening waiting to see what the golden Frayan would do.

He merely extended his arms.

The Gorgath crashed into the Golden Frayan who dug his feet into the ground and with all his might stopped the creature in its tracks. But the Gorgath reacted quickly, it swung its boulder like head and knocked the Frayan aside. He struck the wall of the arena and fell to the floor. Crushed stone ran off his armour, next thing he knew the Gorgath and piled into him ramming him once again into the wall. Ryan was at first worried that the man had been crushed but Frayans obviously had strong bodies and the gold fighter punched the creature in the snout. The rocks that grew on its head shattered and the creature howled in pain.

Another punch and the creature was knocked out cold.

Another deafening roar filled the arena and Ryan actually had to clasp his ears with his hands because he thought his ear drums might actually burst.

"Wah Whoooo," he shouted with the crowd. The gold fighter raised his hands to encourage more praise.

However, no praise was forth coming, the crowd fell silent.

From one end of the stadium dark, green skinned Frayans in armour led five more of the giant lizards into the stadium.

"What's this?" Threngst said.

Cheering was replaced by whispering as the whole crowd started to discuss and frown upon this new development. "What's happening?" Ryan said to Torngs.

"Don't know this isn't right, the Patriarch only fought one Gorgath," he said looking puzzled and staring down at the arena to watch the Gorgaths being led in.

The gold armoured Frayan in the arena still recovering from his recent battle looked around at the crowd, completely unsure about what to do. Ryan wondered if he was worried that he would have to fight five of the angry lizards.

It was only when one of the Frayans leading the Gorgath into the arena removed her helmet, that the crowd seemed to know exactly what was going on.

There were screams as revealed underneath the helmet was a face that was just awful, with a black face like burnt wood and tentacles that ran down its back like hair. Ryan recognised them instantly they were the same creature that attacked him and the other Swift children back on the farm. The other four Tredicim took off their helmets and then chaos reigned.

The Tredicim released the lizards they had been holding and the Gorgath were free to run wild. The crowd started to move as whole families clutched their children and took off away from the arena and the Gorgaths now starting to tear up the place.

Threngst was up and away running down to the arena towards the chaos, "Get the children home," he bellowed over his shoulder.

Other Frayans were moving down the arena as well to curtail the pandemonium going on. The gold fighter in the centre of the arena was once again taking on one of the Gorgaths and he was losing, too tired after the previous fight.

The Tredicim then went into action. Five Frayans surrounded one of them on the floor of the arena they cracked their knuckles and balled their fists in anger at the damage the Tredicim had unleashed.

Ryan suddenly felt his collar yanked as Torngs pulled him up from his seat, "Come on we have to go," he said. Ryan was only half paying attention, slowly rising from his seat but keeping his gaze levelled on the arena. The big green-skinned Tredicim wouldn't stand a chance it may have been a foot higher than the Frayans around it and looked just as strong, but Ryan knew that wouldn't help the Tredicim.

He was wrong.

The Tredicim they had surrounded leapt into action first. It was lithe and graceful as it attacked one of the Frayans locking into combat with it. Another Frayan approached from behind arms outstretched to pluck the Tredicim off his comrade. The tentacles on the back of the Tredicim head suddenly rose up and wrapped around the Frayans head like an octopus'. Then the tentacles boldly flung the Frayan to one side.

Then the Tredicim did something awful, it bit into the arm of the Frayan it was facing drawing blood and in Ryan opinion seemed to be drinking it. It released its mouth from the arm and let the Frayan it had bitten fall backwards onto the ground.

"Come on Ryan, hurry," Torngs shouted in his ear and he pulled Ryan with his own great strength up the steps of the arena towards an exit.

The last thing Ryan saw was the Tredicim grow in size as it bulked up on the blood it had swallowed. It roared into the air, one that was so deep and so wild Ryan was really afraid as he was looking not a person, but a beast.

Then he was dragged out of the arena. Going the other way were more adult male and female Frayans dressed in more fierce looking armour.

"The military, those Tredicim are going to be outmatched," Torngs said.

However, the screams from behind Ryan did not convince him this was true.

Ryan suddenly remembered the others, he had to find them and get them out of here.

He stopped following Threngst's family and let the crowd smother him separating them from him.

"Ryan," he heard someone shout after him.

He ran quickly through the crowd towards where the trio should have hidden themselves.

He entered the passageways.

"Guys?" he said.

There was no response.

"Guys?" he repeated.

Then for an awful moment he thought they had been found out and this was not the best time for him to be in trouble.

"Ryan," Nur said speeding up to meet him followed by Deeskly and Reesa.

"What's happening?" Reesa asked.

"The Tredicim have launched an attack on the games," Ryan said, "Come on we're getting out of here," he said.

"Get back," Reesa suddenly said and pulled the group into the passage, away from the stadium.

"What?" Nur said.

A Tredicim emerged from the stadium having somehow survived the conflict in the arena. He was joined by another Tredicim and Ryan saw that this one was like the one he had seen on the farm after the battle. Its tentacles were dreadlocks of bone and its nose had increased in size.

The strange Tredicim sniffed the air.

"Is he anywhere nearby?" the first Tredicim asked.

The second Tredicim shifted his gaze to the passage way where they hid and pointed.

"Run," Ryan whispered and they took off down the tunnels.

"They can't chase us, they wouldn't be using super speed to fight the Frayans," Nur said.

But he was wrong as the rapid footsteps of the Tredicim followed them down the passageway.

"This place is a maze they can't follow us," Ryan said.

"They've got a Stimuli they can track us easily," Reesa called back.

"What's a Stimuli?" Ryan asked.

"Another tribe," Reesa answered.

Finally, they made it to the door Ryan had used to let them into the mountain.

"We can get out here," Nur said.

Ryan unlocked the door again and attempted to push it open but his strength had left him and in his fear he could not call upon it.

"Come on, come on Ryan," Nur said anxiously.

"I want to go home," Deeskly cried out.

Ryan looked over his shoulder as he struggled with the door and realised that he wanted to go home too, not earth but back to the farm, as the Tredicim who had found them surrounded him and the others, one of whom had crystals growing from his head like a member of the Astral tribe.

The crystals glowed and Ryan's mind went blank.

Chapter 27

Ryan squirmed about in the hold of the Tredicim vessel trying to break his bonds, but they were too strong, even for him.

He rubbed his head on the floor and managed to work a blind fold off his eyes.

He blinked to clear his vision and saw the others similarly lying around the room. Most surprisingly of all though was the fact that his dad was there too.

Ryan sat up, "Guys."

"Ryan?" Reesa said and she started to move, as did Nur and the others.

"Hang on," Ryan said and he brought his bound legs up to his chest and tried to bring his hands out in front of him. After a bit of squeezing, he managed to get his legs through the loop his arms made and become more mobile. He crawled over to Reesa, Nur and Deeskly and removed their blindfolds.

"We're on a Tredicim ship," Reesa said.

Why did they kidnap us?" Nur asked, "why didn't they just take you," she said.

"Thanks," Ryan said sarcastically.

"Hey I didn't mean it like that," Nur said.

"They want hostages," Ryan's father said.

"Uncle Edeps," Nur said in surprise. "You're supposed to be in jail."

"The Tredicim broke me out," he replied groaning as he righted himself. "Hello son," he said.

Ryan did not reply.

"How did they break you out, you would have been guarded," Deeskly said.

"I was being transferred and although security was higher than normal, somehow they defeated an entire company of Frayans, that should have been impossible," he said.

"Well, it doesn't matter now, they just attacked a prison and a major Frayan settlement, no doubt the security forces will be trailing them," Reesa said.

"They might be too late," Edeps said.

"Too late?" Nur replied.

"They grabbed me and you children at roughly the same time very quickly, there's only one reason for it," Edeps said.

"What?"

"They're taking us to the Prison Island, to release their brethren," Edeps said.

"They won't get close, my dad said the facility that maintains the shield is protected by a battalion of Frayans, and numerous defences, they only have a few Tredicim," Nur said.

"If they could defeat a company as easily as they did when they got me, they probably have a plan for getting rid of the defences," Edeps remarked.

Suddenly the door to the room opened and standing there was a Tredicim.

"TRETTAN," Edeps snarled recognising him. "You won't succeed, you'll be caught between two forces, the defences and whatever is pursuing you."

"I think it will be easier than you suppose," Trettan replied. "The council have been rather too sure of themselves regarding the defences of the control centre. There's only a company of Frayans protecting it nowadays.

"A company?" Nur said, "my dad said..."

"Your father is uninformed," Trettan interrupted. "The council have been reducing the number of troops stationed there over the last five years believing them a wasted use of troops. They believe the shield is still sufficient," Trettan added.

"How are you going to open the shield, you don't have the key," Ryan said.

Trettan stepped back up from the doorway reached down to the left then lifted a small box into view.

He opened it and the light source from behind him shone through the Red Crystal he held, which scattered light throughout the room.

"We stole this ages ago and replaced the one in the museum with a fake," Trettan said.

"Why do you need us then?" Nur said.

Trettan held the crystal over his head as if to examine more closely and then threw it to the floor where it shattered like glass.

Fragments of red crystal scattered across the room and everyone flinched away from the flying pieces.

Trettan scowled down at the pieces.

"That should not have been possible," he said.

"Was that a fake?" Ryan said motioning towards the remains of the crystal.

"No, it never was the key," Trettan said.

"What...? But the red crystal was used by uncle Edeps to seal the prison of the Tredicim," Nur said.

"It was all a ruse, a piece of trickery to distract anyone who might try to open the prison," Trettan explained.

"Then what does open it?" Deeskly asked.

Trettan turned to Edeps, "Tell them," he ordered.

"Tell us what?" Ryan asked.

"How your mother died Ryan," Trettan answered.

"I don't want to hear this," Ryan said.

Trettan reached forward and grabbed Ryan under the chin and held his face close to his, "Oh I think you do," he replied.

"Tell them," he barked at Edeps.

Edeps sighed, "I tried to tell you before Ryan," he said.

"I know, Mum died because of you," Ryan hissed through gritted teeth. "Isn't that right?"

"Yes and No," Edeps said.

"What does that mean?" Ryan said.

Edeps opened his mouth to speak and the truth spilled out.

Chapter 28

11 years ago, on planet Earth

   Edeps waited in the human restaurant all alone. It was an Italian place and he liked the Italian tribe's style of food very much. He was drawing the attention of a few human patrons to the restaurant. After all he was wearing a loose jumper and baggy jeans in the middle of summer, while everyone else wore smart but casual shirts and shorts. Unfortunately, he could not risk exposing the bony plates on his arms, legs and back. Therefore, he had no choice but to wear the thick jumper even in sweltering heat. Thankfully though he was not hot, his body was designed to reduce heat so that when running he was not baked by his own physical exertions.

   He checked the watch Emma had given him. Despite all his time spent on Earth he still had trouble with the local system. His watch said 19:30. He knew that meant 7:30 in the evening and he cursed the human 24-hour clock, it had made him late on a number of occasions particularly when his own son had been born.

   However, he knew he was where he was supposed to be, at the right time. This was his and Emma's five-year anniversary since their secret marriage. Ryan would be in the hands of his human grandparents, and they were going to enjoy an evening alone together.

   There was no sign of Emma though and his watch moved to 19:31, she was a minute late. Edeps then began to fidget, as a Swift Tribe member sitting still and waiting was not one of his skills, he preferred things to happen quickly.

   He looked at his watch again, 19:32, now he was worried, Emma was not usually late.

   Then the mobile phone he had started to vibrate in his pocket. It was another gift from Emma so they could keep in contact. He felt reassured now, only Emma had the number to this phone and therefore she must be the one calling.

   He took it out and looked at the screen, it said number withheld.

Number withheld, that is not possible, he thought.

He felt anxious, no one else should be calling him on this number, and then he remembered that humans sometimes dialed the wrong number and so therefore this was a mistake. He rejected the phone call and went back to waiting for Emma and contemplated ringing her himself.

His phone rang again and it was another withheld number, he rejected the call.

When it happened a third time he thought that this was no wrong number, even humans did not dial it wrong three times in a row.

He accepted the call and held it to his ear.

At first it did not register with him what he was hearing, then he realised someone was breathing heavily next to the mouthpiece on the other end.

"Who is this?" he asked.

"I presume this is Edeps Swift?" the voice asked.

Edeps blood froze; he knew that voice very well.

"Trettan," he cried out and received annoyed looks from the restaurant staff and guests at his outburst.

"Oh good, you still recognise my voice," Trettan replied playfully.

"What do you want, how did you get this number?" Edeps said, rising to his feet.

"It's not about what I want it's about what you want, for example do you want your wife to be returned to you in one piece," Trettan said.

"Emma!" Edeps breathed.

"What have you done with her?" he asked.

"Come to the Whitby Abbey and you see for yourself," Trettan replied.

"Sir is there some sort of problem? Only you're disturbing the other guests," a waiter suddenly said, materializing at Edeps' table.

Edeps did not answer he simply shot out of the restaurant at full speed, plates and tables were over turned as he rushed out and people screamed as food toppled onto them.

In one second he was out of the restaurant in another ten he was across the river and another five he reached the edge of the Abbey grounds.

It was dark and cloudy and therefore no moonlight. The only illumination came from security lights facing the crumbling walls of the ruin.

It was as quiet as the grave.

Edeps cautiously walked further into the grounds

He passed a heap of collapsed stone to his right and left. His eyes scanned the Abbey ruins. He sensed an ambush, however he was certain that he could out maneuver anything with his speed.

Suddenly the two piles of stones he had passed stood up. Their grey stone surfaces changed and dark, green limbs extended outwards grabbing him and soon, as the rocks continued to change, standing right next to him were two Tredicim.

They forced him to his knees before he could do anything about it.

"Morphosis gifts," Edeps said.

"That right," Trettan said, stepping into view from behind an crumbling wall.

"Where's Emma?" Edeps asked.

Trettan reached out from behind the wall and pulled Emma Barnes into view. She was bound and gagged. Her hair was a mess and covered in mud and with tears rolling down her cheeks.

"Let her go," Edeps said.

"Do you really think I will?" Trettan said, "let's not bore each other with trivial conversations at this point, you know what I want and you will tell us," he added.

Edeps would have to stall for time, "What do you want?" he asked.

Trettan's claws that held Emma by the arm tightened and she screamed in pain. Blood started to soak the shirt she was wearing as the claws dug into her flesh. She looked Edeps straight in the eye and shook her head he heard he muffled words behind her gag.

"Mmm don't, mmm don't," she said.

"You will not stall, you will not try and trick me like the last time we were in this situation, if the next words out of your mouth are not the crystal key is protected by, etc, etc, then she dies," Trettan threatened. "I want the truth. I am surprised that the council haven't hidden the location of the crystal from our people, but I know there must be defenses around it. Tell me what they are."

Edeps looked at his wife, he could see real fear in her eyes. He loved her so much it was more than he could bear to watch her suffer. He then thought of his family and friends on planet Ontaria enjoying peace because of the key that kept the Tredicim locked away, so many people that relied on him and he had a duty to do.

…

…

194

But as he continued to look into his wife's eyes and could not bear the thought of living without her or at least knowing she was safe. For years he had held on to a secret of supreme importance and now finally he was going to tell.

"It's not what you think Trettan..." he began and took a breath before he continued.

Trettan did not let him get that far.

The Tredicim roared in anger and plunged his other clawed hand into Emma's side.

Five claws dug their way into her flesh where her lungs were.

Emma gasped in pain.

"I told you," he said and released Emma from his grip.

She fell to the ground, blood was seeping across her jumper around her chest.

Edeps screamed, "NO, NO," he said and tried to leap forward towards her but the Tredicim holding him kept him still.

"Your fault," Trettan said.

"Edeps," Emma whispered.

"Emma," he said and tried again to break free of his guards.

"Look after R...," she said then the light in her eyes was gone and she did not move.

Edeps hung his head in grief and tears flowed down his cheeks.

"If only you had told me," Trettan said. "Oh well at least I've had some revenge."

Edeps suddenly came to life.

"YOU STUPID CREATURE I WAS GOING TO TELL YOU," Edeps said struggling even more.

"No, you were lying of course. You brought the key to this world you know how to get to it," Trettan said calmly, "I was there, remember! You dropped it off here to keep it from us. But you should have left and returned to Ontaria. These relationships you've formed," and he gestured to body at his feet, "are weaknesses."

"There is no Key you fool, you vile thing, there never was, the shield is kept locked by a code, one I entered in the fortress and in the control room. The crystal was a diversion, the code is the real key, you killed her for nothing," Edeps spat.

Trettan's expression turned ugly, "How clever of you, to miss-direct our attention like that. In that case tell me the code," he ordered.

"You just killed my wife why should I, I'm going to kill you," he said.

"What If I brought your son here? Would you be willing to let him die?" Trettan threatened.

For a second Edeps stopped struggling, he was shocked to hear Trettan knew of his son, his half-human son.

Edeps suddenly jerked his back in a spasm, he did it so fast it nearly broke his back. Instead, it broke the Tredicim's hold on him. He used the opportunity to get to his feet and he swiftly kicked both creatures in their legs breaking them and pulverising the knee caps.

Then he leapt at Trettan and started beating him savagely and at super speed.

His fists rained down him and he did not stop even as Trettan clawed at him, Edeps grabbed and tore out the tentacles on his head.

He screamed and shouted the whole time.

Trettan was finally able to gain his composure for long enough to throw the raging Swifter off him and his head hit a wall.

Edeps blacked out at that point both in anger, pain and sorrow.

He drifted off into unconsciousness, crying the whole time.

Chapter 29

"That's what happened," Edeps concluded.

Ryan was shocked, the hatred of his father was still there, but the blame was evaporating, it was not his fault, it was Trettan who had killed his mother.

"YOU…" Ryan began and leapt at Trettan who swatted him away.

"Know your place," Trettan said.

Edeps tried to struggle under his bonds.

"Don't touch my son," he said.

"It's a code, a code only you know," Reesa said to Edeps.

"Yes there never was a key, only a password to the shield generator. My mission, was to activate the generator with the code and seal the shield with the same code. The crystal was a distraction so that no one would suspect I was the one who knew how to unlock it. Every Ontarian knew where the crystal was on Earth. We thought the Tredicim would waste time trying to get there and steal it." Edeps said. "It would keep me and my family safe as well, why chase me, when you had to chase an object, one that could be passed around. We would have the Tredicim following the crystal not me. Or my family."

"But we found out, your moment of weakness," Trettan said. "How sad. Now we're minutes away from the shield control room and when we have gained access you will unlock the generator," Trettan said, "and you know you will do it," he added.

Edeps did not say anything in response he just went pale.

Trettan left the room and sealed the door.

Father and son looked at each other across the room, there were no words to say, they both knew what Trettan meant.

Ryan would die if Edeps didn't tell.

His life and the lives of millions of Ontarians, now hung in the balance.

Chapter 30

Only a few minutes passed before the door opened again. Trettan led two more Tredicim into the room and they got everyone off the floor. Trettan took control over Edeps and Ryan stayed with the others.

"We can't walk with our legs bound," Nur said.

"Link them," Trettan ordered.

One of the Tredicim look a length of metal cable and linked it to the cuffs binding Ryan's and the other's hands and then their legs were freed.

"You won't be able to run fast tied up like that, if you think of trying to make a dash for it we'll easily be able to chase you down," Trettan warned.

The ship then shuddered, "We've landed, let's go," Trettan said and he led the group out of the ship. Ryan's eyes squinted in the daylight as he stepped out of the vessel. The landscape was desolate. Ash was everywhere and black, hexagonal pillars sprouted from the earth. Cracks in the surface released gas into the atmosphere.

"This is a volcano," Ryan pointed out.

"The prison is built into the crater," Edeps said.

"Look, it's the Shield," Nur said.

Ryan looked in the direction Nur was facing and saw a spectacular sight.

Rising high above the lip of the volcano's crater was a dome of energy. It was like shifting glass and crackled with arcs of lightning. Pylons surrounded its rim sending beams of energy at the shield, which punctured it, reaching out towards the centre of the crater.

"Get moving," Trettan said and he pushed the group forward.

Other Tredicim ships had landed nearby and fifteen of them disembarked and joined the group as they set out towards a hill not far off.

Trettan led the way and when they reached the lip of the hill he motioned for the rest to stop. He then peered down the other side.

"The Frayans know we're here, they're preparing fortifications," Trettan said to his men.

"You can't beat them Trettan," Edeps said.

"That is where you're wrong," Trettan replied and he nodded to a Tredicim standing nearby Ryan.

The Tredicim immediately stuck a syringe into Ryan's arm and he cried out in pain. The Tredicim drew blood into the syringe and after he removed the needle another attachment was put in its place.

"Share it round," Trettan ordered.

To Ryan's disgust, but no one else's, the Tredicim each received a drop of blood.

Trettan was last and he let a drop touch his tongue. He worked it around his mouth savouring its taste.

"Having speed won't help you," Edeps said. "Those Frayans received training in order to combat our speed, running fast doesn't help you smash through a brick wall."

"It's not just speed though is it, we will have strength too," Trettan said.

"You can't have two powers at the same time," Edeps mocked.

Ryan peered around expecting the Tredicim to produce another vial and give more blood out, but none was forthcoming.

Trettan kneeled before a nearby boulder then smashed it with his fist shattering it as easily as the crystal had been shattered.

"Strength and speed," he said.

"Ryan's blood," Reesa breathed.

"Impossible," Edeps gasped.

"Two powers for the price of one, made possible by the half human who also uses two powers of the tribes," Trettan said. "Are those Frayans trained to combat that? Move out and destroy that company of soldiers," Trettan ordered his companions and him and ten of the Tredicim suddenly dashed over the hill. The remaining Tredicim started moving Ryan and the others forward.

After a few seconds screams and shouting came from over the rise.

Ryan and the others then crested the hill and witnessed the battle below them.

Frayans were everywhere, the Tredicim who were fast and strong, easily dodging attacks aimed at them and fought back with their own, which normally would have been useless against a Frayan, but delivered now with super strength, were taking them apart.

"No," Ryan said.

"It's not your fault Ryan," Edeps said.

"We have to thank you human, without you this wouldn't be possible," one of the Tredicim said, smiling at the carnage going on before him.

They all then descended the hill. Ryan felt his blood go cold as they passed dead or defeated Frayans. The Tredicim had been merciless. The Frayans had broken bones and twisted necks. They had torn off their armour or dented it by ferocious punches. The Frayans had only managed to take out a few Tredicim.

Deeskly started crying. Reesa and Nur faces were pale and they looked like they were going to be sick.

The Tredicim just laughed at the dead as they passed by.

Trettan and his little war band were waiting for them at the entrance to shield control centre. He pointed to five other Tredicim, "Get back to your ships and patrol the skies, attack any vessels that approach the control centre," he ordered, "give us time."

Those Tredicim sped away.

"Let's get inside we have a job to do," and Trettan led the group into the control centre.

Ryan did not know much about volcanoes, some vague geography classes bubbled to the surface of his brain, and told him he was wandering through lava tubes, tubes normally filled with near liquid rock.

They passed out of a tube into the control centre, inside were more dead Frayans and Intelligen, who had been monitoring the controls. Armour, helmets and equipment were strewn about the place, useless in protecting their owners.

"Go guard the entrance," Trettan ordered, all but one of his fellow Tredicim left the control centre.

Trettan turned his attention to one end of the room and a circular door way where the room tapered to. There was no door just the shield wall where it extended from the centre of the crater.

Trettan seemed to regard it with awe, "Finally," he said. His palm moved across the bubble, a dark shape was standing on the other side, like a reflection.

"Is that you?" Trettan said to the shape. His tentacles shuddered and he stared with a hopeful smile on his face at the dark shape beyond.

The shield then gave him a small shock and Trettan hissed and pulled his hand away. He looked back at the shape, then Edeps.

"Now then for the reason we are here, Edeps open the lock."

"I will not," Edeps said as defiantly as he could, but there was a lack of conviction in those words.

Trettan was instantly by Ryan's side, he cut the link holding him to the others and dragged Ryan to Edeps. Then made him stand in front of him. Trettan's claws held Ryan just below the neck, he could feel their sharp points dig into the skin on his shoulders.

"We've been here before, but I don't have time to remember old times, give me the code. I can't use Astral powers to get it from you, tell me."

Edeps eyes were wide in fear as he looked Trettan in the eyes then his own sons.

"No," someone said in a whisper.

Everyone's attention turned to a Frayan who was crawling his way towards the group. Everyone had assumed he was dead and he very nearly was.

"Don't release the Tredicim, please," the Frayan begged, "My family."

The remaining Tredicim in the room shot forward towards the Frayan and kicked in him the head at super speed and with super strength. There was a loud, horrible crack as his neck broke and the Frayan slumped forward, dead.

Ryan taste vomit in his throat, he had just witnessed someone die for the first time in his life.

"Now where were we," Trettan said. "The code for your son's life," and he grasped Ryan's neck again. "You know I will do it," Trettan said.

Edeps was shaking, his eyes flickering as different scenarios and options flew through his mind.

Ryan ignored all this, staring only at the now dead Frayan. It was the most awful thing he had ever seen, the breaking of the neck, the utter brutality and ease at which the Tredicim had ended his life.

He looked around and saw the other dead Ontarians around the room, he thought about the families they might have had, now broken by the actions of these Tredicim.

He thought about death, how it was all around him and possibly going to come for him any moment.

Then he realised something else, others were going to die too, his family. Nur, Reesa his father they would still die even when the Tredicim gained their freedom. The war would start again, a repeat of all those battles he had seen in the museum.

He did not want to live knowing more Ontarians would perish if the Tredicim escaped.

"Now Edeps," Trettan said.

"I can't," his father said. "Emma," he whispered in affection.

"Yes you can," Trettan said. "Your son will die otherwise, remember your wife," he said.

Edeps stared angrily at Trettan all his fear replaced for an instant by his anger towards the Tredicim who had killed his loved one.

"Don't make me," Trettan said and his claws dug a little deeper and Ryan felt blood trickle down his neck as a few tiny cuts appeared.

"If you kill him I will never give you the code," Edeps spat.

"THIS IS MY LAST CHANCE," Trettan suddenly screamed, and then he managed to compose himself. Trettan then fumbled with something in a pocket, his arm came up holding it outstretched past Ryan's ear, right in Edeps' face.

"It's my son versus your son, I will do it."

Edeps stared into Trettan's hand, Ryan saw the golden edge of some sort of locket.

"I can't release your people Trettan, I care for my own family."

"Your family that you doomed with your foolish decisions on Earth. Who don't speak to you? Your family farm was small Edeps, how much did the council take? How about I give it back when the Tredicim rightfully rule the planet again. You don't even have to feel bad about releasing us. By Patriarchal Right we are your rulers, we could forgive you for trapping us."

Edeps slumped further, his eyes darting around looking for a solution.

"Your son doesn't want to die," Trettan added. "Tell him Ryan, make your father see sense. I tell you what, if you convince him, you can go back to Earth."

Ryan frowned, not because the offer was a random offering, but because it didn't evoke the reaction he expected. There was no cry in his heart for Earth. In fact, he wanted to go back to the mountain and have another friendly exhilarating fight. He wanted to be on the farm. He did not want to go to school, he wanted to stop, look up from a plant or crop and watch the sprinklers create rainbows across the fields. He missed Earth, but there was still so much to see here.

This felt like a home now.

He looked at his father and saw that he had cracked. His head hung low and he was sobbing.

Trettan smiled when he saw it too.

Ryan gasped as he watched his father break. It occurred to Ryan he was going to get everything he wanted if his father gave Trettan the code. The Tredicim might honour the agreement, he could still stay and his family could get their farm back.

Plus, it wouldn't be his fault, it would be his father's for being weak.

Weak for risking his life to safe Ontaria in the first place, weak trying to protect his wife, weak facing prison and weak for trying to bond with his son?

Ryan felt tears roll down his checks.

His father was about to save him, however it wasn't weakness. He was wrong.

His dad had just been pushed to the breaking point, because the thing he valued most, was in danger, his family.

Ryan asked himself if he could live with that, not just the son of a criminal, but also the son of a traitor.

He could not. Death though did not appeal to him either. They just needed time, soon the other Ontarians would be here, Ryan had to stall for time, do something Trettan did not expect.

"Your son wants to live, he had a life on Earth he was popular he was going places, let him go back to it," Trettan said. "I've watched him, he wants to live and get wealth and fame, something humans crave. Save him so he can have them. Give your son a future so I can give mine one too."

Ryan gritted his teeth and almost snarled at Trettan's words. Hatred boiled within him at this creature reminding him who he used to be. His eyes widened and his mouth fell open. He knew now what Trettan would not expect. He was going to have to try something risky, it might get him killed, at least he would die for his home and family.

"No dad," Ryan said.

"Huh," Trettan uttered.

His father raised his head and he met the gaze of his son.

"Don't do it."

"What?" Trettan snapped.

"It's alright dad, don't give them the code. Mum was prepared to die to keep the code and this planet safe, I am too," Ryan said.

His dad looked confused by his words.

"I am prepared Dad, don't give it to him."

"Son I…your mother would want you to live. If he killed you, I'll be the father who did nothing to save his son, Emma wouldn't want that."

"No dad she would understand, and I forgive you for it, you can't let him win," Ryan said. "He'll kill us anyway, you must have a seen a human film at least once, you know how this works, the villain never lets them go when he has what he wants."

Trettan started spluttering. "No Edeps he doesn't, he'll die and it will be your fault." Trettan turned Ryan to face him. "Do you really think a father can just watch a son die? Do you really want to die for this planet you don't know?"

Ryan wanted to break down and cry, he was fifteen years old and dying for your planet was not something anyone should face. He pushed it down and stood straight. "How could I let you win, you killed my mother," he spat back.

He heard the sounds of battle outside getting closer, the Tredicim were finally being over powered, and soon the soldiers would arrive. He needed more time.

Ryan used his own strength to turn his head towards his father against the vice like grip of Trettan's.

Father and son gazed into each other's eyes.

Ryan winked…how much did his father know of human culture?

His father for a moment looked confused, then a microsecond later he understood and hid it before Trettan could see. "No," Edeps said and he stood tall and proud.

Even though that word would seal his death, Ryan felt his heart leap, he felt energised and glad to have a father like Edeps. He was standing up for something bigger than him, making a tough choice, Ryan could see he had a brave and strong willed father, whom he wished he had known for longer.

"What?" Trettan growled.

"I will not give you the code," Edeps said.

Trettan was flabbergasted and he spluttered incoherently, unable to accept what was happening.

Another Tredicim entered the room bloodied and bruised.

"We're being out numbered," it said.

"NOT NOW!" Trettan said dangerously and the Tredicim bowed weakly and decided to hurry back into battle.

"Tell your father to give me the code," he said to Ryan.

"No, I am ready to die," Ryan said. "You've lost Trettan, your people will never be free," he said. Out of the corner of his eyes he saw looks of admiration and respect on Nur and Reesa's face.

Trettan looked like he could not comprehend what was happening he turned to Edeps.

"He WILL die," Trettan emphasised.

"You heard the boy," Edeps said.

"YOU WANT TO DIE?" Trettan asked Ryan, with spittle flying from his mouth and desperate eyes boring into Ryan's.

"No, but I prefer it to betraying **my** home-world." Ryan replied.

"This isn't your world," Trettan said.

"It's one of them," Ryan said.

Trettan did not know how to respond.

Suddenly the crater shook as something impacted the outside walls.

"The Ontarian ships are here," said the other Tredicim, "We're running out of time, our ships can't hold them for long."

Trettan stared at Ryan and Edeps trying to find proof that both of them were lying, but there was nothing for him to find.

Trettan took a step back in shock, "You were supposed to give me the code, I broke you last time," he said.

He turned his head towards the shield wall, to the single dark shape beyond. A tear rolled down Trettan's face.

For a second his grip on Ryan slackened.

"This is the most difficult decision I have ever made, I..." Edeps began, "...RYAN, DUCK!" he then shouted not in Ontarian, but in English.

"What?" Trettan said.

Ryan understood and crouched down just as his dad propelled himself forward towards Trettan.

Trettan side stepped right as Edeps charged.

Edeps went sprawling on the floor expecting resistance and finding none.

"Nice try Edeps, but I don't fall for the same trick twice," Trettan said, in English.

Edeps got up, "Ryan take out his knees," he said not in English or Ontarian...but in Spanish.

"Huh," Trettan said clearly not well versed in **that** language.

Ryan smiled at his dad, pirouetted on the spot and lashed out with a fearsome kick fuelled with speed and strength at Trettan's nearest knee.

The Tredicim's kneecap grinded against his leg and he howled in pain just as Edeps came bowling in, shoulder first, straight into his face.

The other Tredicim roared in anger and stepped forward to help his companion.

Ryan noticed a discarded Frayan helmet at his feet. He grabbed it in both hands and imitating the perfect rugby pass launched it at the Tredicim at super speed and struck him in the head knocking the creature out cold.

Edeps and Trettan rolled about on the floor. Edeps managed to get on top of the Tredicim then started rapidly beating him in the face at super speed.

Trettan knocked him off, flinging him across the room with the strength he still possessed.

Ryan ran to the other three, "Run, get going," he said.

At Ryan's urging, they tried to run, but they fell to the floor as soon as they went to super speed finding it too awkward since they were linked together.

"It's no good," Nur said holding up the rope that bound them.

"Stay here," Trettan ordered getting up and holding his face, which was bleeding profusely.

Edeps came from his side and kicked him in the stomach and Trettan doubled over.

"Get them out of here Ryan!" Edeps said.

Ryan decided there was only one way to accomplish that.

"Get on my back," he said to the trio.

"What?" they answered.

"Just do it," he said.

They obliged and awkwardly climbed up on his back and mustering all the strength he had he carried them out of the room, not at super speed but at normal running speed.

"Can't you go faster," Nur said from his right shoulder.

"No," Ryan said.

"Not that way, that leads to the surface," Reesa said, "That's where the Tredicim are."

Ryan choose another lava tube that disappeared into darkness.

"COME BACK," Trettan yelled and the control centre shook again as more impacts from above stuck the crater.

"Go," Edeps said and attacked Trettan again.

Edeps grabbed Trettan just as Ryan disappeared down another tunnel.

Trettan wrenched Edeps free from him, and held him aloft. He growled and slammed him down on a control panel, denting it with Edeps' body and choking him.

"I will kill you," he said.

"Do it and you kind will be trapped forever," Edeps gasped. "This was your last chance and it's fallen apart I bet you never thought that my son, my Half Human son, would stand up to you," he said.

Trettan growled in anger, "I really thought you would break, you know," he said and increased the pressure on Edeps. "The council chose wisely in giving you the code, but now that I know I cannot get it out of you, your son, he is useless," Trettan launched Edeps across the room and there was a crack as something of Edeps' broke.

"And you didn't even get a chance to say goodbye," Trettan said and ran off after Ryan.

Edeps went to give chase, but his leg was broken and he fell to the floor.

He watch the Tredicim go and did the only option available to him, he started to pray for his son.

•

Ryan ran as fast as he could go carrying the others with him down the lava tube. They soon came to a junction where the tube broke off into two tunnels.

"Move, move cousin," Deeskly said, hitting his back like he was a horse.

Ryan stopped and let them down, "No more," he gasped.

"Ryan you were prepared to die," Nur said.

"Sort of, we need to go help my dad," he said.

"We can't like this," Reesa said indicating her bound hands.

Ryan grasped her bonds and with all his strength broke them.

"Aaarrh," he said bringing his hands together.

"Again," Nur said holding out hers.

Ryan's hands shook but he was able to repeat the process. Deeskly was the only one left with his hands bound, with the remains of the cable hanging off his bonds.

"Hurry up," he prompted.

Ryan felt like his hands were broken so he was reluctant to try for a third time.

They then heard footsteps; someone was rapidly approaching down one of the lava tubes that led to where they were.

"It's one of the Tredicim," Reesa said.

"What do we do?" Ryan asked desperately.

Nur grabbed the end of the cable still connected to Deeskly, "Hold him down," Nur pointed to Deeskly and drew the metal wire across the tunnel.

Ryan and Reesa saw what her plan was and grabbed the wire and Deeskly.

"Hey wait," Deeskly said in protest.

"Here it comes," Nur said.

The lava tube bent off around a corner and as the Tredicim rounded it the wire, which it failed to notice, caught one of its legs high up on the shin. The Tredicim tripped, screamed like a child and hit the wall of the lava tube at full speed.

It fell to the floor.

"Well done Nur," Ryan said.

"Well..." Nur said and smoothed her hair back.

"HUMAN," someone bellowed down the tunnel.

"That's Trettan, go that way I'll lead him away from you," Ryan said.

"No Ryan," Nur said.

"We've no choice," Ryan said and shoved them away.

Trettan came into view.

"This way ugly," Ryan said and disappeared down the tunnel.

Trettan eyed Reesa, Nur and Deeskly but turned to Ryan speeding away and ignored them, running at super speed after him.

Ryan was alone now he heard the footsteps of Trettan behind him chasing him down deeper into the earth. He wiped his head of sweat and tried to pull his soaked clothes off his skin. As he breathed in the air felt dry. It occurred to him that maybe this dormant volcano, was not.

He ran for a while and no one chased him.

Had he out run Trettan?

The tube he was in then opened up into a cavern and Ryan's immediate attention was drawn to the lava leaking out of the walls. This cavern was no doubt still in the active part of the volcano.

Trettan bowled into him out of nowhere, and threw Ryan to the floor.

He rolled over with Trettan standing over him.

"You ruined everything, you filthy Human." Trettan said. "Your father was going to crack and give me the code but you had to get all heroic," he added. "Are you still keen to die?" he asked.

In truth Ryan was not, if he died now it was for Trettan's revenge. He scrambled away.

Trettan smiled and barked a laughed as he stalked Ryan around the cavern. He stood over him and punched down at Ryan.

Ryan raised his hands in defence and when Trettan's blow struck, something threw him backwards and he crashed into a nearby wall.

Ryan was dazed, his vison went blurry. He managed to get to his knees, but he felt like he had just run a marathon.

Trettan scrambling onto tow feet, panting, clutching a broken arm. He at Ryan seething through gritted teeth. "Motus Powers," he said.

"What?" Ryan said.

"That was the powers of the Motus tribe; you raised a telekinetic shield around your body by instinct."

Ryan struggled to rise.

"It takes a lot out of you doesn't it," Trettan said. "Too much it seems, you can't get away now."

Trettan ignored his arm and took a step towards Ryan.

Reesa and Nur suddenly charged in.

They both stuck him on his broken arm and he squealed in pain.

"Get away from my cousin," Nur shouted.

"Get away from my friend," Reesa added.

They both circled him at high speed and rained down punches on him. Trettan cowered away from them. He lashed out with a free arm and managed to grab Nur by her shirt and used her like a mace clubbing Reesa to one side.

"The only thing I have left now is the pleasure of killing you," Trettan muttered, discarding Nur, who landed in a heap.

Trettan reached into a pocket and flung something in front of Ryan. It was a golden locket and it snapped open as it landed.

He looked down at it and saw what was a Tredicim baby, an ugly baby in Ryan's opinion.

"My new born son became trapped under that dome, he's only a few years older than you now. He was a new born when that happened. I have not seen him for seventeen years. He has never seen our beautiful planet. Because of your father. You could have helped him Ryan, I could have seen him again. You can still free that child from his imprisonment."

Ryan got up the floor, "You killed my mother," he said to Trettan.

Trettan's face fell, then he smiled a cruel, vicious smile. "I did, stabbed her with my claws," and he flexed his good hand in front of Ryan.

Trettan snarled. "Do you want revenge? Is that why you won't free my family and people."

Ryan squared off against Trettan raising his fists, but wobbled on tired legs. "I'm doing this for my family and people."

"So brave," Trettan mocked and lunged forward with a super strong, super-fast punch.

Ryan was barely able to dodge it, leaping aside as Trettan's fist impacted the wall cracking the stone.

The Tredicim shook his fist and soothed it, "You can't dodge forever. I'll kill you and your friends, just for fun," he said. "I'll enjoy it. I waited seventeen years to reunite with my son beyond the shield. You cannot imagine what it feels like to have him so close yet so far."

Ryan heard a rumble behind the wall Trettan had punched. Lava started leaking from the walls. Ryan's blood went cold despite the intense heat, fearful of the red-hot stone all around. Goosebumps rose all over his flesh.

Then his eyes widened, he still had a chance.

He raised his hand and poured into all the energy into it just like before. He fired a telekinetic blast, not at Trettan, instead at the wall next to him.

Trettan laughed at his inaccurate shot.

Then the rock cracked and split.

Trettan turned his head just as a burst of lava shot out of the broken wall.

He screamed as the molten rock struck him full in his chest and burned his body.

Trettan reached out with his good hand and clawed at the ground trying to pull himself away from the lava leaking slowly from the tunnel wall.

He disappeared from Ryan's view as smoke from the lava and pressurised molten rock spewed out of the hole. He heard Trettan scream as the lava burned him.

"Reesa, Nur!" Ryan yelled.

The girls started to stir.

He crawled towards them. The effort of using those Motus powers had totally worn him out.

His chest had shooting pains, his limbs felt like his very bones were on fire.

He suddenly had a new respect for member of the Motus tribe, expelling tremendous amounts of energy just to do their jobs.

Nur stirred and rose, she helped Reesa get moving, they both came to Ryan and picked him up.

"Breathe Ryan," Reesa said.

Ryan took their advice and breathed deeply. He felt power returning to his body.

"What happened?" Nur asked.

"The lava got him," he replied waving vaguely where Trettan's body was obscured by lava. He choose not to reveal he had developed the Motus powers. Using them was the worse feeling in the world, like a crazy PE teacher had forced him to do a hundred press-ups sits up and burpees. He wanted to vomit, his flesh crawled at the thought of ever using those powers again.

If he told someone, no doubt they would make him train with them, something he did not want.

Ryan managed to stand.

"Where's Deeskly?" He asked and swayed a little.

"With your father, Trettan roughed him up bad," Reesa said.

Ryan turned to her then to Nur. "Thanks for coming back to me," he said.

Nur sighed, "You are my cousin." Nur said. "My only one actually, wouldn't want to lose you."

"Thanks," Ryan said.

"What you did back there in the control room was very brave," Reesa said.

"Not as brave as when you two attacked a Tredicim," Ryan replied.

"Yeah I guess people will be more interested to hear about that," Nur said to Reesa.

"The valiant heroes who fought a super-fast and super strong Tredicim," Reesa replied smiling at Nur.

Nur clasped her hand and held it in the air, "To the heroes of Ontaria," she declared. "Don't worry Ryan we'll still make sure you get invited to all the good parties."

Ryan laughed, "Ow," he then said. "It hurts to laugh," he added.

"Run," Nur said.

"What?" Reesa replied.

"Run," Nur repeated pointing at the wall Ryan had cracked.

Ryan and Reesa looked and saw more cracks appear and lava poured in a torrent.

The three of them bolted.

The lava started chasing Ryan, Nur and Reesa, down the tunnel out of the cavern.

Ryan tried to keep up, but he was going slower than normal worn out by his use of the Motus powers.

"This way Ryan," Reesa called out and he followed her voice down a passage and saw daylight.

The lava rumbled down the tube behind him nipping at his heels.

He felt the heat on his back and it got hotter.

He was not as fast as the others; there was no way he could out run the lava.

He saw Reesa and Nur at the end of the tunnel, "Run cousin," Nur called out, "come on."

Ryan reached the tunnel exit, a splash of hot rock caught his foot and he felt it burn, in one last gambit he dived forward using his strength to give him an edge. Hoping to clear the tunnel exit.

Everything seemed to slow.

He flew through the air out of the tube.

He smelt the burning rubber on his shoes.

Nur's hands flew up to grab Ryan, yanking him to one side and held him against the rock face of the crater, as the lava spewed out of the tunnel.

Reesa and Nur kept him pinned against the side of the rock as the lava poured out right next to them, roaring like a dragon breathing fire. All three of them screamed in terror. After a minute the pressure eased off and the lava spill ceased. The trio kept screaming long after it had died down.

The screaming then turned to laughter.

Chapter 31

The trio trudged across the landscape towards the entrance to the control room. Reesa and Nur held up Ryan as he staggered forward with painful steps. Their faces were covered in ash, their hair grimy, and their clothes sweaty and singed.

"I want to lie down," Ryan said.

"I want a bath," Reesa said.

"I never walked so slow in my life," Nur added.

"I still can't believe you did that," Reesa said. "Standing up to the Tredicim."

"I thought you didn't like our planet?" Nur stated.

"It's my planet too," Ryan replied.

"Yeah, I suppose it is," Nur said. After a pause she looked at him, and then lifted Ryan up a little bit more, taking a bit of extra weight off his tired legs. "Look cousin, I apologise for the way I treated you since you arrived. I guess it's easier to be angry at you than uncle Edeps."

"That's fine," Ryan replied. "I didn't want to be here at first, I wasn't exactly making a good impression."

"It's just you know, your dad gave my dad some problems. However, I can see now that uncle Edeps isn't so bad," Nur added.

"Yeah, I agree," Ryan replied, and he patted his cousin on the back.

They finally reached the entrance to the control centre where a massive ship hovered above the site. Frayans emerging from drop pods secured the area. Three Tredicim who had survived the battle were in custody, their blood powers having worn off. A party of Frayans spotted the trio who were surprised to see the children there. "They need medical attention," one of the Frayans said looking at their disheveled appearance.

"We're fine, just tired," Nur said.

"Come with us," the Frayans said and lifted them off the ground. Ryan nor the others made any move to resist in fact Ryan like being carried.

When they entered the command centre they were plonked down in front of the Admiral and Ryan's dad who was still in chains. Deeskly was sitting in one of the operator's chairs spinning in the seat, mostly out of sheer boredom.

Admiral Tarms surveyed Ryan and the others. "You," she said pointing at Ryan, "Smuggled three Swifter's into the tribal lands of the Frayans, you are in a lot of trouble."

Ryan wondered if there were some Frayans somewhere waiting to enact some sort of punishment, it made him shudder.

"However, I think that in preventing the deactivation of the shield generator your crimes can be forgiven," the Admiral said.

"Thanks grandmother," Nur said.

"Grandmother, she's your grandmother, but that makes her my grandmother," Ryan said.

"Quick isn't he," the Admiral said to Edeps rolling her eyes.

"No, but he is strong," Edeps said chuckling.

"You've got five minutes," the Admiral said and ushered Reesa, Nur and Deeskly away leaving Ryan with his father alone.

"Five minutes?" Ryan said.

"I'm still a convicted criminal I have to go back to jail, but for now we've got some time to talk. Edeps eyes then fell on the small section of the shield that was visible from the control centre. They through into the shield and saw dark shapes on the other side, members of the Tredicim trapped beyond the bubble of energy.

"I sorry for what I said during my last visit," Ryan said.

"I understand Ryan, what else were you to think," Edeps replied.

"I sorry about mum too," Ryan said.

"She loved planet Ontaria as much as she did Earth. When she died, she died the way she wanted, defending it. That was one of the many reasons I loved her so much. I have to ask, were you really prepared to die?"

"You know I was trying to trick Trettan," Ryan said.

"I guessed, but it could have gone wrong, he might not have believed you. You threw him with that bluff."

"What else was I supposed to do?" Ryan asked. "You looked ready to break."

Edeps swiveled in his chair and looked at the section of the shield. "You know when I set the trap all those years ago, I had a similar choice, same as the one I faced with your mother. Save your great grandfather or complete the mission. I saved my grandfather. I was prepared to save your mother despite the risks. I was willing to save you despite the fact the Tredicim would once again be unleashed."

"Sort of an easy decision when you think about it…" and Ryan swallowed and starred off into the distance. "Trettan would have killed both of us anyway after you did what he wanted."

"I know," Edeps said. "But do I want to be the father who let his grandfather, wife or son die?" He mused. "Would you accept my choice?" he asked Ryan.

He stared at the shield wall, watching the dark shapes beyond pound on the shield in vain. "I don't know dad," he replied.

"Well don't worry son, you're a farmer now and you don't get called to make those decisions. How are you finding life there now?"

"I think I've made some new friends," Ryan said turning to Nur and Reesa. He noticed impatience about them as if they were waiting for him.

"Proper friends," Edeps commented. "That's good."

"What do you mean?" Ryan replied.

"Your uncle and I still talk, he said you were desperate for attention, to be the centre of what's happening and showing off," his dad said.

"Yeah, I guess I kind of was," Ryan said.

"That was never the way to make friends Ryan. Sacrifice and courage and loyalty. That's what builds deep and meaningful friendships, exactly the kind of traits you showed today. Try not to mess up what you've laid the foundations for."

"Thanks dad," Ryan said with a smile.

"I mean it, and while you're at it try and get faster, your old man was once the fastest Swifter ever, you've got a lot to live up to."

Ryan smiled, "I will try."

"That is all I ask."

Then for the first-time father and son shared a hug.

Epilogue

Ryan grabbed the fallen tree, steadied himself with his knees bent and launched it to one side using his super strength to toss it aside like it was a mere twig. It flew for twenty metres then crashed back down with the sounds of snapping timber. It settled amongst lots of other trees and few boulders.

There were impressed whistles and nods of approval from the other Swifters nearby. "Now we can finally have new tracks," Nur said to her family and those representing the other Swift families nearby. "We've asked for years for all that stuff to be moved. Thanks to Ryan, we've moved it."

Saft looked at the tossed tree with grudging respect. "Ok, he can race," he said.

Ryan opened his mouth to make comment that would make everyone laugh, then stopped himself for a brief moment, smiled to himself and said, "Look I'm sorry for the last time we did this, I just want to get faster," he said to all those who had watched him do some landscaping.

Saft sighed. "That makes sense, you are slow for an Ontarian…but you can be faster. Grab a helmet you're up, but no super strength," he warned.

"Deal." Ryan strolled past Nur and Reesa and others from his family to where the racing helmets were stored.

"Remember what I showed you," Nur said.

"I will," he replied.

"Just come in the top three," Reesa added.

"I'm just here to have fun and make friends," Ryan replied, *real friends* he added to himself. He went to his place on the line and took up the professional Olympic runners' stance once again. When the other Swifters looked at him he said. "I think I need all the help I can get," he joked.

There were some smiles and laughter, then everyone steeled themselves for the beginning of the race.

Saft on the sideline raised his hand.

He paused for a moment.

The hand dropped, the race started and Ryan gave it his all.